LESLIE O'SULLIVAN

HOT SET

BEHIND THE SCENES BOOK 1

HOT SET

LESLIE O'SULLIVAN

CITY OWL
PRESS

HOT SET
Behind the Scenes, Book 1

CITY OWL PRESS
www.cityowlpress.com

Cover Design by MiblArt. All stock photos licensed appropriately.

Edited by Theresa Cole.

For information on subsidiary rights, please contact the publisher at info@cityowlpress.com.

Print Edition ISBN: 978-1-64898-186-9

Digital Edition ISBN: 978-1-64898-185-2

Printed in the United States of America

ALSO BY LESLIE O'SULLIVAN

Rockin Fairy Tales:

Pink Guitars and Falling Stars

Gilded Butterfly

Wild Azure Waves

Crimson Melodies

Emerald Spire (Winter 2024)

***

Behind the Scenes:

Hot Set

Press Release

Not to Scale (Coming Fall 2023)

PRAISE FOR LESLIE O'SULLIVAN

"*Hot Set*, by Leslie O'Sullivan, is a contemporary love story that creatively infuses modern concerns with the nostalgia generated by a period television show. The Irish setting was fantastically romantic, and I thought the cast of characters was refreshingly practical for a group involved in show business." — *Reader's Favorite 5-star review*

"As full of heart and soul as the music it describes, *Crimson Melodies* drew me in with a fresh take on a classic tale, masterfully combining celebrity and monster romance vibes to give me everything I wanted and more!" — S.C. Grayson, author of *Beauty and the Blade*

"Submerging readers into a fantastical world, *Wild Azure Waves* is a love story swimming with music, mysticism, and magic." — *InD'tale*

"*Pink Guitars and Falling Stars* is a fast paced and very engaging read, with a constantly evolving main character and a colorful cast. The adventure wraps up nicely, and ends with a hint of what is next in the Rockin' Fairy Tales series. This is a great read if you are looking for an action-packed modern fairy tale with aspiring rock stars who fall from the sky." — *Paranormal Romance Guild*

"*Gilded Butterfly* is a unique and magical mashup of fairy tales, Shakespeare, and lore, unlike anything I've read before. At its heart, is a beautiful story about family, the destructive power of chasing fame and money, and the healing power of love. The twists, turns, and magic sprinkled throughout create an engaging story that brings a new kind of fairy tale to modern Hollywood." — *Megan Van Dyke, author of Second Star to the Left*

To Cameron Rose, a wildly creative artist who never stops pursuing his dreams

CHAPTER
ONE

I f dread is ground glass shredding your stomach, then I'm digesting a set of eight crystal goblets. As I ready my opening shot on the seventeenth hole, Lanie Blesch's giggles rise from the golf cart parked alongside the tee box. Aglow in her fifteen minutes of fame as the spokesmodel for everything from moisturizer to orthotic inserts, Lanie flirts with abandon. Her target and cart buddy this morning is my boyfriend, Treat Graham.

This woman who holds the gold medal for stellar BMI is everything I'm not—tall and curvy with negative body fat in all the right places. I flick one strawberry blond braid over my shoulder and wonder if I could pull off Lanie's fluffy chocolate bob with strands of amber peeking through at strategically stylish locations. Next to her overflowing sexuality, I come off like Treat's tomboy sidekick.

When Lanie adds another lipstick smudge to the collar of Treat's gaudy, neon pink polo, I take a step back from the tee and drop my lethal glare to the grass before anyone notices. It's hard to justify visually disintegrating Lanie since she has no clue the man next to her is off limits. Per an agreement I'm rapidly losing patience with, my two-year relationship with Treat is a secret.

Bobby Provost, who shares my golf cart, takes a break from

destroying every blade of grass on the tee box with his practice swings. He sidles up next to me. "Gillian, you okay?"

Ironic question from the man who's responsible for half the pulverized goblet glass sitting in my digestive system. I toss Bobby a smile that would register as less than ten percent genuine to anyone who knows me. "Rethinking my club." *And the gag order on my relationship.*

A gust of wind knocks my newly acquired *Chieftain's Son* baseball cap off my head. As the showrunner bringing the most anticipated series of historical romance novels in a billion years to television, Bobby is a swag dispenser. Everyone in this charity golf tournament is outfitted with *Chieftain's Son* logo caps, jerseys, and metallic water bottles.

"I've got it," says Bobby, chasing my cap as it skids down the rise next to the tee. Definitely a gentleman, for more reasons than one. Thankfully, for the last sixteen holes he has diplomatically ignored the giant elephant riding between us in the golf cart. Nearly a year ago, our mutual literary agent approached me with Bobby's interest for me to possibly join the writing staff of *The Chieftain's Son*. An opportunity so unexpected and frightening it came from whatever territory is out beyond left field.

Treat's words ring in my head from our discussion about whether or not I should even entertain Bobby's request to take a meeting.

"Why put yourself through it, Babe? You've never written a script in your life. Face it, Gilly, you are master of the short game. Copywriting for my company is your sweet spot."

Treat is blunt, but I know he only has my best interest at heart. Raw truth—my agent couldn't sell my book; therefore, I live in the stable reality of being the reigning queen of clothing blurbs for Lawson Graham Premier Sportswear.

I shake out my hand, numb from gripping the club too tight. If penning catalogue copy is my career, at least it involves writing. Is the definition of a career what you do to pay the bills when you're two years shy of thirty?

When Bobby Provost, gentleman, and I did meet face to face this morning, I managed what I hoped was an appreciative "thank you" for even considering me for the position on his show, followed by an apology that things didn't work out. We shook hands and Treat whisked him away to talk business, but something about the look Bobby's jade-colored eyes shot in my direction didn't feel like a period at the end of a sentence.

Thankfully, in less than an hour, Treat will finish selling Bobby on the crossover marketing benefits if our companies pair up. The Irish Country Lass clothing line will shoot on Bobby's company property in Ireland, featuring show locations. *The Chieftain's Son* will get some dandy print exposure for its premier season.

Bobby waves my rescued cap like he's starting the Indy 500. "Victory."

"Good catch," I say, fitting the hat back on my head as Bobby salutes.

I clear my head by ripping a handful of blades from the grass and let the wind carry them to calculate my shot. The faster we play these last two holes, the faster I'll avoid any talk with Bobby about his offer, and the faster I can pull the pin on the *what the hell* grenade I plan to heave at Treat for his flirting overdrive with Lanie.

My tee shot hits the fairway dead center. To my delight, momentum carries it forward a gratifying distance.

"Brilliant," says Bobby, applauding. "One fairway shot, a chip, putt, and you're the birdie queen of the day." He pulls off his own logo baseball cap and trains his hair back. "How many so far?"

"Nine birdies," I say, and head back to our cart. I'm behind the wheel before Bobby finishes his tee shot.

He pops onto the seat next to me. "I chunked it. Is it driving you nuts to play with a duffer like me?"

I muster a smile. "You're far from a duffer. If we didn't have Lanie and Treat dragging us down, we'd own this tournament."

Bobby is the type that perpetually moves and chatters. Luckily, a sweet, candy-coated personality keeps his hummingbird vibe from being irritating. He's the geeky big brother that all my friends would confide in. Treat actually expected me to flirt with him. I'm a good little soldier for Lawson Graham Premier Sportwear and loyal girlfriend, but I have my limits. It's awkward enough spending this much time with Bobby after rejecting his job offer. Given our age gap, which has to be at least ten years, any attempt at flirting would reek of insincerity. Treat's the game player, not me.

Treat and Lanie blow by in their cart, barely missing ours. She drives like an idiot, trashing shrubbery as she rips down the cart path. The flirty laughs between them threaten to bring up my breakfast burrito. Treat doesn't even wave at me.

The jerk can't spare one measly, reassuring smile. Less than six months ago, we were together in Oregon eating his mother's homemade chicken marsala while his stepdad reminded him daily that he'd be a fool to ever let me go.

On the drive back to L.A., Treat professed a dozen times how much he adored me. *Adored*, not loved. Here in reality, *adored* translates to undercover relationship. Treat made it clear from the beginning that if our situation ever became breaking news at Lawson Graham Premier Sportswear, we'd get the axe. I'm certain that axe would only swing my way since Lawson Graham is Treat's father. Lucky me. I get to carry on a hush-hush relationship and watch my boyfriend play gigolo every time Daddy needs someone to court a spokesmodel or female designer.

A pang of disappointment stabs as I relive the joy of living as a non-secret couple with Treat up in Oregon. People take handholding and quick kisses for granted.

After his next shot, Bobby lopes over to me like a deer. The entire cart lurches when he leaps in. "Well, that drive made up for my previous chunkage."

My face heats. "Full disclosure, I missed it."

"I'm sure I can repeat it—never." He laughs.

Before I step on the gas, he raises a hand. "Hold up. I don't intend to waste the serendipity of sharing this golf cart with the author of *Traipse of Moonlight* because her boss wants to use my property."

The serious look and tone of his voice set off a warning klaxon in my brain. *No, not now. Don't do it, Bobby. Throw the elephant in the cart some peanuts and call it a day. Please kill off any mention of our awkward history when we're so close to the finish line.*

"Why in the hell is Gillian Bettencourt wasting her talent writing banal clothing descriptors for a Ralph Lauren wannabe company?"

I'm not sure how many times per minute one is supposed to breathe, but I don't make the quota.

Bobby continues. "In the spirit of full disclosure.. "

I remember to breathe but forget to blink.

"My offer still stands for the author of *Traipse of Moonlight* to join my writing staff for *The Chieftain's Son*."

I swallow a very unladylike gulp. This is not a conversation I ever wanted to have, but he's got me cornered.

"*Traipse* never made it."

He stares me down. "Awards and landing the literary agent that we share say otherwise."

I attempt to match his intensity. "It's a decent novella that became a novel she couldn't sell."

Bobby holds up a hand to stop me. "It sold me. From the day Jen passed it to me last year when I was reading everything in sight about Irish history and folklore, *Traipse of Moonlight* has been a major tonal inspiration in my development of *The Chieftain's Son*."

He gestures so wildly I have to lean away to keep from getting whacked.

"The way you juxtapose the despair of the villagers with the unrelenting possibility of hope is gorgeous. Your story shares DNA with Deidre LaRochelle and her *Chieftain's Son* series."

"*Traipse* isn't a romance."

I must present like a shock victim because Bobby speaks with slow and succinct phrasing. "It is a love story. The passion those parents feel for their sick child and the bargain they make with the Otherworld... grand stuff."

His energetic dance calms. "And my dear Miss Bettencourt, *The Chieftain's Son* series is so much more than a romance. It's got historical gravitas and a timeless message." He runs a finger across his chin. "As does *Traipse of Moonlight*."

I rub my hands together, shoring up courage to reject Bobby a second time. His offer is nuts. I barely survived converting *Traipse* from a novella to a novel.

Bobby knocks on the roof of the golf cart. "I don't invite people lightly to be on my creative team, Gillian. Your story has stuck with me. I see raw talent in you. Talent to be cultivated."

"My novella version of *Traipse* is likely a one hit wonder."

He points at me. "How will you ever know if you don't take a shot?"

My damp hands slip off the steering wheel. "I'm not good enough for something this huge."

"'Not good enough,' says the woman whose prose about trekking in flagstone jackets raises Lawson Graham stock prices."

"I'm good at the short game." Treat's words feel sour on my lips. "I'm not a fool, Bobby. I know writing for your show is a once-in-a-lifetime offer. It's just one that would be a better fit for someone else."

Bobby dismisses my embarrassment with a flick of his wrist. "I disagree."

I can't deny the rush I get from this guy addressing me as a writer. My pilot light to become a novelist sputtered out shortly after *Traipse* fell flat and I landed the blurb writing gig at Lawson Graham Premier Sportswear. Bobby's offer makes my light spark for a moment but then die. Except for witty descriptors, my writing muscles have atrophied, and I know zilch about screenwriting.

My mind flashes on the trio of manuscripts I wrote in grad school hiding on my hard drive. The stories I never raised enough courage to even show my agent.

"What can I say to make you reconsider, Gillian?"

I fidget instead of answering.

Bobby leans in closer. "I dare you."

I slide away. "I don't know the first thing about writing a screenplay...teleplay? See, I don't even know what to call it."

"No one knows how to write one until they do it. We'll teach you. My writing staff is as generous as they are talented, and I'm betting you're a fast learner."

I can only imagine how big of a thorn a green writer with no experience would be in the side of a staff trying to condense a twelve-hundred-page novel into thirteen episodes. I'd resent the hell out of me. I'm not eager to flaunt any more insecurity, so I go with the practical argument. "You shoot in Ireland. I live in L.A. Bit of a commute."

He shakes his head. "You're a hard ass, aren't you? I'm used to people begging to get a foot in the door of *The Chieftain's Son*. We're on the brink of a five-season pick up, and I've no doubt we'll add five more to that, a season per novel. What's not to love?"

"The offer is flattering, but I just don't see myself joining a television writing staff. Too intimidating. I'm sorry."

A muscle on Bobby's jaw twitches, and his fingers tap the dash of the golf cart. The hummingbird perks up. "What if I find a way to ease you more slowly into the picture?"

I nearly take the bait but stop myself so I don't give the impression of false interest. I need to veer away from this subject and resuscitate the Lawson Graham Premier Sportswear agenda.

"Continuing our trend of full disclosure, what will it take for you to agree to Lanie Blesch over your leading lady as the spokesmodel for our line?" I ask.

Bobby's eyes narrow at my skittish change of subject. The way he appears to be reading me like a cheap novel is disconcerting. I fully expect him to reject my new choice of topic and launch back into his campaign to unhinge my life.

"My green Irish hillocks are ripe for the picking if Mr. Graham signs my star, Niks Tellefson, as spokesmodel."

Relief softens my stone-hard muscles. The elephant has been evicted from our cart as we shift back into conversation that doesn't force me to take stock of my existence.

The corner of his lip sneaks up and his pupils flare. "Hmm? Then again, Mr. Graham wants my land, and I want his writer. Dare I say there may be a bargain in the making?"

And Jumbo plonks back onto the seat between us. I sputter like a kitchen faucet coming back on after the water's been turned off. Treat will have an apoplexy if my repeat rejection of Bobby's job offer gets in the way of his plans for the Ireland shoot.

Someone hollers behind us, and I realize we're stalling the tournament. I hit the gas to drive the cart up to where my ball landed. "That's not where I was going with the conversation," I say as I hop out and grab my six iron. "You know that one has nothing to do with the other."

Bobby chuckles. "I didn't get where I am without testing every available angle."

Every available angle to bait me again. His business with Treat and his job offer to me exist on two entirely different planes. There's no leverage crossover between them, and Bobby Provost will not bamboozle me into thinking there is.

As I line up my shot, I notice Lanie and Treat are nowhere in sight. *They must already be on the green. Damn, how long were Bobby and I yakking?* I'm equal parts flattered by his kind words and jittery from his pressure. A golfer's worse enemy, distraction, clutches the back of my neck, and I slice my shot into the trees.

"Damn it."

It takes my entire reserve of self-control not to stomp back to the cart or snap my club in two. That was my worst shot of the year.

Bobby leans with his back against the cart. "So, you are human."

"Tragically human." I pick out a few clubs. "I'll go find my ball and meet you on the green."

He tugs at the sleeve of my newly acquired *Chieftain's Son* jersey. "New deal. If I can't convince you to join my team, which I'm not giving up on yet, how about this? I'll agree to let Treat Graham use *The Chieftain's Son* property for his shoot and go one more round with him over the spokesmodel stand-off, if"—he holds up a finger—"you join *The Chieftain's Son* foursome in our charity golf tournament at the end of the month."

"Which course?"

"Gal Tré in Kerry."

I stumble on the cart path. "As in Ireland?"

Bobby nods. "Expenses paid by the network. It's a good cause."

I should say yes. The showdown for the Irish Country Lass model will be over by then, and I can settle back into my clandestine but adoring relationship with Treat.

The thought of putting the Atlantic between Treat and me feels perilous. The shattered goblets in my stomach tinkle a warning, but I shake it off. A night in my apartment in front of the fireplace with Treat and a bottle of wine will wash away this rising sense of doom. He cozies up to women for business, but at the end of the day, it's my bed he's in. Or *was* in. It's been over two months since he's been in town long enough to spend couple time with me, our longest separation so far.

Unwelcome thoughts percolate in my head. What scares me the most? Treat not showing up at my door or seeing his face next to me on the pillow while I continue to invest in a relationship that only goes in circles?

"You're sweet, Bobby, but this is a crazy time for me with looming Irish Country Lass deadlines. I can't get away." With what I intend as a kindly wave, I head into the trees to find my errant golf ball. It sits on a tidy patch of grass between two sycamores in a direct line to the green. I may pull off a decent score on this hole in spite of my godawful slice. As I address the ball, a familiar giggle fouls the air to my right. Shadows dominate this makeshift forest but don't obscure everything. As I turn toward the sound, golf becomes the least of my problems.

Shafts of sunlight filter through the trees to feature Treat pressing Lanie against a nearby trunk. His hands twist her hair in a way I know all too well. My boyfriend's lips devour Lanie's mouth, neck, and single exposed breast. Treat's hand travels down her ribcage, over a hip to disappear under a Lawson Graham Premier Sportswear golf skirt. The two rock and slide together in a rhythm that fills me with the chilling certainty that this isn't their first encounter.

When she hooks her leg around his hip, I bite back a scream. To make the nightmare vanish, I whip around, execute a violent backswing, and strike my ball with gale force intensity.

Frantic commotion explodes from the green. I lift my head in time to see Bobby Provost, showrunner of *The Chieftain's Son*, crumple onto the grass.

CHAPTER
TWO

In my fantasies, an entire boy band or Hemingway were the men sharing my teenage bed. It was never a slightly scrawny hummingbird of a guy. A hummingbird whose wings I clipped with a crazed golf shot.

They'd only release Bobby from the hospital to people who would wake him up every hour for the next twelve. I figured the best place for a concussed showrunner is my parent's place. There, I'd have backup for waking Bobby throughout the night. Most of all, I needed my mom. As soon as Bobby was snoozing under no less than three quilts, all lifted from television shows my parents designed the sets for, I unraveled in her arms.

The hallway light is burned out, so my mother and I stand in the dark outside my bedroom. The odd thing is my tears are akin to mourning the loss of a death you knew was coming, not the kind where you get an unexpected, tragic phone call. How long have I been subconsciously preparing myself for the demise of Treat and Gilly?

Mom squeezes me tighter. The advantage of having a chubby mother is the ability to bury your woes against a squishy, comforting shoulder.

She holds me at arm's length. "Sweetheart, if it's any consolation, I do believe Treat loved you as much as a spoiled princeling can love anyone besides themselves."

"No more bashing."

"I'm sorry, but I'm not going to pretend it doesn't irk me you invested over two years in that man while he insisted on a secrecy manifesto."

I rip fresh tissues from the box in her hand. "But—"

She raises a hand to shush me. "I'll stop bashing if you refrain from excusing him."

My standard defense for Treat's lack of commitment bubbles up then fizzles. I feel more duped than dumped, but if I paint him as the devil, I'm an even bigger loser for sticking with him all this time.

"*Hush-hush doesn't mean it isn't real.*" Treat sang that song every time I fretted over our secret. And I believed him. I accepted his cadre of reasons our relationship had to fly under the radar as logic.

Mom straightens the collar of my golf shirt. "Now buck up, honey. It's almost time to wake Bobby again." She sets the tissue box on a table in the hall. "I'm going to go make our guest some soup."

"Soup for a concussion?"

"Soup for anything." She sweeps down the hall, leaving me to reset.

Mom never liked Treat, but until tonight, she tolerated my obviously misplaced loyalty to a man who adores instead of loves me. After unleashing her pent-up dislike for him, she promised we'd eat caramel truffle ice cream straight out of the carton.

On the other side of my bedroom door, my responsibility gently snores. I slip into the room. Bobby doesn't move. He's curled onto his side with a hand by his mouth. I'll bet he sucked his thumb as a kid.

I gently shake his shoulder and whisper. "Bobby?" He's not waking up. *Oh, God. What if his brain is swelling or some other cranial malfunction?* I've damaged the showrunner of the most anticipated television show in a decade. Fans will kill me.

"More oomph, Gillian," says my mom, barging into the room. "Wake it up there, Bob."

Bobby's eyes open and widen like Mom and I are oncoming headlights, but then he settles into a moan.

I offer a couple of capsules on my open palm. "For what ails you."

He wiggles into a sitting position. "I'm trapped in a coven of merciless women. A man needs his sleep."

Mom clicks her tongue. "After near murder by golf, that's off the table. Do you prefer chicken noodle or Italian wedding soup?"

I want to drop my head into my hands at this blatant reminder of the disaster my rage-fueled golf shot created. "If you're a good patient, I'll let you sleep an hour and half before I wake your concussion next time."

Bobby assesses my red face. "Don't cry, golf buddy. I promise not to sue."

I turn and blot my eyes with a crumpled tissue.

"Tell me, Amethyst," says Bobby to my mom while he pops pills and chases them with half a bottle of water. "How many of Gillian's golf kills have you buried in the backyard?"

Mom smiles. "Is Forensic Files on your IMDB or are you just a fan?"

Bobby points a finger at her. "It's always the husband." He and Mom share a laugh as Bobby eases back onto the mound of pillows.

Mom drags the white toll painted desk chair she made for my eleventh birthday next to the bed. "Are you up for a little *Chieftain's Son* dishing?"

"God, Mom. Let the man concuss in peace."

She leans closer to Bobby. "I won't spill any classified information. I've worked in television long enough to sign a trail of NDAs. I can be trusted. This is personal curiosity. Is that Jack O'Leary doing justice to the role of Donal Cam? I've never heard of the guy."

Bobby rubs his temple.

I stand and crook my arm through my mom's. "I'm sorry, Bobby. I'll escort the crazy woman off the ward."

He holds up a hand to stop me. "No, it's fine. Talking about the show will bring me back from the brink of death." He gestures downward with his hand. "Maybe at a slightly lower volume."

Mom gives me a triumphant waggle of her head and leans back in the chair. "So, Jack O'Leary—discuss. Is he worthy to bring Deidre LaRochelle's heartthrob off the page?"

"Throngs of women following him everywhere say yes." Bobby

shakes his head. "Poor guy can't sneak out to buy toothpaste without inciting a fan tsunami."

My mom clucks. "So, he's pretty. Can he act?"

"Jack's been a fixture on the Dublin stage for a few years now." He snaps his fingers. "Have you ever caught *Randy in 6B* on BBC? He's the fitness obsessed neighbor."

"Nope."

Bobby raises his eyebrows to me. "Are you a Randy fan?"

This actor who may be facing gum disease due to popularity piques my curiosity. "I've never seen it."

"Jack was pretty damn hilarious. He pulls off an A-game airhead."

Bobby starts to wilt.

"Okay, Duffer, back to the land of nod. Just don't go in too far past the border." I shoo Mom toward the door and call over my shoulder to the man in my bed. "See you in an hour."

"And a half," he says.

I chuckle. "And a half." I would have enjoyed a big brother like him.

"Maybe by that time, Amethyst will have convinced you to join the *Chieftain's Son* team."

An annoying big brother.

I close my eyes for a long beat. When I open them, Mom gives me the single eyebrow raise. Bobby has a shit-eating grin on his face. Double-teamed. I face my mother. "Bobby wants me to golf with some *Chieftain's Son* folks in a golf tournament."

He shakes a finger at me. "I see you're as wily as you are stubborn." Bobby turns doe eyes on my mother. "Did Gillian tell you *Traipse of Moonlight* has been a major tonal inspiration for my show's vision?"

Mom shoots me a glance. "No, she did not."

"So, I suppose she also neglected to mention my offer for her to join the writing staff of the show."

"Holy mother of God," squeaks my mom. "You said yes."

"No, she did not," says Bobby, parroting my mother.

Mom's eyes widen.

"The offer is way out of my league," I mutter, caught like a rat in a trap with no juicy chunk of cheese for consolation.

Mom holds up a finger and disappears.

Bobby's gloating turns to chagrin. "You're never going to wake me again, are you? I'm about to be set adrift in concussion limbo forever."

"Siccing my mother on me is not playing fair."

"I suck at golf etiquette too."

I drop into the chair. "It's crazy flattering my story meshes with your show—"

Bobby lays the back of his hand on his forehead. "As my dying wish, don't turn me down again. Come to Ireland. Play in the charity tournament. I'll give you a tour of *The Chieftain's Son* complex in Kerry. It's 'pretty brilliant', as the locals say. We'll take your picture next to the board in the writer's room where we proudly display our staff copy of *Traipse of Moonlight,* and you'll see why you belong with us."

A book comes sailing through the doorway and lands on the foot of the bed. *The Chieftain's Son.*

"A little something to kill time between wake ups," says Mom, baring teeth in her wiliest grin.

Bobby throws her a thumbs up. She bows and leaves us alone.

"You do sort of owe me after…" Bobby points to the bruised bump on his temple. God, if my ball had hit a few inches to the right, he'd be the late showrunner of *The Chieftain's Son.*

I drop my head back to stare at my lavender ceiling. The color is supposed to be calming. It ain't working. A concoction of pissed off and regret slosh inside me. Part of me wants to confront Treat, another says never look back. Saying yes to Bobby is running *to* something instead of just running away from the man who crossed the line from wooing a client to being a cheating bastard. God, this is such a leap.

"Nap time." I reach over and turn off the bedside lamp without answering him.

Bobby's eyes close before he sinks all the way into the pillows.

I retrieve *The Chieftain's Son* from the bed and run a thumb over the well-worn cover. I've read this book a dozen times. Inside the front cover, an illustration of a powerfully built blond fellow in a tunic and other assorted draped fabrics stares at me. Donal Cam stands beside a snow white horse. The man's cheekbones alone are the stuff of dreams.

This Jack O'Leary fellow has a lot to live up to. Atop the steed sits an ethereal beauty in a long green dress with a fur collar. There's something about the way they look at each other than flattens what's left of my heart. That look says love, not adore.

Is Treat even thinking about me? Is he with her tonight? A sob busts out with such force I slap a hand over my mouth and shoot a glance at Bobby. He's out cold. It's twisted, but I'm grateful for his concussion. Taking care of this friendly stranger gives me purpose, at least for one night. Tomorrow is not something I'm looking forward to. After witnessing Treat's lusty slobbering over Lanie, how am I going to walk into the offices of Lawson Graham Premier Sportswear and pretend nothing has changed?

I hope knocking back *The Chieftain's Son* will be a distraction. I set a phone alarm for ninety minutes, as promised. A niggle of self-satisfaction that the showrunner of this phenom personally asked me to join the team stokes a small flicker of adrenaline inside me. What if I did say yes? Bobby knows how inexperienced I am. It's not as if I'm misrepresenting myself. Am I up to the challenge? Fear mixes with the adrenaline, and I feel wobbly. Kicking off my shoes, I snuggle into my favorite armchair.

The Chieftain's Son, Book One, by Deidre LaRochelle

Time and love are the strongest forces a human heart must endure.

A tear sneaks all the way to my chin. *You got that right, sister.*

"Color coded Post-its. I'd expect no less."

Bobby's voice snaps me out of a doze. "Technically, they're Post-it flags." I rub my eyes to pull myself through the threshold of sleep. "Hey, you woke up on your own."

Stripes of morning sun wash the stubble on his face into a walnut sheen with a few hints of gray. Treat's beard is as black as coal. Harsh and prickly.

"I may survive yet." He swings his legs, clad in my father's sweat pants, off the side of the bed and stretches each arm across his chest.

He wobbles and gingerly probes the impact zone on his temple.

"Slow and easy there." *The Chieftain's Son* plops onto the carpet near Bobby's foot when I reach out to steady him.

He retrieves it. With his thumbnail, he fans the line of Post-it flags sticking out of the pages.

Waves of shyness and embarrassment collide in a cross current as my cheeks heat up. "I had to do something to occupy myself while I made sure you didn't go to the great golf course in the sky." I shrug. "Text analysis is my drug of choice."

His lips curl into a *caught you* smile as he thumps the cover. "Will you share your system, or must I crack the color code unassisted?"

"You'll laugh. I'm over-the-top systematic."

"I didn't get where I am without reveling in the glory of systems."

I indulge in a moment of envisioning Bobby as my mentor.

I take the book from him. "Green is everything that makes Donal Cam tick, motivations, quirks, his big want—the usual nuggets." I open a page wearing a purple flag. "Purple is the love interest because green and purple are complementary colors."

A crease etches a path across Bobby's forehead. "No, red and green are complementary. Thus, the harmonious décor of Christmastime."

"Not on the color wheel of light. And in the world of romance, isn't love all about the light?"

Bobby studies me.

"Red for the main plot points. And I twist them"—I point to one of the crumbled red flags—"when there's a plot twist or a red herring." I stick four fingers into the book, dividing it into five sections. "*Sign Here* arrows for act breaks. Five, not three. Three is too watered down. It doesn't give enough traction to story shifts."

Bobby sets his hands on the edge of the mattress and leans closer, studying my face. "I forbid my staff to write in anything but five act structure. Shakespeare was on to something." He jerks his chin at the book. "You organized the whole book in one night?"

I nod at the clock. "I'm quite familiar with the material, and you've been in and out for twelve hours."

"And?"

"And what?"

"Have you fallen in love with Donal Cam all over again?"

I toss the book on the bed. "Maybe, even though he's a teeny bit too good to be true."

He leans back, hands behind his head. "It seems a shame to waste twelve hours analyzing the hell out of a story and do nothing with all that brainwork."

If he only knew the real work going on in my brain. As each hour ticked by, I had to face the fact that the life I've settled for has been blown to bits. A life that slowly broke my heart.

I check in with the mauve carpet to gather my nerves then meet Bobby's targeted gaze. "When you said, 'ease me into the picture,' what exactly did you mean?"

The grin on his face is hard not to answer with one of my own. "Holy shit, Miss Bettencourt, has the tide turned?"

New layers I hadn't noticed earlier under his easy-going, nice guy attitude show themselves in Bobby Provost's expression. He's waiting me out. Calculating the penultimate chess move in his game.

Once, when my Dad was fried after art directing six seasons of a grueling crime drama, he'd said to me, *"Gillian, every director is part Doberman, and every showrunner is a gambler. One bites, and the other never completely shows his hand."*

What the hell do I have to lose by saying yes? Bobby's dangling a shot for me to make art through storytelling instead of selling clothing. "Why did it take seventeen holes for you to revisit your job offer to me?"

I see the all business, showrunner side of Bobby come online. "Since you turned down a meeting with me, I never got the chance to read *you*, just the work. Gillian Bettencourt might have been a bubble-headed wannabe novelist who thinks she's this century's Jane Austen. Yes, *Traipse of Moonlight* is something unique and original, but a roomful of monkeys with typewriters may accidentally write Macbeth. If you turned out to be a zero, I'd have assumed you stole the story from your agoraphobic college roommate. In which case, I never would have repeated the offer."

When Bobby stands, the rigidity of his posture borders on imposing.

"I don't play fast and loose with my show or the people I allow to work with me. I'm potentially investing a decade of my life and my livelihood into *The Chieftain's Son*. It will not be less than exquisite. Before I opened the gate of my kingdom even a crack, I had to get a valid sense of who you are."

Am I flattered to have passed Bobby's test or insulted he thought I had potential to be a bubbleheaded, Shakespeare-typing monkey?

"Look, Bobby. I don't know the form. I have no experience telling a visual story. That's what I was trying to do last night with the breakdown. See if I could imagine lifting *The Chieftain's Son's* words from the page and turn them into a movie in my head."

"And?"

I look away from the eagerness in his eyes to the glare bouncing off the window. "I liked it."

He retrieves *The Chieftain's Son* from the quilt and plops it back into my hand. "I've been where you are, Gillian—at the beginning. It's scary." Bobby chews on his lip. "As far as easing you into the picture, does the title of Assistant to the Writers sound less intimidating? I'm offering you the chance to take this season to learn the form, the process, the new way of storytelling, and apply your talent. The ball is on your tee, Gillian Bettencourt."

I nod to Bobby, and using *The Chieftain's Son* as my club, I swing.

CHAPTER
THREE

wo hours on Irish soil, and I understand why Deidre LaRochelle set the ten books of her *Chieftain's Son* series here. The beauty is addicting. The people personify charm. Everyone I've met, from the taxi driver to tournament folks, bubble with warmth and humor.

Gal Tré Golf Course surpasses the most luscious places I've ever played. Grass appears to have been replaced with emerald velvet. The rise and fall of the hills echo the waves cresting below the cliffs. Greens and fairways flow into one another with the grace of clouds lightly blown by the wind. The Atlantic itself shushes and hums as a backing track.

I saw Bobby briefly before I was whisked in a golf cart to the eleventh hole where our foursome will start the tournament. My coffee and I are first to the tee. I didn't get to play the course before today because I had to finish the descriptors for the entire Irish Country Lass line for Lawson Graham Premier Sportswear before I left L.A. I'm operating on maybe four hours sleep since I've yet to master the art of snoozing on planes.

I pat my cheeks. "Wake up, Gilly."

Wind off the Atlantic packs a bite, so I slip on a jacket. With my trusty seven iron, I begin a regime of stretches.

Across the tee box, movement catches my eye. A man large enough to snap Treat in half wheels his golf bag on a pushcart up the small rise. He's wearing a baseball cap with *The Chieftain's Son* logo embroidered on the front. I should probably dig mine out to represent.

What department did Bobby recruit this guy from? The man's build screams scene shop, possibly electrics. I can easily picture him climbing a ladder with a monster stage light in each hand.

When my teammate swivels to position his cart at the edge of the tee box, the back of his cap comes into view. It rides too high on his head, forcing the brim down at a steep angle. A bound lump of straw-colored hair bulges out of the opening in the back of the cap.

"Man bun alert," I whisper low enough so the wind doesn't carry my voice.

Treat gave that particular look a go last year. Godawful. His coiffure read more barista-in-training than senior manager of an international sportswear company. My fingers were sticky for days from the copious amounts of hair spray and gel it took to keep Treat's saggy sack of hair on trend.

"Chieftain's Son!" booms a voice from behind me. Bobby fist pumps and kicks a leg out the side of the golf cart he's driving like a maniac up the path. A man I'd peg to be around my dad's age with a dour face and iron gray hair rides beside him.

Bobby leaps from the cart, leaving his passenger to slide across the seat in order to hit the brake. He sprints over and crushes me in a hug. "Here's our birdie queen."

The goofy hummingbird I met in L.A. sheds the all-business, executive producer skin he wore back at the clubhouse.

"Come meet Doolin."

A closer look reveals Doolin as a nice-looking man who wears golf clothes well on a slender physique. He offers a hand. "Doolin Byrne. You're very welcome here to our team. Rumor has it you'll be putting Bobby to shame." I love Doolin's Irish accent. Bobby should trade his California sound for Oirish.

Bobby rubs his right temple. "Stay away from her drives, and you'll survive the round." He nods at Man Bun, who turns his back to us. Our silent teammate arranges the clubs in his bag on the pushcart. "You've met J, I see."

"Actually, no."

Jay selects a club and takes a few practice swings, still not facing us. He's wearing jeans and a *Chieftain's Son* logo baseball jersey. Someone thinks appropriate golf dress code does not apply to him.

"Already in the zone, I see," says Bobby. "J is into this book called *The Inner Game of Golf*. It's some type of Zen in your core approach to the game." A phone alarm buzzes in Bobby's pocket. "And we're off."

Jay tees up a day-glow yellow ball, steps back, and points his club toward the fairway. Without a glance in our direction, he addresses the ball and executes a tee shot with hesitation and a hitch at the top of his backswing that sets my teeth on edge. The sheer power behind his motion launches the ball high in the air and, lucky for the Zen master, centers it nicely on the fairway.

Only then does he look at us. "Morning," he says with a wave. The tilt of his cap brim shadows his face. I catch a glimpse of a strong chin with a cleft in the middle. Instead of coming over, he wheels his pushcart to the path and stands apart.

Something about his brush-off behavior harkens back to Treat. Despite my disgust with his Lanie cheat, I felt two years of investment in him called for discussion about my relocation to Ireland. How much would it even affect Treat if I vanished from Lawson Graham Premier Sportswear?

Said conversation died on the vine. Since the L.A. tournament, my so-called "boyfriend" has been nothing more than an out-of-office reply on email with two exceptions. First, a bouquet of tulips appeared on my doorstep with a note.

G-

Kudos on being my wingman for the Irish Country Lass shoot.

No signature. Did Treat think the florist was in fact a P.I. charged to fly back to Lawson Graham with the scandalous reveal the boss's son sent his fashion copywriter flowers?

The only other contact was a brief text volley where Treat explained he was off with Papa Lawson to court fall retail placements for the Irish Country Lad and Lass sportswear lines. I mentioned the renewal of Bobby's offer to me, to which Treat replied, *"Some guys need to hear no twice. You're right where you belong."*

Where I belong. Where Treat wants me to stay because it suits *his* needs, not mine.

It was in that moment I realized how low my supply of trust in Treat had already waned. Watching him slam Lanie Blesch against a tree felt more like confirmation than shock. No doubt he's off with his dad, but my gut tells me Lanie is also in the mix. I'm dying to casually work the spokesmodel question into a conversation with Bobby. How many levels of petty have I sunk to by hoping Lanie lost the gig?

"Ladies first," says Doolin, fanning his arm across the tee.

I tee up and send my ball soaring through a cornflower blue sky.

Behind me, Doolin lets out a long, slow whistle. "So, Bobby wasn't blowing sunshine up our asses. That's one grand shot."

Bobby applauds. "Wait 'til you see her putt. Poetry, my friend."

Doolin says something in Irish and gives me a broad grin. "Yep. You're very welcome here."

I glance over at Jay, but he's already making his way up the path toward his ball. For nine holes, he plays his solitary Zen game. It drives me crazy that Jay putts out before Doolin, Bobby, and I join him on the green. For those same nine holes, Bobby stays in the cart with Doolin, so I don't get the chance to quiz him for details about my new job. All he's tasked me to do so far is work on my relocation to Ireland and "reread the hell" out of *The Chieftain's Son* books one and two. I will be buying stock in Post-it flags.

I call out my score to Doolin. "Five on that hole."

As I reread the hell out of book one, I played around with dividing it into episodes as a writing exercise. I'm damn proud of the way my breakdown honored the romantic heart of the piece without sacrificing the wealth of history. My imagined episodes build enough tension to make an audience dig their fingernails into the palms of their hands. I feel I've uncovered the connective tissue of *The Chieftain's Son*, but

Bobby's right about my lack of screenwriting knowledge. I could have missed some essential strokes to tell the visual story. I'm dying of curiosity to see how Bobby and his staff broke down the book. Is it close to what I did? If my take on chopping up the story is even in the same zip code of what the staff is doing, this rising fear of being out of my league might ebb a smidge.

When we finish our tenth hole, I point to the retreating figure of our elusive teammate. "How do we know Secret Agent Jay is being honest with his score?"

Doolin and Bobby let loose twin explosive laughs.

Doolin lays a fatherly arm over my shoulders and flicks a finger in Jay's direction. "You're looking at the most honest man in Ireland. That one there's got integrity tattooed on his bum."

I smile at Doolin. "Just no people skills?"

We catch up to Jay two holes later. In an unspoken pact, we give him exclusive rights to the tee box. He begins his requisite three practice swings. *Oh, God.* That backswing, that hitch at the top. What the man could accomplish if he'd just add fluidity to his swing.

At the apex of his third backswing, I knock my head against the steering wheel of the cart and groan. "I can't watch anymore."

Bobby, who's selecting a club from his bag saunters over to me. "What?"

I turn my back on the tee. "Jay's backswing. He's got this funky hitch at the top that totally kills his momentum. If he wasn't all muscle, his ball wouldn't get any distance."

"That so?"

The voice behind me is not Doolin. *Oh, crap.* Jay heard me. Slowly, I turn toward him. He's so tall he bends quite a ways to peer into the golf cart. I get an extreme close-up of the muscles bulging under his baseball jersey. His build isn't gross like weightlifters in TV competitions. Jay's body is solid and formed in a way that would make a sculptor weep with joy to have him as a model. Before my gawking becomes embarrassing, he slides into the seat next to me and pulls off his cap. The hair lump, now free from elastic, cascades in golden waves to his shoulders. Man bun down. Who is this guy? Freakin' Achilles?

"What would you have me do?"

His Irish accent is as lyrical as Doolin's is crusty. The strong chin is just a tease of a man so gorgeous God could have retired after creating this guy. From high, broad cheekbones, his face tapers gracefully down to that dimple. Along his jawline are three identical, tiny moles right in a row. I want to touch them and count one, two, three. Jay's lips are the color of a blush and full enough to be inviting, but not so big as to produce sloppy kisses. I am staring. I want to stare more.

"It's my backswing, is it?"

I bite hard on the inside of my cheek to avoid falling into a trance. "Uh, yeah."

"Care to show me?"

Bobby knocks on the top of the cart. "Zen timer run out, J?"

Jay wags a finger at Bobby. "The new system's shaved six strokes off my last round so far." He knocks a fist to his abdomen. "It's all about the core." He points to the sky. "And connecting to the world 'round you. Put them together, and you lose six strokes."

I have an urge to pound on Jay's abdomen to prove it's as solid as it looks.

"Shall you doctor up my backswing, Gillian?"

Hearing my name spill from Jay's lips jars me. "You know who I am?"

"Yeah. Bobby here hasn't stopped gushing about the new writer since he got back from L.A. Welcome to *The Chieftain's Son* family." Jay takes my hand in his. It's big and so warm I feel heat through my golf glove.

Bobby smacks the top of the cart. "We'll all celebrate Gillian over a pint after the round."

Doolin hollers from the tee box. "Will you break up your chat fest and tee off, for the love of Saint Michael? It's getting too cold for my bones out here."

Jay pops out of the cart. "I'm at your mercy, Gillian."

My brain snaps into teacher mode. I've coached a dozen high school kids straight into golf scholarships. This is no different, as long as I can stop staring at eyes that match the blue of the Atlantic so perfectly the sea and the man are reflections of one another.

I step up to the tee with a seven iron. "Now watch. Here's what *you* do." I pull off an exaggerated version of his hitchy swing.

He cocks his head to one side. "Well, that was far from lovely."

"See, because you have that weird pause and wobble at the top of your backswing, you lose momentum. It's power you rely on to finish the job. Let it all flow together, the power and the swing. Like this." I feel the wind dance through my hair as I sight the exact dimple on the golf ball I plan to hit and blast the sucker toward the green. It hits the edge and rolls a short distance from the hole.

All three men applaud.

I wave a hand at them. "It's only a par three. Don't be too impressed."

"If you write as pretty as you swing, Bobby here might be out of a job," says Doolin, whacking the showrunner on the shoulder.

"Okay, coach," says Jay. His swing is as smooth as a bird lifting into the sky. The ball rides the wind and finds a home inches from mine on the green. Jay's face glows as warm as his hand. "That felt grand."

"You pass," I say and then hold up a finger. "Now, duplicate that swing ten times in a row, and you'll own it."

Instead of walking to the green, he straps his clubs to the back of my cart and hops in. "I never knew I paused like that. God, it was like slicing through butter coming down that time."

"There is nothing like a good swing—the fluidity, the swishing sound, all of it."

He's practically bouncing up and down on the seat. "I owe you a pint. If Bobby doesn't bury you too deep in work, I want you to give me lessons. Smooth up all my rough edges. I'm determined to beat this bitch of a game."

I pull the cart up to the edge of the green. "Jay, haven't you heard? No one ever beats this bitch of a game."

He looks at me for a long moment. Too long. It takes all my willpower not to squirm in my seat. His hair shines saffron in the midday sun. The corners of his lips hitch into a smile. "If anyone could, I have a feeling it might be you, Girl."

Bobby clears his throat next to us. "J, you're farthest out."

Jay grabs his putter. "Will you join me, Gillian? I think our balls are taking a meeting." Sure enough, his day-glow yellow and my white ball wait patiently side by side to finish their foray into the hole. "I'll bet you a second pint that I'm in before you."

"Two pints on your dime. I'm in." I pat the grip of my putter and stride past him. He catches up and we both squat to read the green.

"What are you seeing?" Jay asks.

I laugh. "Oh no. You're not getting a free read off me."

He rises, marks his ball, and steps back. "After you."

I see the door into the hole. The green runs straight and then breaks slight right. I take my stance.

"Are you sure you want to go that way?" says Jay, his breath tickling my ear.

I lay a hand on his shoulder and guide him away from me. Yep, solid as the marble statue he will become in a gallery someday. "Sir, a little courtesy while I'm putting."

"I mean, one of us has played this course a far sight more than the other."

"Jay, let the woman putt," calls Bobby, pulling the flag from the hole.

Jay's moved in again. Heat radiates off him like he's got a barbeque in his pants. "I'm just returning the favor for the brilliant swing correction. You think it's breaking right, but if you squint, you'll see it's up and around, back to the left."

I pretend to ignore his proximity, but the smell of salty air and freshly mowed grass coming off him is more intoxicating than any pint.

"I stand my ground." The blasted ball rolls straight, breaks right, and curves away, coming to rest six inches from the hole.

Jay steps up and taps his ball so it rides the contours of the green straight into the hole. Grinning like a pup getting a belly rub, he yanks my ponytail. "Somebody owes me a pint."

CHAPTER
FOUR

T here are many kinds of drunk. Buzzed, your basic drunk, punch drunk, sloppy drunk, passing out drunk, and a new category I'd like to introduce—fantasy drunk. That's what I am. Hunk rhymes with drunk, and I'm sitting across from a man who qualifies on any scorecard—male or female—as a hunk. Being drunk in a country as friendly and lively as Ireland adds sparkle to the fantasy drunk category. Factor in the tournament win for team *Chieftain's Son* over the local favorite, *Kilkenny Kitchen Blunders,* plus a job that promises to change my life, and you get fantasy drunk.

Jay's hands travel across the table to check in with mine the way they've been doing for the length of time it took us to get to our third pint of Guinness. A tractor company is footing the bill for an open bar at this post-tournament shindig, so Jay and I settle our bets free of charge.

"Treat Graham, what is the man, a cracker? No. I've got it. He's the chocolate and marshmallow sandwich you toast over the campfire."

"A s'more."

Jay pounds the flat of his hand on the table. "Yeah. Treat S'more Graham Cracker."

"The best part is that it isn't even his real name. He swapped Ronald for Treat." I crimp my fingers into air quotes. "Ronald isn't sexy enough."

Jay nods. "Why use your given name when you can sound like dessert?" We laugh so hard I almost knock over my half-drunk pint. "And the bastard has no idea you've left him?"

I raise my glass. "Nope." I take a long drink, then whip my head side to side, searching the pub with a baffled look. "Where's Gilly? Where's the girlfriend I cheat on and adore but don't love? Ireland, you say."

Jay leans across the table to look me eye to eye. "Tell me you realize S'more doesn't deserve official notification you've sent him out to sea. If the bugger was blind to the value of what he had in you, then you walking away without a word is grand." He tucks a strand of hair behind my ear. "And just the right amount of wicked." He shoots me a calculating look. "Be the cat and he the little mousy. Bat him around a bit before you go in for the kill." His grin is as dazzling as the rest of his face.

"And this coming from a man who, according to Doolin, has integrity tattooed on his ass."

Jay's *whoop* is loud, hearty, and full of fun. I can't remember the last time I laughed this easily with a guy. I can't remember the last time I laughed with Treat at all.

"Doolin never lies. Here, do you want to see?" Jay stands, lifting the tail of his jersey to stick his bum in my direction.

I fan my hand at him to sit down. "Maybe later."

He sits, laying those big warm hands over mine. "It's best you've sailed over the wild Atlantic. Never look back."

Jay is someone a girl could melt into. My hands turn to soft clay under his. "I do enjoy the concept of Gilly the Wicked," I say, fascinated by the way his blue eyes turn slate gray in low light.

"Gilly? You don't call yourself Jilly for Gillian?" Jay runs a finger across my knuckles, igniting a series of electric shocks that travel up my arm, down my body, and land in the place where tingles get you in trouble.

"Blame my dad. It's a mash up of silly girl. I'm his silly girl. Always have been. My daddy's Gilly."

Bobby sidles up to our table when his PR rounds with the charity reps finish. "Keep her trapped here in a dark corner until she agrees to join us for more than a season." He's none too steady on his feet.

Pressure punches through my fantasy drunk and builds in my chest. "I call foul. That doesn't jive with the 'easing me in' you promised." *Wait*. Has Jay been appointed to sweet talk me into extending my trial run before I've dipped a toe?

Jay pulls a chair over and sits Bobby down on it. They both stare at me. My fuzzy brain drinks in the anticipation on their faces. These two super nice men are inviting me to play on their big-league team. It is a refreshing change to be the prettiest girl at the party for once instead of someone's dirty little secret.

Oh, Treat. Why'd you have to grope Lanie Blesch in the woods? Why couldn't you be okay with everyone knowing we are together? *Were* together. I haven't used past tense out loud yet. My trigger finger itches to send a definitive "We're done" text to Treat. Not exactly the high road.

Bobby takes my hand in both of his. "Face it, Gillian. I read that episode breakdown you shared with me, and here are my notes. You belong with us on a show where thousands of women want to claim the treasure beneath the leading man's tunic."

"Whoa, Bob," says Jay, extracting my hand from Bobby's. "We've got a lady here."

"I'm just quoting what Deidre says about Donal Cam, the Chieftain's son, loyal lover and all-around great guy." He sits back in the chair. "My apology, Gillian. I didn't mean to be crass."

I pat his hand. "I'll give you one pass since I coldcocked you with a golf ball, but next time, I blow the sexual harassment whistle."

Bobby bows. "Most gracious of you. Apologies if I crossed a line. Now seriously, your instincts about the show are dead, dead, dead on." He knocks on the table three times. "I knew you and Deidre LaRochelle were connected on some cosmic level. Holy God, the way you morphed the characters of Mac and Mary into one. Never occurred to me, but it completely solves the snafu we're heading into." His voice rises in volume and draws attention to our cozy little table.

A buzz of self-satisfaction swirls through the Guinness in my veins. "I'm glad it passed muster."

Bobby clamps a hand on my shoulder. "I'm rarely wrong about people. Fair warning, I will campaign to keep you."

"Before I've written a single word for you?"

My new boss pairs a slightly off-target finger point with a drunken, lopsided smirk. "Wondrous magic weaves through family that surpasses even the machinations of gods..."

This is the first time anyone has quoted words I've written back to me. Like the Grinch when he hears the Whos down in Whoville singing their Christmas song despite his chicanery, my heart grows three sizes.

Jay's smile is as warm as Bobby's is sly when he picks up where Bobby left off. "And spills a traipse of moonlight across the crests of a blackened sea." He threads his fingers through mine and squeezes. "Grand stuff, your words."

My eyes lock on our joined hands while I soak in the compliments. It's been so long since anyone has praised my writing. Any confidence I had in the quality of my original work is long buried under the pyramid of rejections after my agent, Jen, tried to sell my story. The kindness of these two sweet souls spills a few drops of moonlight across my own personal blackened sea. "I'm barely off the plane. A girl needs to acclimate."

"You've got your golf clubs," says Jay with a wink. He catches Bobby staring at our joined hands and pulls his free from mine. "What more acclimating do you need?"

My fingers are immediately lonely for his. I shake off the feeling. He's one of three people I know in Ireland. I don't want my drunken attraction to mess with these new friendships. "A place to live, for one. I don't even know where to begin looking."

Bobby waves me off. "Stay as long as you need in the company housing in Waterville near The Clan. On our dime. Problem solved."

"The Clan?" I imagine myself camping in the woods with a hoard of wild, Celtic men.

"It's what we call the studio complex." Jay gives me a sneaky, sideways look. "Keeps things private."

Bobby scoots his chair closer and dons a business persona. "I promised to ease you into the job, but that doesn't mean I'll ease up on tapping into your talent."

It's a whole new reality, this confidence Bobby has in me. My mind flicks back to my cubicle at Lawson Graham. I took a leave. I still have a backup plan if I can't cut this new step in my life. The beautiful thing about a backup is that it allows you to take a risk. My lingering doubts about diving into this world begin to flatten like the thin layer of foam left on my Guinness.

Bobby snatches my nearly empty glass and holds it up to the light. "I've got you locked in for this season, and I'm betting you'll be in for the series."

"Let me guess. You never lose a bet."

Bobby finishes my drink and bangs the glass down. "Exactly."

I grab the edge of the table to keep from swaying in time with the room spinning around my head. Bobby said the show had a five-year pickup to cash in on the blockbuster status of the book series. That would mean staying in Ireland for the better part of the next five years. *Wow.* I will basically be moving to Ireland.

I've always wanted to see Europe. This is a great jumping off point to see Versailles, the Hebrides, and to visit my dad's family in the Azores. The thread holding me to life back home stretches like a loose strand of spider silk in the wind.

Bobby lays a hand on the side of my face. "Gillian, are you still with us?" He doesn't radiate heat the way Jay does.

I pat his hand and lean back. "Just trying to wrap my head around all of this."

"Get wrapping. We have a table read tomorrow morning." Bobby makes a clicking sound and nods his head. "You're on the clock, Gillian Bettencourt." He's up and away so abruptly his chair rocks back on its legs.

I watch him cross the room. "Did I say something wrong? Is he pissed?"

The corner of Jay's mouth rises. "As in drunk or angry?"

"Either."

Jay crosses his arms. "You'll get used to it. Our chieftain can click from pub guy to business in the twitch of a whisker. Bit of a Doberman, that one."

I pull my hair out of the ponytail and twist it into a loose braid to keep busy. The pros and cons I've been weighing since I accepted Bobby's offer flit through my head.

Jay grasps my hand again when I finish my braid. "Will you do mine?" He flaps a hand under the hair flowing across his shoulders.

Thanks to the perks of still being slightly fantasy drunk, running my fingers through that golden hair is an invitation not to be passed up. I walk behind his chair. "One or two?"

"A manly one."

His hair is as silky as it looks. Any tangles relax into straight strands at my touch. I purposefully drag the task out as long as possible.

Jay lets out a soft purr. "Golf isn't all you've got a fine touch with."

I pull one of the elastic bands from my pocket and secure the tail of his braid. "Very manly." My arms ache to wrap around his broad shoulders to feel the power I witnessed on the golf course. I force myself back around the table to my seat.

"Thank you, Gilly." When he stares into my eyes, I see thoughts streaming behind his. "As far as wrapping your head around joining the team for the short or the long of it, I see your subconscious saying 'I'm in,' even if your words haven't caught up."

"I didn't realize the volume of my subconscious was up to full."

His gaze falls to my lips, then he leans in and kisses me so lightly it's barely more than a tickle. A warm, soft, *do that again* variety of tickle.

"Did you just kiss me?"

"Well, if you can't tell, I made a bad job of it."

I touch a fingertip to his mouth. "Let me rephrase. Why did you kiss me?"

Even in the low light of our corner, I see his face pink up. "I have no idea." He captures my finger in that amazingly warm and gentle palm of his. "Please accept my apology for the unprovoked and unappreciated kiss."

I lay my hand over his. "Not unappreciated." Looking deep into his eyes, I feel as if I'm sinking into that dark blue sea that rages around his pupils. "That was the sweetest kiss I've had in a very long time."

He slides his chair around so he's next to me instead of across the table. "Is there anything you want to ask me about the show before you dive in tomorrow?" Jay slings his arm over the back of my chair.

I want to lean into him. Rest my head in the hollow of his shoulder while he strokes my hair. This big, warm, sweet man feels like a haven in the swirling confusion my life has become. I've known him less than a day, but he gives me the sense that if I fell, he'd catch me. Treat never made me feel that way.

I lean on the tabletop, head resting on my hand. "Tell me what you like best about working on *The Chieftain's Son*."

He mirrors my position so our noses almost touch. "The story. I want to believe a love like the one Donal Cam and Nieve share exists. A love time can't destroy no matter how hard it tries. Bobby said you're a fan of the books, am I right?"

"Yes. The characters get to me, especially Donal Cam. I guess I need to believe there's a man, even a fictional one, that sticks to his principles, his truths." It might be the Guinness or Jay's benevolent steadiness, but I feel completely open to him.

"Ya. The bugger's got his flaws to be sure, but goodness drives him. Every book, the man gets thrown into a different time, and his Nieve doesn't know him. Donal Cam's got to be a loyal warrior son to his latest chieftain while he wins her love over and over. It kills me that she never remembers him until he's earned her trust again. And then, as soon as he manages, *poof,* Deidre LaRochelle sends the poor bastard off to serve a new chieftain. Back to square one—his eternal gut punch."

Soul mates. This series is about soul mates. I wanted that with Treat. *Silly girl.* Gilly the silly girl.

Jay is so close his breath warms my face. I bump his nose with mine. "Poor bastard indeed."

I'm just about to move in for another taste of those blush-colored lips when the haze of my fantasy drunk buzz clears. I ease away from him to recoup some sense without completely closing the door to whatever the heck is going on between us. Jet lag and Guinness are not a good pairing for spontaneous decision making. I'm going to be working with this guy. I have the luxury of not cashing in on this attraction immediately as if this were our only night together. "What is it you do on the show?"

He sits straight in his seat, looking at me like I just asked him to buy me a unicorn. Jay recovers, and a sly expression sneaks over his face. "Have a guess."

I study him. I'm amending my initial impression of carpenter or electrician. The man's long locks say artsier type. Maybe he's in set dec or props, possibly a scene painter. After his butterfly kiss, I figure I've been granted permission to touch, so I squeeze his bicep. The muscle flexes beneath my grip. It's not the only part of him I'd like to explore. "Something athletic. Hints please."

Jay leans in conspiratorially. "Bows and arrows, swords, and the occasional mace are involved."

I use our guessing game as an excuse to let my eyes explore his gorgeous bod. *Weapons, huh?* After taking a cursory inventory, I clap my hands. "You're the fight coordinator or a stunt double." What else would this body of an Irish chieftain be doing on a show about Irish chieftains?

Jay slides a hand to the small of my back. "Glad you're coming aboard Gilly, and I'm saying that for purely selfish reasons."

I slide to the edge of my chair. "Which are?"

"I get the chance to know more about this silly girl who can dive into the soul of book like *The Chieftain's Son* and swing a golf club like a madwoman." He trails a gentle fingertip on the skin beneath my lower lashes. "Your eyes are the strangest reddish-brown color I've ever seen. Not quite a rust. Maybe if I study them in sunlight, I can name it."

I lay my head on his shoulder then, to escape the intensity that's building as we stare at one another. As much as I want him to kiss me again, I don't want it to be because Treat isn't kissing me. Jay strikes me as a decent guy—too decent for a rebound romp. Working on the show together will give us a chance to become friends. This evening with him has been great. We both golf. He can be my new Irish friend, Jay. Friends can be a dandy place to start.

"That's the nicest thing any guy has said to me in a very long time. Thank you. By the way, I was beginning to consider the long game with the show even before the eye comment."

"That's grand." He takes my face in those warm and wonderful hands. If I let this follow-up kiss happen, it will be more than a fly by.

"Jack!" A compact woman about my age in a tidy, dark brown suit that matches her hair perfectly sweeps up beside Jay and grabs his arm. Panic brightens her eyes. "Into the snug, now!"

The sensation of being pulled under by a wave when you can't find up or down washes over me as the woman yanks Jay who in turn yanks me, into a small, partitioned space at the end of the bar.

"I'm sorry for this. I told them we'd be in Tralee, not here in Blennerville. Someone in the pub must have tipped them off." The woman peers back into the main room.

I tug at Jay's arm. "What's going on?" He locks like he ate bad clams.

"Reporters, paparazzi, the whole mess," whispers the woman, then she eyes me skeptically. "Who are you?"

Jay's face is bright red. "Meg, this is Gillian, the one Bobby's been on about, the new writer's assistant."

She gives me a sharp nod. "So, you are. Meg McGrath, publicist. Welcome aboard." Her gaze rakes the room. "Here's what we're going to do." She pulls out her phone. "I'm texting Bobby to corral the reporters over for an interview. Jack, you duck behind the bar and out the back door. Patrick's waiting to drive you." She assesses me. "It was dark enough at the table, so I don't think they saw you with Jack, but stay here until Bobby dumps the mob, or they'll crawl all over you." Meg plays her cell like a slot machine. "I'd hate for your first night in town to be a nightmare."

I narrow my eyes at Jay. "Jack?"

He clutches my hands. "I thought you knew. I'm Jack O'Leary. Bobby calls me 'J' for Jack."

Meg shoves Jack, busting us apart. "Okay, go! Go!"

He turns to me just before disappearing behind the bar and mouths, "I'm sorry."

Five seconds later, the press swarms Bobby. Jack O'Leary, star of *The Chieftain's Son*, bolts out the back door with Meg on his heels, leaving me alone in the shadows of the snug.

CHAPTER

FIVE

Momentum is a funny thing. We pretend to have control over it, but that's a wish, not reality. The moment *The Chieftain's Son* entered my life, I became a captive of momentum.

There was never a defining moment when I officially began this new life. It wasn't when I said "yes" to Bobby or that first step off the plane at Shannon Airport. Momentum gobbled me up at some point last night in the pub. Jack—aka Jay or J, per Bobby—introduced me as the new writer to Meg, and she made sure I got to my hotel in Tralee. This morning, Patrick, a production company driver, is bringing me to *The Chieftain's Son* studio complex called The Clan near the town of Waterville.

What I said to Jack last night is true. Tiny seeds of entertaining the possibility of an extended future here lay in my hand. I haven't shown them the Irish soil yet, but they're with me. Those seeds appeared, first one then the rest, as I assigned myself the task of breaking book one of *The Chieftain's Son* series into hypothetical episodes. I did the exercise to prove to myself I may be able to do this. I'm not ready to admit to the seeds, but I will keep them safe. Maybe I should thank Treat for being a cheating asshole and throwing me clear of the car crash that my life with him had become.

Patrick nods out the window. "That way's Waterville, where you'll be staying, but Mr. Provost wants you at The Clan straight away."

I recognize Patrick's name as the driver who rescued Jack from the press last night. "Do you usually drive for Jack O'Leary?"

"Nah. Miss Tellefson's my ongoing concern." He lets out a percussive laugh. "That one'll never take to driving herself. Her assistant, Marisa, isn't fond of our narrow roads."

If I'd been tossing back pints last night with Niks Tellefson—Nieve, the female lead on *The Chieftain's Son*—I wouldn't have mistaken her for anyone else. Her porn satires online are snort laugh hilarious. My personal favorite is *Sloppy Serenade,* where she plays a hooker with a list of clientele she has no desire to sleep with. Disgusting examples of humanity show up to her fluffy, pink boudoir to collect their pleasures. Niks makes them wait while she chows down humungous, four-patty cheeseburgers, sending pickles, tomatoes, and secret sauce spilling all over her would-be lovers. One by one, they stomp out in disgust, which we learn was her diabolical plan all along. It ends with her ordering a pizza and tipping the delivery boy with one of the hundred-dollar bills she collected in advance from her men. Classic.

Patrick slows by a tiny guard shack and rolls down the window.

A ruddy-faced man the size of a pro wrestler sits in front of an electric fireplace playing video games. "Ho, Paddy."

"Ho, Dev. Couldja, send word to Mr. Provost that his girl is here?"

His girl? If Patrick hadn't been witty and wonderful on the drive down and given me a list of all the golf courses I have to play before I go home, the title would rankle me. I don't intend to be anyone's *girl.*

There are no signs marking this nexus of *The Chieftain's Son* universe. On either side of the single-lane road, grasses grow so high I can't see beyond them. The further down the road we go, the more violently butterflies flap in my stomach. I try to tell myself the buzz is only eager anticipation over my new adventure, but that would be a lie.

My nerves are on the verge of shorting out because of Jay. Correction, Jack. Jack O'Leary. I'd like to blame our cozying up to each other last night on the Guinness. Blame it on the high of winning the golf tournament. Blame it on Treat for making me crave what he doesn't give me. Where the fault lies doesn't matter. Last night was fun, but it's a one and done. A decent takeaway from my Treat Graham debacle is to stay out of the shark-infested waters of workplace romance.

If only I hadn't liked Jack so much. He's fun, smart, ridiculously handsome, and damn it, a decent golfer.

The land opens up, sheep as far as the eye can see. Spray-painted sheep. Lines of orange, green, and even pink spread across wooly coats.

"Patrick, who tagged these poor sheep?"

"Ah. The orange are Catholic sheep, the green, Protestant, and the pink, nondenominational." He allows me a few beats of silence, watching me in the mirror before he laughs. "The colors tell you who the beasts belong to."

I answer him with a cheeky look. "Is anyone in this country serious about anything?"

"Only on Tursdays," he says with the characteristic "t" replacing the "th" sound that I'm getting used to. "See over tere." He points to a trio of donkeys gorging themselves on grass. "Those are Doolin's ladies. I hear you golfed a round with the man himself yesterday. He rescued these darlings from a bad situation. Now they follow him around like dogs."

Beyond Doolin's donkeys and the sheep, cows roam the lush fields. As we descend a small rise, a gray warehouse complex appears in front of us. It's at least the length of three football fields.

"Here we are," says Patrick.

The massive collection of nondescript buildings plunked in the middle of a pasture is not how I envisioned The Clan.

Cars are scattered over an expanse of gravel that serves as the parking lot. Bobby Provost bursts out of a set of double glass doors and makes a beeline for the car. He throws his arms around me for the closest thing to a bear hug a hummingbird can pull off.

"You're very welcome here, Gillian Bettencourt," he says. The Irish greeting coming out of his American mouth sounds strange. *When in Rome.* "We've got a little while until the table read. Let me give you the express tour."

I turn to Patrick. "Thank you for the ride and the company."

He tosses me a salute. "I'll take your things into Waterville."

"Great." I almost say "grand." It is easy to slip into local speak.

Bobby drags me into the building.

The lobby is quite a contrast to the Irish country calendar scene outside. The theme is leather and black marble. Behind the reception desk is a massive painting that matches the picture from book one of *The Chieftain's Son* where Donal Cam and Nieve drink each other in as if there is no one in the world but the two of them. I suck in a breath when it registers the novel version of the lovers has been altered to the likenesses of Niks Tellefson and Jack O'Leary. His wild Atlantic eyes blaze with eternal love. The same eyes that danced with mine last night in the dark corner of a Blennerville pub.

Bobby introduces me to Murphy, the guard who is even more imposing than Dev, the gatekeeper. We're buzzed through two sets of double doors into a full-blown sound stage complex. I spent my childhood on sets of the shows my parents art directed, but here, the size, the scale, the authenticity of colors and texture are so magnificent, I've stepped back in time. A great hall with massive fireplaces twice my size and faux stonework so real I can almost hear moss growing in the cracks looms before us.

Off to our left is a set with an enormous bed covered in furs. There must be a hundred candles on ledges, tables, and in every niche. On the wall is an enormous map painted on what looks like tanned animal skin. I walk toward the room, drawn by the naturalism of the environment. I want to touch everything and savor the timelessness.

Bobby puts out a hand to stop me from further investigation. "Hot set. We've still got pickups to shoot in there from episode 106."

I stop dead in my tracks. *Hot set.* The ultimate hands-off order from the art department. Everything in this environment has been captured by the camera. Bump one thing out of place, and the continuity of the scene will be screwed up. My parents' mantra has always been *"Respect the hot set."*

"I promise you can pet the furs later." He waves his hands in the air when I wrinkle my nose. "Prop department fabricated furs. We're completely animal friendly, down to stables filled with the most pampered horses in all of Ireland."

I spin to take in this set and the others that occupy the massive sound stage. "This is breathtaking. Are you sure we weren't buzzed through a time portal?"

Bobby beams. This is his baby, and he's one proud papa. "Everyone in our art department is actually a wizard."

"Definite evidence of magic wand work," I say, holding arms out to the studio.

Bobby scurries behind a row of flats, waving me to catch up. "We're all in-house here. We've got a kick-ass design studio, a shop right off the sound stages, and you should see the costume department. Think Willy Wonka with fabric and jewels."

We leave the sound stages and move down a corridor flanked with glass walls. In one pearly gray and plum-themed office, I see a familiar dark brown bob.

"Hey, that's Meg. I met her last night when she yanked me into the snug."

Meg waves as we pass by.

Bobby's chirpy countenance sours a little. "That was a screw-up extraordinaire."

Next down the row is a classroom of sorts. There's a long table in the middle and a wall of white boards. Doolin writes a sentence on one of the boards in a language that must be Irish.

"Hey, Doolin. Nice donkeys you've got out there in the field."

He adds an accent mark to a word and turns to us. "Morning. I'm sure they'd like to make your acquaintance." He looks over his glasses at me. "I'll be seeing you in here soon, Miss Gillian. You've got a bit of catching up to do."

"Catching up?" I look back and forth between Doolin and Bobby.

"Irish language class," says Bobby. "Everyone takes it—cast, writers, designers, even guest directors. Absorbing the language builds the world, don't you agree?"

"Honors the past," says Doolin, pointing a marker at me. "He'll be putting you on a horse as well. Now go away. I've got work."

A thrill runs through me. Free Irish lessons. How cool is that? With Doolin. If his seriousness on the golf course is any indication, he's got to be quite the task master with his language lessons. I wonder if he raps knuckles for mispronunciation.

"Wait, did Doolin say 'horse'?"

"We're all about immersion, Gillian. My writers ride horses and get some weapons training. We even did an overnight in the woods. I want organic writing. This story needs to be told from the inside out. Feel it. Live it. Write it."

"So, we're all Donal Cam and Nieve?"

"And Chieftain Rory O'Connor, his soldiers, and his people, right down to washer women and cooks."

A wave of something akin to dizziness makes me lay a hand against the wall to steady myself. This isn't a job. I've walked into a world, a universe. Bobby Provost's universe. *Holy crap. I almost killed him with a golf shot.*

"And you've invited me into all of this." Imposter syndrome seeps into my bones. I'm in the land of artisans and experts. What the hell is a girl who writes about the way a raincoat reflects rainbows doing here?

Bobby lays hands on my shoulders. "You were already here. *Traipse of Moonlight* helped build our vision."

God. I hope I can live up to his expectations.

Bobby's phone alarm goes off as we turn a corner. "Table read. Are you ready to meet the family?" he asks.

Up ahead, the music of a dozen conversations chases around the room. The hallway ends at a big glass wall with double doors framed in brushed nickel. On the other side is my future. *This is it.* Once I step through that looking glass, there is no going back. My entire body buzzes.

Bobby propels me forward. We navigate a few cliques, heading deeper into the crowd. Running nearly the length of the room is a table massive enough to host an actual chieftain's post-cattle-raiding banquet. In addition to seats at the table, lines of chairs stretch along side walls. Above them are coats of arms with the names O'Connor, MacMurrough, and O'Suileabhain beneath them. At one end, a huge flat-panel monitor is mounted high on the wall.

Bobby nabs a remote from the table and points it at the screen. "Here we go."

When a trailer for the premier episode of the show blasts onto the monitor, the room goes into suspended animation. That's when I see a familiar profile.

Jack O'Leary.

He sits at the head of the table, hair tied back in a low ponytail, much more period than the man bun he sported yesterday. My stomach drops to my knees when it registers his arm is draped around a stunning beauty with hair so white it looks like frosting. Niks Tellefson. I'm witness to Donal Cam and Nieve snuggling in real time.

The room bursts into applause when the clip ends and the logo for *The Chieftain's Son* blasts onto the screen. More hoots and hollers follow as reviews for the series scroll by. They're amazing, all from top-level entertainment news sources and showbizzy magazines. Deidre LaRochelle's bestseller jumped off the page and hit the stratosphere.

Bobby slaps backs and grins. He raises both arms in victory. "We're a hit!" He's answered with a roar that shakes the glass wall.

I sneak another glance at Jack and Niks. He pulls her in for a peck on the cheek and then they're both swallowed up by others for congratulations. No mistaking how very cozy they are with one another. Beyond cozy...connected, like they are actually a thing.

Why did he kiss me last night? I wanted to believe he was as sweet and genuine as he seemed. *Are you that big an idiot, Gilly?* He's an actor for Heaven's sake—a good one, apparently, judging from the reviews. The man didn't even bother to tell me his real name. To top it off, we were both drunk. If Meg hadn't ridden in on a paparazzi wave, who knows what idiocy that kiss could have led to. I'd better remember to thank her for that someday. Time to tread more carefully in this realm where romance refuses to stay on the page.

"Come with me," says Bobby, dragging me toward the head of the table.

His movement is a signal, and people settle at the table or the chairs along the walls. Scripts open, pencils appear, and laptops spring to life as the table read is about to begin.

"Good morning, everyone. Before we get started, I'd like to introduce you to Gillian Bettencourt."

Jack's head snaps up at the mention of my name.

"Author of *Traipse of Moonlight* and our new writer's assistant."

I'm absolutely floored by the sheer volume of applause. A woman with kinky red hair about halfway down the table starts to pump her fist in the air. "Traipse, Traipse, Traipse!" The room picks up her chant. Everything blurs a smidge as I realize how many of these people have read my manuscript. I give a stupid, little wave.

Bobby pulls out a chair for me. "And if you need any coaching on your golf swing, this is the woman to talk to. Right, J?"

If I don't acknowledge Jack now, it'll be weird. There's a beat before we look at each other. His smile is as warm as the hand I held across the table last night.

"Eight strokes off my last round says yes." He throws me a salute.

Bobby goes on about the killer reception the show is enjoying, giving me an excuse not to look at Jack. Despite my better judgement, I dwell on how fast we connected at the tournament yesterday. My lips savor that single sweet kiss from a man called Jay that ignited an attraction in me I thought I was incapable of feeling after years of a worn-thin relationship with Treat.

"And welcome back to Niks and Jack after the insanity of their promo tour."

Niks assumes a pouty face that makes her look a thousand times more sensual. "Never send me to New York in February again, Bobby."

Her Norwegian accent is a jarring contrast to the Irish lilt I just heard from her in the trailer.

At the head of this table sit a pair of gorgeous human beings, oozing with chemistry, who've been thrown together on planes, interviews, and in hotels for weeks. There must have been dozens of possibilities for intimacy on such a junket. I can't think of Jack as anything more than a careless night in a pub. *Move along, Gilly.*

A script for episode 107 slides across the table and lands in front of me. I open it up as if I have a clue what I'm doing.

A shortish man who looks to be in his late sixties stands next to Niks. "Welcome to 107, everyone. We've got a Bobby Provost script this go-round, so let's make the captain proud."

As if this morning can't get any more surreal, it clicks in my overtaxed brain who this man is. *The* Alan Rafier—director of my favorite show from now until the end of time, *The Socrates Chronicles*. I am sitting at a table read with Alan Rafier. My fingernails dig into my jeans. I am so out of my league. How am I going to function in the presence of gods?

Taking in the company, I begin to suss out who's who. The male actors are all bearded with long hair and builds that would fit on the defensive line of any professional football team. Clansmen. Tribesmen. Brutes. Near the center of the table are a pair of network types. The suits are the dead giveaway. I wouldn't be surprised to see True Time Network insignias on the breast pocket of their blazers.

Clustered together in the corner are what have to be the writers. Buried under a fleet of laptops, they'll soon be listening to the tune of the dialogue. These folks will smooth out the flats and sharps of the piece. My favorite playwriting professor, Gary, always said, *"Words are music to shape the story."*

Alan Rafier adjusts his glasses, and everyone quiets down. "You are all very welcome. This is *The Chieftain's Son Episode 107, Blood and Bone*. Our guest cast for this adventure is Morgan O'Toole as Bowstring." There's friendly applause that I can't help but notice is nowhere near the ovation *Traipse of Moonlight* scored.

As he finishes the welcomes, I retrieve my favorite mechanical pencil with the super fat grip to write notes. I have no idea what I should be writing, so I decide to freewheel it for now.

The opening scene is Chieftain Rory plotting and planning with his bros. Donal Cam, the chieftain's son, is still in the process of proving his worth to dear ol' dad. The rest of the clan hasn't decided if the young upstart should get a command for the next foray into land acquisition.

Jack isn't in this scene. When I dare a glance his way, he looks straight at me. Before his lips manage a smile of greeting, I drop my eyes back to the script. An insane urge to doodle around Donal Cam's name on the page comes over me. I quell it by highlighting a line in Irish I'll ask Doolin to translate.

"Jack," says Alan Rafier in a tone reserved for schoolboys who stare out the window instead of focusing on their lesson. By reflex, my head snaps up to look. Jack is flustered and trying to find his place on the page.

"Sorry, Alan."

It's safe to watch him now since that's what everyone else in the room is doing. I swear the bone structure of Jack's face shifts into something hard and savage. "Aye, Father. 'Tis the blood of the despicables you seek, and that's what I'll deliver." Even the pitch and timbre of his voice is altered. Jack O'Leary has left the building. Donal Cam is in the house.

As the scene jumps back to the doubting soldiers, Jack seeks me out again. No smile this time. His look questions, wonders. For the space of a few heartbeats, there's no one else in the room but Jack, me, and our silent exchange. It hollows me out to do it, but I manage a quick shake of my head and return to my place in the script.

Whatever my responsibilities will be on *The Chieftain's Son*, I'm sure they don't include locking eyes with Jack O'Leary.

CHAPTER
SIX

My office is tiny but more inviting to a writer than my cubicle at Lawson Graham Premier Sportswear. It's a cozy nook off the main writer's room stocked with a magnetic white board nearly as big as the back wall, a desktop computer and its huge monitor, as well as a brand-new laptop. On my desk, a silver metallic basket overflowing with packages of Post-it flags wears a green ribbon and a note that says,

I knew we'd get you!!!

-Bobby

My new boss slips a lanyard with my ID card and a key fob around my neck. "All access. I'm giving you the keys to my kingdom."

I inspect the card with my picture security snapped of me, proof I'm all-in with my new reality. Once I agree to something, I stick with it. Sometimes longer than I should. "Many thanks, Your Majesty. I don't know about the long haul, but for now, I'm all yours."

His face relaxes. "Music to my ears. Dinner tonight?"

I almost choke but clear my throat to cover it up. Does he mean *dinner* dinner, as in "I'm asking you out," or "You're new so I'll show you where the good eats are?" I discovered through effective Internet stalking that Bobby is thirty-seven—younger than I guessed but still well out of my personal dating range.

"Bobby," calls the woman with kinky red hair I recognize from the table read. She looks to be around my age. I covet her *Chieftain's Son* logo zip-up hoodie. It's chilly in here and even chillier outside.

The writer's room itself is stuffed with comfy couches and armchairs that make you crave a good book and a fireplace. A giant picture window frames bright green pastures peppered with copses of trees along the fringe. Even the crooked fences are picturesque. At one end of the room is a meeting table surrounded by a dozen green mesh rolling chairs. Every other inch of wall space is covered with massive white boards splashed with color-coded scene cards and episode numbers written above them.

We join the group that I correctly pegged at the table read as the writers. There are greetings all around, then bartering begins for changes and cuts that the writers' tuned ears picked up while the cast read through the script.

Bobby nudges me. "Go get your laptop. I want you to record the session and transcribe so I can review decisions and not lose any decent ideas. Once this group gets going, things tend to fly fast and furious."

I dart into my office and back to the room while the laptop boots up in my arms. Claiming a seat near the far corner of the table, I start recording. I open one doc for Bobby and another for myself to type notes on who is who.

Collin looks to be the oldest of the group. He's got the beginning of a paunch and hair so black it shines bluish under the lights. Danna, one of two women on staff, could have stepped off a page of the Lawson Graham business wear catalog. Her air of authority fits her title as a senior writer with producer status. Benj and Benny look like the jock vs. nerd pair from an ensemble sitcom cast. I make a note to remember that Benny is the larger one because his name has double n's to Benj's single n.

Maureen, the red-haired women in the logo zip-up, is casually splayed across two chairs with her aqua ballet flats resting on the table. Whenever a lull crops up in the debate, she checks in with wry remarks that work to diffuse any rising tension. I wonder if she's a writer or the on-staff therapist.

Collin's elbows dig into the table as he kneads both temples with his thumbs. "I'm just saying the back-and-forth between Bowstring and Rory runs too long. Let's cut half of page thirteen and get to Bowstring's takeover hints earlier to punch up the tension."

The silence is instant. Five sets of nervous eyes are on Bobby. *Note to self: Bobby Provost must not take well to being rewritten.* The muscles in his face have turned to iron, and I swear his eyes actually vibrate. If this is his thinking face, it's super intimidating. Like an ice cube dropped on a griddle, he thaws in the snap of a finger. "Yes. That'll work. Get me the cuts in an hour."

Bobby targets Benj and Benny. "B and B, where are we on 109? It's location heavy. I want to start second unit by next week."

Benj, the cute debate-team-captain type of the pair, gestures to me. "Close. We want to chat up Gillian on her vision of fusing Mac and Mary into one. 109 will be ready for group dissection tomorrow."

The casual comment about my idea starts a flutter in my stomach. How did they know about my theoretical character mash-up? It had to have been Bobby. The flutter shifts into a rush because he gave credence to my suggestion.

Bobby nods rapidly. "Maureen, where are you on the final for 110?"

"Collin's giving it eyes, then I'll add the last coat of polish."

Bobby pops his lips. "I'm off to editing then." He waves me over as he heads out of the room. "So, dinner?"

"Yes" is the correct answer. If Bobby takes me under his wing, it'll be easier to avoid Jack. God, I wish I didn't have to avoid the artist formerly known as Jay, but that connection is fraught with complications. Especially one named Niks. Another naggy voice in the back of my mind warns me not to get too social with Bobby. Until I get the big picture here, I'm better off as a solo act. "I don't mean to be antisocial, but I'm dog tired. I need some settling-in time."

The easy-going duffer I beaned in the head makes an appearance. "Of course. Feather your nest. We're going to work you to the bone." He scratches his chin. "I'll probably be in editing into the wee hours anyway. This is a bitch of a production schedule." A weary smile tugs at his lips. "It's going to be a wild ride for the next twelve months, but we'll be ahead with scripts and shooting on season two." Something catches his eye over my shoulder, and he bobs his chin. "Benj and Benny request your presence. Prepare to have your brain picked."

I lay a hand on his arm. "Thanks, Bobby. For everything."

He gives me a friendly pat. "Let's meet in my office at ten tomorrow morning. I'll go over your schedule and the thousand things I'll expect from you."

"I'll be the one wearing Post-it flags." With a wave, he pivots and rockets down the hall. Damn, that sounded a little too flirty. None of that. I'm going for a clean slate. Fresh start. Reinvent myself. Step one: impress B and B.

An all-access pass and a studio key fob are things of beauty. It's not snooping if you've got permission. *The Chieftain's Son* complex seems to go on forever. I follow the main artery deeper into this playground. Through a set of metal industrial doors, I find the scenery shop. The smell of freshly cut boards takes me back to all the lumber yard runs I made with my dad during summer vacation when he was working on shows.

With the shop crew gone for the night, the buzz of giant table and panel saws are quiet. I'm surrounded by walls of stonework, the façade of a cottage, and even a tree that seems to magically grow out of the cement floor. I lay a hand on the trunk. It's real. There's a conversation starter.

At the far end of the cavernous shop, I hear galloping hoofbeats. Doolin mentioned I'd be getting up on a horse.

All access, baby. I head toward the sound.

Past the shop office, through a wide-open arch, is a huge dirt packed arena. Jumps, tires, and bales of hay set in a zigzag pattern spread out in different parts of the space. There's even a purple plastic wading pool filled with water for God knows what.

Across the arena, I see the entrance to stalls. I clocked quality time at equestrian camp in Ojai for a couple of summers back in high school. I loved it. I only ride a few times a year, but if Doolin isn't foolin', I'll be up on a horse again soon. I giggle at my mental rhyme. Carefully navigating ripe piles of evidence this space was recently occupied by the noble steeds of *Chieftain* and company, I make my way to the stables.

A string of lanterns run near the ceiling to light the dim space. They could pass for old world even though they're definitely electric. I wonder if they shoot in this stable. It's not dressed completely like days of yore, but it's not super modern either. From the quality I've seen so far from this art department, they could turn anything into a page from a history book.

A dappled gray head pokes over the rail to inspect me. "Hey, baby." A questioning whicker greets me as I rub the long nose. "Aren't you a sweetheart." When my new pal discovers I have nothing of the carrot or apple variety to share, she loses interest.

Smells of hay and horse mingle in a timeless aroma. I let my mind fade into a semi-dream state.

A deep, rich male voice flows from the next stall. "Who's my beauty? Yes, you are." I hear soft scrapes of a horse being groomed.

"Do you love me? I love you, gorgeous."

A horse blows and stamps.

"That's my good girl."

A shadow rises on the back wall of the stable. It's broad and tall without detail, but there's no doubt, standing less than ten feet in front of me is Jack O'Leary.

"Don't you blab to Moose about our private workout." He slaps the horse's flank.

I should all-access myself out of this dark stable, but my lips tingle with a memory of a certain brief kiss from last night

I push the thought away. Jack lied to me. The man sweet-talking the horse let me call him Jay without correcting me. Jack O'Leary is an actor. His role last night was to charm the new girl, make her feel like one of the gang. I saw the warm fuzzies between Niks and him. How many times have I heard my parents talk about on-set romances?

This man's job is to capture every heart and lustful urge of the world's female population. That's a spell best avoided. Donal Cam on paper will be my responsibility, not Donal Cam in the flesh.

"You realize I can see you." Jack leans on the rail. "I saw you come in under the arch. Did you figure if you held your breath, I'd mistake you for a wooden post?"

There isn't a damn thing I can say to prevent coming off like an idiot. "I didn't want to scare your horse. Sorry to interrupt." I turn to go, but Jack is fast.

He's got my upper arm in a firm, but non-threatening grip. "Gilly, wait." I stare at the hand holding me captive, and he lets go. Light from the lanterns shines off his golden hair tied back in a ponytail with a frayed piece of leather. "I owe you an apology."

"Nope. Everything's cool. Great job at the table read this morning." I back away from him, trying to look casual.

Jack holds a hand out. "I truly thought Doolin and Bobby told you who I was straight away, or that you'd seen ads for the show."

"Nope again."

"I thought you were playing along with me at the pub."

The back of my neck starts a slow burn. "Me, playing?"

He shakes his head and tries to speak, but nothing comes out but a few sputters.

"Look, Jack, the first time I even heard your name was the night Bobby stayed at my parent's house because I gave him a concussion. I've never seen you in anything, and I don't read fan magazines while I'm waiting in line at the market or scroll entertainment sites on my lunch hour."

He steps closer to me. "Please, Gilly. I am sorry I made assumptions about you knowing who I was. Call me an ass and be done with it so we can get on together."

The warm, honest face looking down at me is as guileless as any horse in this stable. "I'd like to think you're not an ass."

His smile is as intoxicating as the Guinness from last night. "So, what do you think I am?"

I play with a halter hanging from a peg. "You struck me as a sweet and genuine guy." I press my lips together. I remember the way his hands kept traveling to mine last night. The kiss. I flash on those same hands all over Niks at the table read. "And then I find out you're this whole different person."

Jack leans his back against the rail. "How do you know I'm not as you say?"

I study his face. "You flirted with me, then at the table read, I saw some very familiar physical interplay going on between you and Niks." He looks genuinely confused. "Arm around her, a kiss, basically some snuggling."

"Niks is a pal. We're on this crazy ride together."

"Are you referring to the multi-week ride in three countries you just finished with her?"

"I give you my word, there's nothing more than a close working relationship between Niks and me." The start of a grin eases up the corners of his mouth. "Familiar physical interplay, huh? You were watching me that close? And I couldn't even catch your eye. Nearly strained my neck muscles trying."

"Why were you trying?" The question is out before I can filter it.

He moves so close heat rising from his body wafts over me. "Listen, I'm not one to kiss a woman the first day I meet her. I didn't kiss you last night for nothing." Jack's fingers slide up my arm. "You fascinate me. Have for a while." A blush turns his skin the color of my mom's tangerine rose. "I think I started falling for you a bit when I first read *Traipse of Moonlight*."

"How can that be? You had no clue who I was."

"Ever heard of the source of all knowledge in the known universe, Google?"

"You Googled me?"

"I thought it best. Didn't want to risk my heart on a granny or someone's wife."

"So, you found out I'm not fifteen or sixty." I haven't Googled myself in a while, but I'm well aware of what tops the links, and it's not my handful of awards for the short story version of *Traipse of Moonlight* from back in the day.

"And you write grand and fancy words about clothing."

There it is. My tenure at Lawson Graham Premier Sportswear still dominates any Gillian Bettencourt search. I wince, thinking of the laughable descriptions he must have read.

"After Bobby gave me your manuscript to read for character work and tone, more pieces of Gillian Bettencourt fell into my hands." He plays with a loose strand of my hair. "I drove Bobby near mad asking about you, then this spitfire of a girl gives me the business about my golf swing and tears up the Gal Tré course like she's played it a hundred times. You knocked the breath from me."

I'm in the vortex of a bizarre juxtaposition. How many women have Googled Jack, binge-watched his BBC sitcom, and fallen for him? He's previewed me, and all indications point to no disappointment on his part. It's a strange reality to be on this side of the equation. Strange, but at the same time, fascinating.

I stare at the stray curls of chest hair sneaking over the top of his T-shirt. I wonder if they're soft or wiry. "I had a really good time with Jay last night. Beyond the Guinness."

He lifts my chin so I'm looking up at those sculpted cheekbones. "I *am* Jay. It was easy being with you as well. Easy to laugh. Easy to talk. Easy to want to know more." A gust of Jack's warm breath raises a loose strand of my hair. "I'm not blind or stupid. The smart choice is to sweep anything between us into the bin." His hip brushes mine, sending tiny rivers of electricity up my side. "But I can't keep myself from wanting to know you better. Can you give me that chance?"

"God, Jack." I study the hay strewn floor of the stable. "I don't know." It would be so easy to melt into his arms. I'm dying to run my hands under his shirt and feel his body, made for furs and leather and weapons. But the way he touched Niks nags at me. How many other women know the feel of those hands?

He guides me into the stall with a shockingly white horse. "This is Streaker, Donal Cam's horse. She's the only being who can travel through time with him and not forget who he is."

Before I know what's happening, fingers clamp on either side of my waist. Jack lifts me like I'm as light as pillow fluff to set me on Streaker's back. "What are you doing?"

"Shh. Don't spook my horse." He leans against my legs, throwing one hand around my back to hold me in place. "I believe I'll leave you up there until you decide I'm worth investing a little time in."

"God, you're pushy." A big part of me wants to give in, but Jack is the star of *The Chieftain's Son*. His career is in the process of exploding. I've barely dipped a toe into my new position with the show. Hell, this is only the second day I've even talked to the guy.

He points a finger at me. "You're thinking we're a bad idea. I see it."

I look down at him. "Aren't you?"

"Some of the most amazing stretches of life start out as bad ideas."

I look away. "Stop doing that."

He gently coaxes me to face him. "Doing what?"

"Making me want to say 'yes' to you."

He makes no pretense of hiding a victorious smile. "You did promise to shine up my golf game." His hands slide up my sides and ease me off the horse, pulling me close enough for my body to slice along his. "Let's see if kissing you again tips the scales in my direction."

Pushy may be too mild a term for Jack. I lay a palm against the monolith of his chest. "I thought you wanted to start by getting to know me better."

Fingers find the nape of my neck and then thread up into my hair. "That's exactly what I'm doing." He tilts my head back and slowly lowers his lips to mine. It's a kiss as light and sweet as our first. I'm the one who answers with zero restraint. Our mouths open to one another, and the heat of his breath burns away the last of my objections. Jack guides me back against the rail as his body presses into mine. My hands lose themselves in the silky waves of his thick ponytail.

"Who's there?"

Jack's body deflates against mine. "Damn." His tongue flicks my bottom lip with the promise of more getting to know each other. "It's Jack, Moose. I just gave Streaker her rubdown."

"Jack O'Leary, I warned you no workouts with my darlings this late in the—" Moose flashes us a bug-eyed stare when he catches sight of me. The man is a walking tree with a sturdy trunk and arms the size of logs. His hair is a mass of tight, woody brown curls. He's dressed in jeans, a flannel shirt, and a padded down vest.

"Moose, meet Gillian Bettencourt. She's the new writer's assistant. Bobby'll want her up on one of your darlings as soon as possible."

Moose's accent is a thousand times thicker than Jack's. "As you say." He gives me a nod. "You're very welcome here to my stables, Gillian."

"Thank you, Moose. I'm looking forward to riding."

He squints at Jack. "Make sure she's got a good helmet."

Apparently, that's all the goodbye we're entitled to because Moose strides past us and never looks back.

Jack waits until Moose disappears into the shadows at the far end of the aisle before he takes my hand.

Alarm bells go off in my head. I lift our twined fingers. "You don't want Moose to see this." I pull away. "Not that there's a 'this' to see." A feeling of skipping very essential getting-to-know-you steps with Jack nags at me.

A guilty look fades across his face. "Before I ask any more of you, it's only fair I lay out the way things have to be with me." He takes a few steps away, drops his head back, and sucks in a very loud breath before leveling his gaze. "Meg McGrath, who you met last night in the pub, has a very clear vision of the Jack O'Leary"—he flicks his ponytail—"Donal Cam she plans to show to the world."

"Which is?"

He pulls off a damn good impersonation of Meg. "Let me paint a scenario for you. Jack O'Leary is a man with no romantic ties. I'll have every woman who falls for Donal Cam fantasizing they have a shot with Jack." He lets loose a percussive groan before inhabiting his own skin. "It's mad, but Bobby and the True Time network types support that mystique as well."

"And you're okay with being a product?" If Jack is forbidden from romance, why is he kissing me? Why is he asking to slip into my life barely twenty-four hours since we met? Why am I not running?

He rakes fingers through his hair, mussing it. "I was." That crazy, intense gaze of his holds me like a freeze ray. "Then I met this girl with rusty brown eyes at a golf tournament who turns me inside out."

No one has ever accused me of turning them inside out.

There's a low rumble in Jack's throat. "I don't take my opportunity on this show lightly. God, what *The Chieftain's Son* can do for a career, I can't piss away. For the next five years, and most likely five after that, I've got to project an image that keeps people coming back for more season after season." He slaps a hand against the closest rail. I hope he doesn't get splinters. "They won't even let me cut my damn hair. They're hell-bent on painting a Jack O'Leary that's as fictional as Donal Cam."

For a man who is riding the crest of a colossal break in his career, Jack looks miserable.

I lay a hand on his arm. "I've lived in a show business family my whole life. I'm aware how thin the line between real and unreal can get."

His look of relief softens my heart toward him. I start to suspect the PR-painted Jack O'Leary is not the man I just kissed.

"If I can convince you to get to know me better, it'd be a bit of a cat-and-mouse game with Meg. She's brilliant at what she does and only wants the best for the show, but there's not a lot of flexibility there." He kicks at a clump of straw on the floor. "I know what I'm asking you is this side of mad, but patience is not something I'm good with."

I close my eyes and feel a wave of unease. For the love of God, what am I doing? This intriguing man is intrigued with me. He's being honest about the potential ugly underbelly of getting closer to him. Jack O'Leary, the star, must be unfettered by emotional attachments, yet here I am on the brink of taking him up on his offer to know each other better.

"What do you say, Gillian? Are you up for some time with me?"

"I'm up to you driving me back to Waterville. Even though it feels like I'm cheating on Patrick."

After checking that we're alone in the stable, Jack presses his mouth against mine for a quick kiss, then whispers in my ear. "We'll figure a way round the Donal Cam muck, Gilly."

He sounds confident, but I already feel my shoe sinking in that muck. Does he fathom how much pressure he's putting on me? The man is pushy and, by his own admission, impatient, but despite my better judgement, I'm powerfully drawn to him.

We walk side by side out of the stable and across the arena, chatting like any two regular work chums at the end of their shift.

Chums who just happened to have shared a kiss or two.

I've flown five thousand miles to escape one secret relationship that's slowly been crushing my heart for months. This is my fresh start. How many degrees of stupid am I to jump back into the same situation? More degrees than I care to think about. Isn't this how Treat and I started, electric kisses and calculating every rendezvous?

I head back to my nook to get my purse before I meet Jack in the parking lot, which I've learned is called the car park. Am I falling into a classic rebound? Or is it only a rebound when you are actually looking for someone? I am most definitely not looking. Jack just happened. The guy Googled me for heaven's sake. That's a first for me. And look at the man. The ratio of women who Google him to whom he Googles has got to be very out of balance.

A fire in my gut reminds me that any loyalty I may still harbor for Treat died a splintery death on an oak tree against Lanie Blesch's back. There's absolutely nothing wrong with kissing Jack. I've locked lips with plenty of guys on first dates. How is he any different? I'm not a freakin' nun.

I kissed Jack out of curiosity. Well, curiosity and an attraction that feels like a super-sized electromagnet.

Through the main double doors, I catch sight of Jack scratching a donkey behind the ear. One of Doolin's, no doubt. My curiosity is strong enough to take the small step he's asking for. I'm up for fun, but I'll be damned if I'll let anything happen between us to send me back into a situation filled with deceit and disappointment.

CHAPTER
SEVEN

W hen the time came for me to drive in Ireland, I expected a steering wheel on the opposite side of the car and keeping to the left side of the road to freak me out. I did not foresee the harrowing experience of being a passenger on the wrong side, especially when the driver fancies himself a Formula One racer. Toss in roads barely wider than a single car with no streetlights, and I'm trapped in a recipe for automotive terror.

Jack points across me into the darkness. "Down that road is the primary school where my mom teaches."

I want to yell at him to keep both hands on the wheel. Huge chunks of rock and barely clipped hedges are so close to my side of the car I'd sheer off an arm if I stuck it out the window.

"Your mom's a teacher?" Talk about grounded. It's cool that his mom is regular folk. Jack may be an actor that needs to be rescued from pubs, but at the end of the day, he's not the son of a corporate mogul who thinks his shit doesn't stink. Wow, I've gone close to thirty minutes without thinking about Treat. Well done, me.

"Yeah, first class."

Ah, first class. That's so sweet. I love my mom, but I've never called her "first class." What time is it back home? I have an urge to call my mom just to tell her I think she is first class. If Amethyst Bettencourt hadn't bequeathed her love of romance novels to me, this life-changing twist may have passed me by. I wouldn't be in a car with a man whose profile looks like the woodcut of a Norse god.

There's adoration on Jack's face as he talks about his mom. "She used to teach fourth class but says there's nothing better than being with kids starting to read."

First class? Fourth class? Oh, he means first grade and fourth grade.

"Mom's always got a book in her hand. She read *Lord of the Rings* aloud to my sister and me when we were still in primary school. My nieces'll be eight and ten this year, so they'll be getting the same." He glances over to me then right back to the road. "They'll be quite impressed with their Gran's Gimli the dwarf."

"Sounds like you're lucky not to be named Elrond."

He chuckles. "Truth be told, it's the Jean Valjean bullet I barely dodged. *Les Misérables* is an annual read for Mom."

"Jean Valjean O'Leary. Very international."

Jack thrusts an imaginary sword toward the windshield. "I'd prefer D'Artagnan O'Leary." He holds his hand up as if taking an oath. "Bit of a Dumas fan here." Jack clenches his teeth. "My rotten sister, Bonnie, used to call him Alexander Dumbass to provoke me."

My mind wanders to an image of a family in a quaint, whitewashed Irish cottage reading together from the light of the hearth. Jack lies on his stomach with his book open on the floor a little too close to the fire.

"What's your dad do?"

"Sheep."

I can't resist letting Wicked Gilly out of her cage. "Your dad does sheep?"

Jack screeches his silver and blue Renault to a stop. Uplight from the dash deepens fury lines on his face. "Gillian Bettencourt, get out of my car. No one insults my Da."

For a horrible moment, I'm sure he means it, but then Wicked Jack busts out a laugh so hearty the entire car shakes. *Well met, Mr. O'Leary.* Our dark sides complement one another.

"My God, your face." He lays a hand on my cheek. "Swear, I've not yet booted a girl out onto a country road in full dark."

Irish Thor leans my way over the stick shift, but the kiss attempt is thwarted when headlights blast behind us. He puts the car in gear, and we surge forward to avoid getting rear-ended. High beams reflect off my side mirror, blinding me. "I take it speed limits are only a suggestion in Ireland."

"Wrong," says Jack. "They're a challenge." He guns the gas to leave the other car far behind.

"So, sheep?"

"Yes, mainly sheep, chickens, a handful of cattle. The farm's not far from here. The beasts with blue streaks in the fields near The Clan are O'Leary sheep. Bobby encourages locals to graze there as a perimeter buffer. Keeps snoopers away."

I lean my back against the door so I can take in everything that is Jack O'Leary. "How does a farm boy grow up to be a heartthrob?"

"It's all the tractor driving." He flexes his bicep. "Turns ordinary fools into the beautiful people." Jack lays a hand on my knee. "Actually, it's shoveling shit that builds the muscles."

I hope he can't feel my skin quiver beneath his touch. "Don't you say shite over here?"

"Shit, shite, cac—it all smells the same."

We trade the countryside for a town road that skirts the Atlantic. Groups of people cluster at tables outside a pub with a mural of a giant compass floating in the midst of baroque-looking waves splashed across the building. It's got to be near freezing out there, but people mill and visit like it's a Fourth of July picnic. Neither rain nor snow nor spray from the wild Atlantic keep folks from hanging out with friends at the pub. It's a party I'd love to join.

"You are very welcome to Waterville on the Wild Atlantic Way," says Jack. "Former summer home of Charlie Chaplin and now Gilly of *The Chieftain's Son*." To prove his statement, we pass a statue of Charlie Chaplin, complete with bowler hat and cane, poised on a miniature plaza with the ocean as a backdrop. "A pal from school, Michael, pushed hard for that statue. He even got to meet one of the Chaplin family in the bargain."

Jack talks so casually about his past it almost makes me forget I'm in the company of a rising star.

"Do you live in town?"

All the while he talks, Jack darts quick looks between the road and me. "I've got a little place in Sneem less than an hour from here, but Bobby puts me up in Waterville during shooting."

My heart starts clanging like a bell in a church tower. Does Jack live in the same studio housing where Bobby put me? That could be some dangerous proximity, not to mention a complete lack of privacy if everyone in the place is connected with the show. Any comings and goings between Jack and me will be well documented.

"This is you up ahead," says Jack, nodding to a row of buildings all matching in design but varying in color. Suddenly, he slams on the brakes, fishtailing to cut down a small side street. After putting a few blocks' distance between us and the main drag, he pulls over in front of a low stone wall and kills the gas. There's a sheen of sweat across his forehead.

It takes a moment for my stomach to drop out of my throat back into its proper place. "What the hell?"

He pounds his hands on the steering wheel. "I didn't think." His eyes are a little on the crazed side when he looks at me.

"What is it, Jack?"

"Did you see the crowd back that way?" He gestures so wildly he bangs his knuckles on the window glass. "Christ, it's tripled since the last time I was by here."

Pressure builds in my chest. "Those people know *The Chieftain's Son* housing?"

"It's Meg's doing, I'm sure. She calls it building a buzz."

The pressure turns into my own buzz of anger. "Meg told people where you live? That's such an intrusion."

He presses his lips together. "There's the place I live and the place where the fans think I live." Jack snatches a water bottle from the drink holder and downs it. "Water Villa, Bobby's term, is where you'll be living, along with assorted guest artists. Meg's had me pop by a time or two to sign autographs and take pictures with folks." He crushes the bottle and heaves it over his shoulder into the back seat. "That's why they think I live there. Lately, she's takin' to tossing out show T-shirts and saying I'm on location to get the fans moving on so they don't block the road."

Hitching a thumb over his shoulder, he says. "I stay in a little cottage on The Clan property about halfway to Waterville. It was an Airbnb before the True Time folk snapped it up. A private road connects my place to the studio, so there's no need for me to drive through town. No one's tracked me there yet."

I'm not sure if I'm relieved or disappointed Jack and I aren't cohabitating in Waterville. The storm cloud of a thought blows into my mind.

"Does Niks have a cottage, too?"

"Naw. She tucks in at the big hotel there on the water." Jack lets out a loud hum. "Niks functions best with room service and dog walkers." He rubs hands over his face. "I dealt with fan jams after *Randy in 6B*, but that was small potatoes compared to what this show's bringing about. Niks isn't used to the crazy, so she insulates herself at the hotel." He blows out a long breath. "It's the books, you know. Whatever feller found himself in Donal Cam's boots would be dealing with this."

I rub his arm. "It's not just the books. You're a pretty amazing lightning rod on your own. Better than a golf club in a thunderstorm."

Jack drops his forehead onto my shoulder. "It's grand you think so." The sound of a motorcycle nearby brings him to attention. He scans the street and his shoulders relax. "I should bring you to my place, and Patrick can drive you here after the watch gives up."

The reason I can't go home with Jack is because I really want to go home with Jack. This is all too fast. It's only the second day I've known him. My primary goal is to make an impression on Bobby and the other writers. If I lose focus because of whatever seems to be starting here, I could blow that.

"Do you know which of the houses I'm in?"

"The yellow one with the stone duck out front. There'll be someone on duty at a desk inside to get you where you need to go." He starts the car.

I put my hand over the stick shift. "You can't take me. If Meg banished me to a snug last night just for sitting at a table with you, I doubt she'll be too keen if I pop out of your car in front of a crowd. Gotta protect the image, Donal Cam." I reach for the door handle. "I'll walk. It's only a couple of blocks."

Jack pulls my hand from the door and kisses it with a growl. "Leaving you off on a dark street is not the way I'd choose to end our first date."

"Oh, is that what this is? I didn't even get dinner."

He pops open the glove box and offers an energy bar. "I hope you like pumpkin and flax."

I grab it. "My favorite." I slip out of the car and shut the door.

The passenger window slides down. "I'll do better next time."

"It's all good." Too good. Too tempting.

"Goodnight, Gilly."

"Sweet dreams, Jack."

He flashes me a Wicked Jack smile. "Oh, they will be."

I do my best impression of a casual wave and walk toward the sound of surf while visions of Jack O'Leary dance in my head.

CHAPTER
EIGHT

Shadows are not to be trusted. Is there anything as fickle as an entity that changes height throughout the day and mimics your every move? The shadows that swallow the last glow of daylight are thieves. They rob us of depth perception, banishing details from sight.

I escaped shadows when I shed Treat from my life. Now, after only two days, I'm teetering on the edge of venturing into a shadow with Jack.

I love my new feeling of freedom, of being able to only care about myself. It makes me giddy. Jumping back into an all too familiar situation holds about as much appeal as a fuzzy plum at the bottom of the fruit bowl.

This would be a much easier call if I wasn't so attracted to Jack. I'd rather this giant question mark hanging over my head blow away in an Irish breeze. The problem is, without conscious effort, I skipped over attraction straight into smoldering want. I can't stop thinking about the feel of Jack's full, soft lips on mine.

"Stop! Stop! Stop it!" I fan the air in front of me to erase the playback loop of Jack's kisses.

Out the window of my quaint, little studio apartment, I have a clear view of the Charlie Chaplin statue by the beach.

"What do you have to say about all this, Charlie?" I rest a knee on the window seat and stare at the waves as they swell and race toward shore. "What's that?" I cup a hand to my ear. "You're putting the cart before the horse, Gilly. Stop stressing about shadows and lies. There's no relationship between you and Jack O'Leary."

I plunk onto the seat and drop my head into my hands. All that Jack asks is the chance to get to know me better. He says he doesn't kiss women right off the bat. Given that he kissed me the first day we met, I don't know whether I buy that or not.

Everything I've learned so far about Jack O'Leary tells me I can believe him.

Common sense advises a retreat from the breakneck speed at which Jack and I are getting to know each other better. I can easily achieve that today. Meet Bobby at ten, find out what my responsibilities are, and do them. If I see Jack at work today, I'll keep it casual. No inadvertent meetings at the stables or any other dark corner of The Clan. If he wants to hang out, I'll make sure we're not alone.

I toss Mr. Chaplin a salute. "You're right, Charlie. Avoid kissing situations." It's always smart to get a second opinion, even it's from the bronze statue of a silent film star.

Professional distance is best for both of us. Jack can play the dutiful hot bachelor for Meg's PR-painted scenario without any complications or deceit, and I'll avoid feeling like I swallowed a beehive. From what I've seen so far, Jack is a great guy—a little pushy, but not obnoxious. I'd love to have him as a friend, someone to golf with, laugh with. The right move is to stick to my plan of an untethered Gilly.

Regret tugs at my heart. I've always wanted what my parents have. A pair of creative souls finding each other and navigating life through that filter. Treat was a bottom-line profit guy. His thinking had no color, no composition. My love of telling stories was something he never understood.

"I buried that part of me for you, you unworthy bastard."

It's been more than a year since I indulged my own creativity. It's as if something vital of who I am withered. *The Chieftain's Son* is bringing that part of me back to life.

Jack lives in a creative reality. He would understand how sublimating a part of who you are slowly kills you.

The knock on my door makes me jump. Patrick isn't supposed to meet me out front for another hour. *Oh, God. Is it Jack? Did he do something stupid like climb a trellis to sneak in without anyone seeing him?*

"Gillian, it's Bobby."

Bobby? The showrunner of *The Chieftain's Son* should not be knocking on my door at eight o'clock in the morning. *Shit. Did Moose tell him Jack and I were together in the stable?* I've ruined my shot before I even started. For messing with the talent, Bobby is here to send me to Shannon Airport for the first flight back to LAX.

"How about breakfast to make up for dinner last night?"

Oh, thank God. "Sounds great. Just a sec." I grab my purse and vow to commit to common sense from here on out.

Bobby's phone is glued to his ear. "Fine. Put the first take back in." He holds up a finger. "I'll be in around half-ten."

"What's half-ten?" I ask when he slips the phone in his pocket.

"Ten-thirty, Yank."

"So, I'm a Yank until I learn to tell time Irish-style?"

"As you say." He yawns. Shadows beneath his eyes suggest a late night.

I turn to lock the door behind me. "I feel guilty for getting a good night's sleep."

He waves me off. "Someone should. Once I put this episode to bed, I can do the same."

"Anything I can do? Assistant on duty."

"As a matter of fact..." Bobby launches into the laundry list of my duties. During a breakfast involving lots of meat and potatoes at the pub painted with Baroque waves, he amends the list at least five times. He chews on his bottom lip. "I'm loading you up too much. I will not waste your talent. I want you pitching and evaluating ideas. You've got to meet Deidre. She's the pulse of the show."

His casual mention of Deidre LaRochelle, the icon, the author of a book series I've read a dozen times and am on my fourth listen of the audiobooks, knocks the wind out of me. "She's here?"

"Of course. I'd never try to breathe life into *The Chieftain's Son* without its heart in residence."

"Was she at the table read?" How could I not know I was in the presence of greatness?

He shakes his head. "No, I've got her chained to a desk writing the penultimate episode for season one. It's her first foray into a script."

The image of Deidre in irons conjures the scene from book four in the series, *Witch on the Wind*, where Nieve confesses to witchcraft, and it doesn't go well for her. Bobby frowns.

"Where's my head at? I should have connected you two right away. She's the perfect person to talk to about making the leap from novel to script."

Add yet another out-of-body moment to this whole experience. Not only am I going to meet Deidre LaRochelle, but we're going to jabber over shared insecurities. I waffle between *Out of My League* and *In Over My Head* as the title for my upcoming day.

When we head for his car, from force of habit, I walk to the passenger side, which in Ireland is the driver's side.

He raises an eyebrow. "Ready to give left-side driving a go?"

"That road out to the studio didn't appear to have sides."

Bobby laughs. "You'll find that a lot. Best advice for a beginner: if someone's coming at you, slow down, move to the left, and let them blow by you."

To my dismay, he settles into the passenger seat and waits for me to get behind the wheel.

He grins. "On my first day here, driving on a country road that makes the one to the studio look like a super highway"—he shakes his head—"I came face to face with a Guinness delivery truck. The guy waved at me to back up."

I slip into the driver's seat. "Did you?"

"If you could call it that. Backing up while I looked over the wrong shoulder and driving a stick shift made me weave like a drunk on a tightrope."

I try to escape the car, but he puts a hand on my arm.

"I angled my way into a shallow ditch smack up against the hedge." He raises a finger. "Not on purpose, mind you." Bobby glides his arm forward. "The truck squeezed by so close, if my window had been down, I could have tapped every silver drum as it passed."

"And this story encourages me how?"

He hands me the keys. "Take your shot, Bettencourt. If we face off with a Guinness truck, we'll switch seats."

Thankfully, Bobby's black Hyundai is an automatic. Given the road to The Clan is private, I pull off a successful maiden voyage as an Irish driver.

As soon as I crunch onto the gravel parking lot—a.k.a. car park—and stop the car, Bobby springs out to examine the paint job on his side. Maybe I did get a little close to the hedges.

"Did I scratch it?"

Bobby licks his finger and rubs a hair-width streak on the shiny ebony door. "All good."

My knees nearly buckle in relief when evidence of my driving "oops" buffs out. I suppose I should consider buying a cheap used car. I can't expect Bobby or Patrick—and certainly not Jack—to drive me everywhere. "Got any leads on a used VW Golf I can blow my life savings on?"

He slings an arm around my shoulder in what seems like a brotherly gesture. "I'll see if Patrick has any connections."

Out of habit, my brain screams for him not to touch me this close to where people might see. For the last two years, I've been on guard with Treat at work or anywhere else we might run into to someone who knows us. An arm around the shoulder probably means nothing to Bobby. I've got to calm down.

I nudge my purse so it slides to my elbow, giving me an excuse to break free and readjust. "May I sit in on your meeting with Benj and Benny? Get the feel of the rewriting process?"

"Absolutely." He holds the glass doors into the foyer open. "You will be the one typing up the changes."

We make it all the way to the writer's room without running into

Jack. Benj and Benny hover by a counter in the corner, doctoring their coffees. Bobby shouts across the room to them. "Okay, you've got fifteen minutes. Sell me."

A tempting spread of super fancy donuts flanks the coffeemaker. There's a particularly delicious looking peanut butter chocolate one. I hope it stays unclaimed until we finish.

We huddle in the corner of the long table while B and B pitch changes. I'm impressed with the efficiency of the quick negotiations between the three. With minimal cross outs and notes in the margins, a new version is born.

Benj plunks the script into my hands. I'm about to make a clean getaway to my niche of an office when Jack strides into the writer's room. The moment we share space, little quivers erupt all over my body.

Bobby glances at his watch. "Cutting it close, J. The van heads out to location in five minutes."

It's then I notice Jack's getup. He's wearing a black parka over a long tunic. His hair is especially blond. It must have been dyed, or at least touched up, this morning for the shoot.

Jack smiles. "The donuts are better in here." He goes straight for my peanut butter and chocolate prize.

Bobby turns to me. "We need ten copies of the new pages, and email the changes to everyone. Get Patrick to bring you up to the location when you've got them. See you in a few."

With waves and thank-yous to me, Benny and Benj head out. I guess everyone is off to the location.

Bobby pauses at the door. "Coming, J?"

Jack waves him off. "Right behind you." He becomes very involved with stuffing the donut in his mouth and grabbing napkins. He's stalling, and I'm not the only one who notices.

Bobby looks from Jack to me, a line creasing his forehead. I brace myself for some comment, but Bobby's phone saves the day. He takes the call and zooms down the hallway.

"Are you nuts?" I ask.

Jack stops chewing. "What?"

"What do you mean 'what'? You came all the way to the writer's room for a donut. Who's going to believe that?"

"Everyone."

I hug the script to my chest. "Did you see that look Bobby gave us?" That cloudy look on Bobby's face is more confirmation that Jack and I are a bad idea.

"I always sneak in here for donuts. Maureen's engaged to the pastry chef at the hotel in town. He keeps her supplied with these drops of Heaven." He licks caramel-colored frosting off his fingers.

The chameleon that is Jack O'Leary has shifted into yet another version of his being. It might be the morning light shining through the picture window, or the whole gestalt of Jack in full chieftain son costume, hair, and make-up, but he's altered. The bone structure of his face is more pronounced. His overall frame looks larger than it did last night in the stables. He's kingly. Majestic. Savage.

He takes a step toward me. I half expect him to scoop me up in his arms and carry me to that fur-covered bed on the hot set. I hug the script tighter to squelch any more dangerous thoughts.

Instead of keeping my hands off him, which is the smart choice, I dab crystals of frosting off his cheek. They shine on the end of my fingertip like fallen stars. I pop the finger in my mouth. "Donut on your face."

His eyes lock on my finger and then my lips. "A bit of sugar won't matter once I've got dirt smeared across my cheeks."

When he steps closer, I move back. "I've been thinking." I blow a soft breath. "Probably too much about what we discussed last night."

Jack scans the room and the hallway beyond before he captures the hem of my shirt and pulls me closer. "We discussed a lot of things."

He smells like the grass of the fields outside the window, uncut and wild. A sensation of lightheadedness wafts over me. What is it about this man that propels me into the land of stupid?

I reclaim my clothing and move around the corner of the table. "The cat and mouse game with Meg..." My gaze drifts to the tabletop to avoid his eyes.

To my surprise, he walks over to the door. "You're right. This is not playing it safe. Anyone could walk in."

"That's not what I mean."

"On the other hand, it'd be stranger if we avoid each other." He taps a finger against his lips, and they go a darker pink. "We'll go to the driving range tonight. You can doctor up my swing and then..." The suggestive smile on this primal being whips my senses into a whirlwind.

"We shouldn't be alone. Your fans or Meg or Bobby will see us and think there's more going on than there is." This is the perfect moment to tell Jack whatever sparks are jumping back and forth here can't flare into something that could burn both of us. Before I get a single word in, Jack snaps his fingers and points at me.

"That's brilliant. I'll ask Meg and Bobby to go with us."

"That's not—"

Jack's pocket begins to ring. Why does it not surprise me the ringtone on his phone sounds like an old-school landline? It's genuine the way he's genuine. "I'll have Bobby drive you," he says, "and we'll all meet up at the driving range." He slaps the phone to his ear, grumbling into it. "I'm coming." Jack stares at me, eyebrows raised in question.

He really is tone deaf to the degree of pressure he's putting on me. "No" is the best choice here. Avoid the whole meeting-up-after-work situation. Apparently, my brain doesn't convey this decision fast enough to my body because I nod to Jack.

His eyes soften, erasing the warring clansman image for a brief second before he's off down the hall. The tunic—skirt, whatever the proper historic name for his low-hanging fabric is—swishes side to side. *Oh, Lordy.* I have got to tell him tonight that this thing between us is not going to happen before I wake up next to him in an Irish dawn.

"Willpower, Gilly. Persevere," I whisper to myself as a feeble pep talk while I choose the second-best donut with chocolate shavings and caramel drizzled over the top. Anything with Jack can only end in a Treat quagmire all over again. Except Jack is not Treat. Based on the way everyone around here talks about him and what I've seen, in the arenas of basic kindness and integrity, Jack is miles ahead of Treat.

A sucker punch of realization catches me in the ribs. I assumed I was in love with Treat, but in truth, I haven't liked him much for a very long time. My reptilian brain must have sensed he was not the long-term emotional investment I should be making. Treat became a habit instead of a passion, and I'd been too lost in routine to recognize that any true sweetness and light had drained from our relationship.

Jack appears to be made up of equal parts sweetness and light—when he's not tempting me into agreeing to things I know I should be avoiding.

I duck into my office and pray my fingers are capable of typing after Jack's lingering look turned me to goo. On my desk is a stack of hardcover books, the entire *Chieftain's Son* series. The corner of an envelope sticks out from under the bottom tome. I slide it free, wondering how much time Bobby has allocated for me to reread these thousands of pages before he expects me to have an intelligent discussion about their content.

Inside the envelope is a note written on what looks like the ripped-out page of a journal.

Gilly,

I'm so glad you'll be on this journey with me.

-J

J. Jay. Jack.

I drop my forehead onto the top book. This man is quickly becoming the hitch at the top of my backswing.

CHAPTER
NINE

I waffle between disappointment and relief that Bobby decided my first Irish language class with Doolin trumps hanging out at the location. A more unnerving thought takes up residence in my brain as I head toward the classroom. Did Bobby's change of my plans have anything to do with that suspicious look he gave Jack and me? Bobby did have a front row seat to our first night together in the pub. Did he see the kiss?

I replay my short but eventful friendship with Bobby Provost. At the tournament in L.A., he was super friendly, but I wrote that off as his plan to woo me for this job. Did I misjudge? He asked me to dinner, but wasn't that just to make me feel welcome? Dang, he showed up to take me to breakfast. Toss in more than one arm around the shoulder or waist…

"Par-a-noid," I sing to myself. Bobby is helping me acclimate to this new existence since he personally twisted my life inside out. Papa showrunner wants all his little chickadees to be happy.

The thought still nags me. Did Bobby's expression have a shade of jealousy?

Get over yourself, Gillian.

My mind flashes back to the pub. Bobby was very attentive that night too. Did I imagine a vibe hinting he wasn't real keen on Jack and I making a connection?

Whether Bobby has an inkling about us or not, I'm pretty damn sure that Jack falling for me or vice versa isn't on his agenda. Or Meg's. Or the legions of female fans that already cast Jack as the lead in their personal fantasies.

What was the word Jack used for "shit" last night?

"Cac."

"If that's all the Irish you've got"—Doolin eyes me from where he's leaning against the wall near an electronic white board, arms crossed—"we've got a lot of work ahead of us."

"Doesn't that mean 'hello'?"

There's a howl of laughter from the end of the table. A woman in a floor-length, cherry and black, batik print dress slaps the table. "Score one for the new kid."

She flies toward me with such force I almost stumble backward. Her mahogany hair, streaked with bright magenta waves, is twisted up in a garish turquoise clip with a few messy strands out of compliance. Bright red lipstick echoes the hue of her dress. I suspect the woman is a product of hippie parents like my own mom and dad a free-spirit type. I wouldn't be surprised if her name is Rainbow Wind or Sunflower. I'm guessing costume designer.

Eyes the color of dark roast coffee grounds widen as she takes me in. "So, you're the girl who slapped two of my characters into one bite-sized piece."

Holy, Mama. I'm face to face with Deidre LaRochelle, authoress extraordinaire.

I must look like a taser victim because Doolin catches my arm to steady me. "She's havin' a go at you, Gillian. Don't mind her."

Deidre swallows me in an embrace. "As they say over here in the land of the good folk, that move was brilliant. I'll be first to admit Mac and Mary are redundant." Her laugh is bold. I believe this woman could save a baby from the jaws of a tiger. "I suppose Mary now has a touch of multi-personality disorder since she'll be filling in Mac's gaps." She swivels so one arm is around my back as she guides me to a chair.

"Honey, you are a real talent. *Traipse of Moonlight* is absolutely gorgeous."

Deidre pulls me down to sit next to her. The woman who has sold more books than anyone on the planet is fawning over my writing. I may never speak again.

"Why aren't you hiding in a garret, writing your own novels, instead of here shredding mine into Celtic grunts and battles?"

Within the first moments of meeting her, Deidre confirms that my years at Lawson Graham Premier Sportswear may have been a colossal waste of my creative life. I told myself so many times that coming up with a dozen kicky new ways to describe the cut of a sleeve kept my spring of creativity bubbling. In reality, the work was thesaurus gymnastics. I want to blame Treat's indifference to my personal writing for causing my creative essence to atrophy, but it was me who allowed it to happen.

I smile at Deidre. I'm certain she does everything in her power to keep her creative well filled to overflowing. "Ms. LaRochelle, I have to tell you that I love the hell out of every book in *The Chieftain's Son* series. I've lost myself in them so many times. Every time I finish book ten, I can't wait to go back to book one." I know I'm burbling, but I can't stop. "The detail, the historical accuracy is a mental feast. I hate the people that accuse it of being a sex romp with lots of hairy men and a plucky heroine. It's the love story we all wish we had."

Deidre leans on one arm, sizing me up. "I think there might have been an insult in there, but you ended it so pretty, I forgive you." I didn't expect Deidre LaRochelle to sound so...well, so American. I imagined her one hundred percent Irish. Her story is molded straight from the soul and spirit of Ireland. Talk about a disconnect.

What did Jack call Google last night? The fountain of all knowledge or something equally hyperbolic. I better dip into that fountain and beef up my background on the people I'm about to spend a serious chunk of time with, starting with Deidre LaRochelle.

I shake my head. "Oh, gosh no. I didn't mean to insult you. I'm sorry if it came off that way."

She lays her hands on my shoulders in a very motherly way. I can't wait until I tell my mom that I'm hanging with Deidre LaRochelle. She may need to be resuscitated. I'll have to get Deidre to autograph one of the books on my desk for Mom. A wave of protectiveness for Jack's gift washes over me. I'll buy Mom a new copy for Deidre to sign.

Deidre leans in so her face is inches from mine. "My characters are my family. I need you to know that before you dig in and start chopping up any more of my story."

Doolin moves in behind Deidre and gently guides her back so she molds into the chair. "Okay, now." He pats her shoulders. "We're all here because we love your people."

Deidre tilts her head to him with an adoring look.

I bite back a squeak of surprise. They're into each other. The crusty Irish teacher and the flamboyant American storyteller. *Perfect.*

"Don't look like you've swallowed a live goldfish," says Deidre. Doolin is my darling." She runs a hand down his arm and grasps his hand. "He's helping me buy an Irish castle."

Doolin frowns. "Find a castle. I'll be doing none of the buying."

Deidre laughs, then refocuses on me. She pulls a strand of my hair to catch the light. "You've got the loveliest strawberry blond locks." She taps a finger on the table. "I toyed with giving Nieve's hair this color, but her name means "bright and radiant". She has to glow with light that allows Donal Cam to find her across tide and time. That translates to silver blond."

"Niamh, a queen of Tir na nÓg, will shine eternal," says Doolin, pronouncing Nieve's name in Irish instead of the anglicized version.

Deidre reminds me so much of my mother a pang of homesickness hits. I'll call Mom tonight. If I get up the nerve, I might even tell her about Jack. *Not yet.* She'll scold me over repeating the situation I just got free of. I don't need confirmation getting tangled with Jack is not a Mensa move.

Doolin walks over to the electronic white board and picks up one of the pens. "I'm gonna start with basic syntax and then we'll get into script specifics." He points the pen at me and then Deidre. "I'm warning the both of you not to write any Irish into a script until you pass it by me first."

Deidre bows. "Yes, oh keeper of language fading into the mists."

"It's not fading anywhere on my watch."

During the lesson, my mind wanders. I wonder if Deidre came on to Doolin first or vice versa. Is he Deidre's love story? I'll get her onto a golf course with the pretense of giving her lessons so she can hit the links with Doolin. That'll give me ample time to milk her for their history. Nothing beats eighteen holes of golf to really get to know someone.

Jack and I only played a few holes together. That was all it took for me to get his measure. Gracious, driven, generous. Whatever he saw in me led to that first kiss in the pub. Creating a divide between us feels wrong. I'm afraid that friendship won't be enough to satisfy either of us. The alternative, a secret forbidden relationship, is a road I know all too well. I can't do it again. I just can't.

As another hour ticks by, I begin to get nervous about tonight. At the range, I'll have to create a moment to have the *if you were someone else this might be possible* discussion with Jack. How will I look into those eyes of his and wish he were someone else when it's the last thing in the world I want?

Doolin' s gruff voice bursts the bubble of my reverie. "This is the point where you repeat what I'm saying instead of staring out into the hallway." I shift my focus back to Doolin as he repeats the phrase for me. "*Uisce na beatha.* Water of life."

"*Uisce na beatha.*" Hey, after a couple of hours at this, my Irish accent ain't half bad.

Doolin nods to me and then wiggles his fingers at Deidre to take her turn.

There's a twinkle in her eye as she leans on one elbow and says, "Whiskey."

Doolin makes a dismissive sound and plunks the electronic pen back on its tray. "We'll call it for today." He bows. "Well done, ladies."

The sound of clapping fills the doorway. "*Maith. Maith,*" says Jack. "Good." He's dressed in jeans and a stylish gray-green jacket from the Lawson Graham Irish Country Lad collection. When worlds collide.

"Yeah, very good," says Doolin. "Gillian here catches on fast." He cocks his head to one side. "Are you sure there's no Irish in your blood?"

"Not a drop," I say, collecting my notes from the table.

Jack beams at me. He rips off a string of Irish. I have no idea what he just said. Out of the corner of my eye, I catch Deidre looking from Jack to me. What did he say?

"Wouldn't the two of you have an adorable crop of ginger babies," says Deidre.

Doolin frowns at her.

My insides churn like crazy, but I decide to play it flippant. "Oh," I say, laying my hands over my heart. "Did Jack just propose to me in Irish?" Jack's face pinks up. I notice the stubble outlining his jaw is the color of my hair, which must have prompted Deidre's ginger baby comment.

"I propose it's time to head out to the range for our golf tune-up. Bobby's waiting to drive you into town so the two of you can pick up your clubs. Meg and I will meet you at the clubhouse." Jack turns to Doolin. "Join us for a bucket of balls?" He nods to Deidre. "And some *uisce na beatha* after?"

Jack plays it cool and careful. He could easily have offered to drive me instead of Meg. Cat and mouse indeed.

Deidre links her arm through Doolin's. "Thank you, Jack, but Doolin promised to teach me how to make Guinness stew."

I'll put money down stew isn't the only thing the two of them will make tonight.

CHAPTER
TEN

I aim for the Waterville Links logo on the golf ball poised on the well-worn tee matt. A three-quarter swing with my sand wedge should land the shot next to the pole of the fifty-yard marker. Jack's ball will have no chance of landing any closer, and I'll be twenty Euros richer.

The overhead lights of the driving range send Jack's shadow ahead of him as he walks up too close behind me. I can't swing without hitting him. "If you blow this shot, you'll only have hit your mark nine times in a row. That'll mean starting over for you."

I straighten up and point to the bench where Bobby and Meg sit watching. "Some golf etiquette please, Mr. O'Leary. I'm visualizing my shot."

His breath is warm against the chilly skin of my neck. "I'm already on seven in a row. Once your next shot goes awry, you'll never catch me."

"He hates to lose a bet," calls Bobby.

"Don't give into his mind game," says Meg. Nothing we did could convince her to pick up a golf club. She's taken on the role of cheering section, fueled by her third whiskey and ginger soda.

Jack smirks as if he's already managed to screw up my shot. "I'm visualizing you missing this tenth-in-a-row shot so you don't own our bet."

"I will make the shot and own you. Get your Euros ready."

"Ha." He struts over to Bobby and Meg. Turning to watch, Jack crosses his arms and takes a wide, cocky stance.

I shut him out, address the golf ball, and visualize it clinking against the pole. My swing is smooth, effortless in its arc. The ball rises, falls, and nestles up against the white metal of the fifty-yard flag.

My turn to smirk. "Tat's ten," I say, busting out an Irish accent to celebrate my victory.

Bobby applauds while Meg lets loose an impressive, fingers-in-the-mouth whistle, earning them an entire row of dirty looks from golfers poised on tee mats.

Jack retrieves a sand wedge from his bag and nudges me off the mat. "Double or nothing."

"Oh, for pity's sake, Jack," Meg says and drains her glass. "I'm not sitting out here in the cold to watch you go down again. I'll be inside."

Jack glances over his shoulder at them. "Bob, you want in on this?"

Bobby raises hands in surrender. "I'm competitive, but you're insane." He pulls Meg to her feet. "We'll be in the clubhouse while you two obsessives finish your duel."

As soon as they leave, Jack pulls off his baseball cap and puts it on my head. My fingers itch to braid his hair.

Delicious, warm breath trickles into my ear. "Finally. I've got you to myself."

I glance at the clubhouse. "Mighty big windows up there."

He pulls me onto the mat until I'm plastered against his back as he takes his stance. "Come on, coach. Wrap those arms around me and guide my club where it needs to go."

Thank God his back is to me so he can't see the cranberry color my face has surely become. I do as he says, imagining a very different club from the one in his hand. "You are a sneaky fellow."

He chuckles. "Isn't this the most conducive position for chipping?"

"Your chipping is fine."

"Fix my putting then. Meet up with me after dinner without that pair." He nods in the direction Bobby and Meg headed.

I pretend to correct his swing, then step away.

Jack twists to face me. "That look is not the one I was hoping for." Lights catch his red beard stubble and the cinnamon of his eyelashes.

The ginger children comment Deidre made comes back to me. "Hey, are you actually blond?"

"You mean saffron, sunlight, and buttercup," he says, naming off a few of the dozens of color references Deidre makes to Donal Cam's hair in the novel.

I can't help giggling. "Or noonday sand, straw, limoncello—"

"In the name of Saint Brigid, stop," he says, laughing with me. "I'm a ginger." Jack scratches the beginning of his beard. "As you see."

Our children would be doomed to red hair. *Our children*. Cart and horse in the wrong order once again. I pick up my golf bag. "Come sit with me."

Jack relinquishes our tee mat and grabs his bag. I lead him down the row to the very last bench. It's in shadow hidden from the clubhouse's floor-to-ceiling windows where Meg and Bobby warm up with whiskey.

I glance at the other golfers, but nobody pays any attention to us. Jack O'Leary doesn't make a stir out here. He's just one more golfer fine tuning his swing.

Jack scoots next to me on the bench and throws an arm over my shoulders. "We've got a knack for finding the dark corners, eh?" Before I can get out the first word of my *slow down* speech, his lips are on mine.

I should push him away. Get him to listen to reason, but I kiss him back. We break away slowly, and I drop the top of my head to his chest. "What are you doing to me, Jack O'Leary?"

He slides his hand around the back of my neck. "If it's anything like what you're doing to me, Gilly Bettencourt, you haven't got a clear thought left in your head."

"We can't do this here." I raise my chin to the clubhouse. "We can't do this at all. Bobby and Meg—"

He pulls the brim of his hat down over my forehead and ducks under it for another kiss, cutting off my words. His mouth is warm and eager, but not demanding. Jack's kisses reflect the person he is. They ask, and when I answer yes, it's as if his light surrounds me, erasing any restraint. His tongue tastes of sugar, spreading sweetness everywhere it discovers a new part of me. Our kiss deepens. I steal a fistful of his shirt to pull him closer. If he laid me down on this bench right now, I'd be powerless to resist. This man turns common sense into confetti.

We finally break, and Jack lets out a quiet groan. "You're going to say it now, aren't you?"

"Hmm?"

My lips tingle. I don't want to speak and dilute the thrill of it.

"Your fully prepared speech of why you shouldn't come to my private, little house after dinner?" He raises one eyebrow, waiting.

I shake my head.

"No, you're not coming, or no, you're not going to argue with me about it?" His hand clamps over my knee. He mimics my voice. "No, Jack. We can't bite the hand that feeds us, poke the beast, put our heads in the lion's mouth."

I lay my head on his shoulder. "That's a whole lot of clichés."

"I've got more. I'll spout them until dawn if that'll bring you to my bed."

"Am I mistaken, or did we skip a few steps of getting to know each other?"

Wicked Jack grins at me. "A few. Do you mind?"

Every one of his clichés has merit, and we both know it. They all pale next to the wanting that may set this bench on fire. Why shouldn't my fresh start have benefits? Jack and I are both adults. We can handle fun without obligation or commitment. *Damn it.* I'm overthinking this. How hard can it be to keep a few great nights with Jack off Meg's radar? I won't be lying because she'll never ask.

"Okay, Jack. Take me to your little house."

Suddenly, I almost fly off the end of the bench when Jack pushes me away. A second later, I spot Bobby on the hunt.

"Shoes." I hiss at Jack and untie my golf shoes. He takes the hint and does the same, giving us an excuse to share the seat.

"There you are." Bobby lifts his chin. "So? Who won the bet?"

Jack stuffs his shoes into his bag and pulls out sneakers, pretending to be miffed. This acting thing can be a real perk. "Who do you think?"

"Ha. Well done, Gillian." Bobby gestures to the path leading up to the clubhouse. "Guess who's coming to dinner?"

There at the top of the small rise is Meg, arm-in-arm with none other than Niks Tellefson.

Jack's voice is low and grumbly. "I thought dinner was off the clock."

"Meg thought we'd tease a little intrigue with you and Niks." Bobby picks up my golf bag. I guess he's being a gentleman, but I would have like to have been asked. "With Gillian and me in the mix, it'll keep the fans guessing."

"I thought Jack was the world's most eligible heartthrob." I was aiming for lighthearted, but a little snark escapes.

Jack's eyes flash a warning.

Luckily, Bobby doesn't pick up on my dig. "Meg knows how to play to the fans. She's a master puppeteer."

Those puppet strings are messing with my life.

Jack searches the area around the bench. "Gilly, have you seen my seven iron?" He jerks his chin down the row.

"Oh, shoot. I think I leaned it on the bench over by our mat." We both make a show of looking for the club.

Jack angles close enough to me to whisper. "I'll pass you my phone at dinner. Put your number in it. I'll call with details when we're done with Meg's fun and games."

I should drink more. One whiskey and ginger soda isn't enough to endure watching Niks hang all over Jack at dinner. When she tugs on his earlobe, I can't decide who to kick under the table—Niks for the tug or Jack for letting it happen. Every time they put their heads together for a private tete-á-tete, I want to wretch.

It takes me by surprise when Niks turns her attention to me.

"Gillian, Bobby says you are from a show business family. Yes?"

Answering her would be much easier if she wasn't hip to hip with

Jack. "My parents are both art directors."

Niks claps her hands. "Oh, when I come to California, I will call them to make my house beautiful." She turns to Jack. 'We go there this summer, yes?"

Jack raises his eyebrows in Meg's direction.

A satisfied smile stretches across the publicist's face. "*The Chieftain's Son* is going to make its San Diego Cali Con debut this July."

Jack leans in my direction. "Have you ever been to Cali Con, Gillian?" Under the table, he slips his phone into my hand.

"A few times. My parents were on several design panels for their shows."

"Do I know these?" asks Niks. "The shows?"

"Did you ever see *The Rhythm of the Beat*?"

I want the conversation to switch focus away from me so I can put my number in Jack's phone.

Niks swats Jack's shoulder. "Yes, I know that one. The cop show." Once again, her gaze settles on Jack. "You watch it, yes?"

I steal a look down at the phone and add my number to Jack's contacts. For a panicked moment, I don't know what to put for the name. I opt for simplicity and enter *G*. Hopefully, he'll figure it out.

When I tap the phone against his leg, he captures my whole hand, sliding this thumb across my skin. It sends pleasant tingles up my arm. We're so sneaky, plotting our rendezvous right under Niks's button nose. All her pawing isn't getting the result I'm sure she wants: more Jack. I envision a thought bubble above my head that says: *Jack and Gilly are happening. Niks and Jack are not. I'm the one with his phone. She isn't.*

Despite our phone pass, I can't shake the tightness in my chest. Jack plays a convincing game with Niks. I don't want to be a game too. He's very handsy with every female within reach, and it bothers me. What's genuine and what's PR?

Jack offers to drive Niks back to the hotel in town. Our restaurant is about half an hour out of Waterville, and the thought of the two of them alone in Jack's car ties my stomach in triple knots. Niks's response, which should be "no," is to kiss Jack on the cheek. Her fingers walk up his neck and play in his hair. The rancid memory of Treat pressing Lanie

Blesch up against the trunk of an oak makes an unwelcome appearance in my head.

Even worse is the *well-done* expression Meg wears. The puppet master is pleased.

When Bobby hints it's time for us to take off, I practically leap from my seat. Jack is on his feet with speed to match mine. He wraps me in his arms with the pretense of thanking me for our friendly competition back at the driving range. The way his fingers press into my back are beyond the bounds of a casual hug. That simple touch reignites my draw to him. I remind myself I'm the one going home with Jack, not the unnervingly gorgeous Niks Tellefson.

Back at my apartment, I take the fastest shower of my twenty-eight years, shave everyplace that needs to be smooth and inviting, and fluff my hair from stringy to sexy. I close my eyes and summon every one of my kisses with Jack. Oh, to be able to take the time to learn what else those lips are capable of. Everything he's planned tonight ends with us together. That's reality, not his flirty façade with Niks. The combination of desire and anticipation makes me giggle. I stare at my phone willing Jack's call to come in. I texted myself from his phone so I'd have his number. He's simply *J* in my contacts. Secret Agent J.

Pacing the perimeter of my small living room only makes my heart race faster and my belly fill with worry bubbles. I want our first night together to be honey, not carbonated soda. The thought of discovering Jack's body while he explores mine starts a slow burn in my chest that's only going to be put out by one thing.

When Jack's contact, *J*, blips onto my phone, I want to dance, but I promised myself I'd show restraint. I run a hand through my hair to let him wait through a few rings on his end. Jumping into anything beyond casual with Jack has red Post-it flag warnings all over it. He already confessed, per the PR department's edict, his brand must be Mr. Available, and I don't want to touch another secret relationship with a ten-foot flaming pole.

Think fun, Gilly. A light and fluffy fling. That's doable.

"Hey."

Jack's whisper is strained. "Before I say what I've got to, know that

I've not changed my mind about you in any way."

My heart squeezes to the size of a lentil.

"I can't come for you tonight."

Shit. I'm going to cry. "Oh?"

"I'm stuck with a drunk Norwegian locked in my bathroom."

Now I'm pissed. "What the hell?"

He growls. "She got to feeling dizzy halfway back to Waterville. I pulled over twice so she could walk a bit and get fresh air." She's at his house. His little cottage. *Damn it.* "If I'd taken her back to the hotel and had to help her up to her room weaving and giggling—"

"There'd be a thousand pictures."

"At least. Niks is new to the game. If I don't protect her, Meg will have my balls on a platter."

Suspicion raises a row of knots along my spine. "How is she now?"

"Dunno."

"Is she vomiting? Collapsed on the floor?" My guess is that she's using his bathroom mirror to freshen her makeup and hair.

There are a few beats of silence and then I hear Jack knocking. "Niks? Everything all right, love?"

Did he have to call her love? I hug knees to my chest and take a mental count of how many times I've heard people use that endearment since I set foot in Ireland. Often. Still, it turns my stomach to hear Jack use it on Niks.

I hear the muted sound of a door opening followed by Niks's singsong voice and giggles answering Jack. Happy drunk then, nowhere near passing out drunk. Happy drunk is horny drunk. I can't shake the suspicion that Niks may be angling for a larger role in Jack's life.

Is this my reward for giving in to the possibility of Jack? For once, I go for what I want, and fate gives me an immediate ass-kicking. *Well, hell.* If I needed any more proof I was heading down the absolute wrong path, here it is. Competing with Niks is absurd. I've got to work with the woman. Instead of being a roadblock, I'll move out of her way.

"Gilly?"

"Tell Niks to feel better. Goodnight, Jack."

"Don't go." My finger hovers over the red disconnect dot on my phone, but I don't touch it. His voice is muted as if he's cupping his hand around his mouth. "Damn it, Gillian." A second later, I hear a door slam followed by the whine of wind. Jack must have gone outside. "Don't you know you're the only woman I want in my bed?"

"She's in your bed?"

A huff of frustration blasts through the phone. "No one's sleeping in my bed tonight but me."

I hear Niks's muffled voice calling out Jack's name.

His response to her is terse. "I need a bit longer out here."

No matter what Jack says, Niks is clearly interested in him. The show has bonded them, and the woman shamelessly came on to Jack at dinner. How can he be unaware that she does want to be the woman in his bed? Even nice needs boundaries. Why isn't Jack setting some with the woman he called his "pal"? Maybe it's time to pinch myself and wake up from this Jack O'Leary dream. Sliding back into any version of the tangled personal life I just crawled out of pokes at the fresh scars Treat left. Self-preservation warns me not to be a fool-me-twice kind of gal even with someone as sweet as Jack.

There's an edge to his tone as he breathes into the phone. "Gilly, I don't want to lose ground with you over this. Niks is here because she feels comfortable with me. Nothin' more."

"You should go deal with Niks. I'll see you tomorrow." I hang up to the sound of my name being hissed into the phone.

I rip off my clothes and throw them across the room. I'll be the only one seeing me naked anytime soon. Without even bothering to wash off my makeup, I pull on flannel sleep pants and a long-sleeved UCLA T-shirt. I curl up on my side under a scratchy bedspread, wishing I was back in my West L.A. apartment wrapped in my own puffy comforter.

I hear the ocean. Wave after wave after wave. I let the rhythm bring me back to some semblance of reason. My life nearly changed tonight. If I'd gone home with Jack, who knows how badly my future with *The Chieftain's Son* might have been screwed up. I should be relieved this one decision was taken out of my hands, but rationale is not preventing me from feeling damn miserable.

Did I just dodge a bullet or take one between the eyes?

CHAPTER
ELEVEN

I'm not used to the short hours of Irish daylight in February. The sun doesn't sneak up until eight in the morning and it departs by four-thirty. I mean half-four.

It's half-six on Friday, and everyone is in desperate need of a weekend. It's also Valentine's Day, as evidenced by the heart-shaped donuts Maureen brought in from her pastry chef.

I've been alone for the last two Valentine's Days. Treat always had a client to wine and dine. I lick my lips, thinking about how close I came to looking across a table, or bed, at Jack this year on the day of hearts and flowers.

Collin and Danna's smackdown in progress drags me away from impossible imaginings. They gesture wildly at the flatscreen in the writer's room. The focus of their battleground is the patchwork of medieval swords I whipped up for them as a visual. Instead of moving them closer to consensus, my research escalates their argument.

Danna jabs a finger at the screen. "They're all sleek and Nordic, Collin."

The rapid, circular motions he makes with a pen on a legal pad produce the sketch of a tornado. I half expect him to draw Danna's face on top. "That does not preclude the blade getting stuck in a briar and destroyed."

Maureen blows on her tea. "Yeah, those Gallowglasses were always snapping their swords in half."

Collin flicks his hand at her. "We need a life or death beat for Donal Cam in the battle. A fall or getting his sword knocked out of his hands kills the aura of his godlike warrior chops."

"I agree," huffs Danna. "But he's got to earn the victory. No sword snapping in two."

Collin brandishes an invisible blade. "Those suckers weren't indestructible."

The emotional landscape in here is fascinating. Details and accuracy throw friendly collaborators into cage matches. On a couch near the window, Benj and Benny have their heads together, fleshing out the climax scene of the season arc into a wallop that will leave fans breathless. It's literally a climax since it's the first time Donal Cam and Nieve tangle naked under the pile of furs in his bedchamber. First of many.

An image of Jack and Niks doing what Jack and I would have been doing last night if she hadn't slammed back a vat of whiskey drives me straight for the tray of donuts. I don't care if they've been sitting out for hours. The sugar content will preserve them until the next ice age.

Jack has not made an appearance today to snag a donut. That's probably for the best since my insides are in a mishmosh over him. I'd be lying to myself if I didn't include disappointment in the mix. Not one text or call from him today. My dark side concludes the silence is guilt based. Maybe Niks didn't stay the night on the couch. She does have the body and face of a faerie queen. What guy could hold back if an ethereal being slipped between his sheets?

Jack said Niks wasn't the woman he wanted in his bed, but she might have been the woman who ended up there.

"Gillian," says Danna.

I swallow my bite of donut without chewing.

She focuses on her laptop, not even looking at me. "Nip over to weapons and bring us one of the Donal Cam swords."

Bobby's vision of a writer's assistant not being a lackey hasn't completely translated to the whole writing staff, mostly Danna. It doesn't matter. I'm fascinated by this cast of characters and how they work. Watching five different temperaments and artistic processes coalesce to bring Deidre's vision to life is a crash course in screenwriting.

"Sure." I welcome the chance to escape the tension in the room.

"Wait a sec." Collin glances at the clock on the wall. "Are props back from location?"

Danna makes a clicking sound with her mouth. "They lost the light hours ago." She points a finger at him like a weapon. "Some people have plans tonight, Collin."

Hours ago. So, Jack did have time to reach out to me today. I slip the phone from my pocket. Still no texts or missed calls from him. What am I doing? I give myself a cease and desist order before shoving my phone into the deepest, darkest recess of my pocket.

"Do you want me to go with you?" asks Maureen, hopefully.

I'm not the only one who'd like a break from the stress in the room. "Thanks, but I need practice finding my way around." As I duck into my office to grab the map I scribbled of The Clan, the conversation shifts.

Maureen throws paper clips one at a time across the table into an empty coffee mug. "Has Bobby named a lead on the finale script yet?"

Collin grunts. "Naw. He's still saying it's to be determined."

"I smell a Bobby Provost script," says Maureen, expertly twirling a silver pen from one finger to the next on her right hand.

Collin plays a drum solo with his pens. "I've got odds he wants to take it on since he gave Deidre the penultimate, but the bugger's a slave to editing."

As I head down the hallway, I wonder how they determine who writes which episode. I have a sense that Bobby runs a creative dictatorship with Danna as his majordomo.

Apart from the writer's room, it looks like Friday/Valentine's Day quitting time is in place. The scene shop is dead, the horse arena empty. I cut over to the design hub and work my way down the corridor where costumes, props, set dec, and specifically, the armory are located.

I make the mistake of poking my nose into a dark room near props and almost scream. A dozen stiff animals and animal heads peer at me. It smells musty and dead. I make a note on the map.

"Taxidermy."

This is one department I'll avoid in the future. Apparently, Bobby's animal-friendly policy doesn't apply to the ones that are already dead.

At the end of the hallway, two crossed swords hang over a doorway. Close up, I see they are wood carvings covered in metallic paint.

"This must be the place." I swing open the door to face racks of swords, shields, maces, and knives. If we're ever under attack, I know where to come. The room is lit by the scant glow of a single overhead light.

"Hello?"

I don't know a specific Donal Cam sword from a food processor. On one rolling rack, character names are written on strips of tape above the weapons.

"Bowstring. Rory. O'Connor Clansman." No Donal Cam.

Off to the side, there's a deserted, glassed-in office lit only by the glow of a bouncing glass of Guinness screen saver on a single computer. I'll have to scan the racks until I find a Donal Cam sword. From my research, I got the gist of what it looks like. Hopefully, any gnarly weapon capable of lopping off a head will do tonight for Collin and Danna.

Moving down the center aisle, I catch sight of a rack of swords that look as tall as I am. Those Celtic chieftains didn't mess around. Warding off other clans or Viking invaders wasn't a friendly game of badminton.

I find a sword most like the ones I put in the collage for the writers and close my fingers around the hilt. When I try to lift it, I nearly lose my balance the blasted thing is so heavy. It drops back into its berth with a clank.

"There's never a burly Celt around when you need one."

When the clang dies away, a muffled sound of metal on metal replaces it. My first thought is *epic ghost battle*, two dead warriors using props to settle ancient feuds. Not so. The clanks are of this world and seem to be coming from behind a line of racks along the back wall of the armory.

"Grand," I say, embracing Irish verbiage and heading toward the sound. Hopefully, someone is here to point me toward a Donal Cam steel special.

As I near a door in the far corner of the armory, the sounds of battle increase. Grunts and curses join the heavy metal harmony. I open the door a crack to peek and not disturb.

The room is a massive gym with mats covering most of the floor. There are treadmills and fitness machines along one wall next to a collection of free weights and kettlebells. The space looks like an Olympic training center. An epic battle does rage in the center of the room. Based on the intensity of the interplay and the combatants, I could be watching Hercules and Zeus duking it out with swords for domination of the universe. Except I know Hercules. The warrior with hair of spun gold dancing wildly above broad shoulders strong enough to lift a mastodon is Jack. The layer of sweat coating his bare upper body catches the overhead lights, setting him aglow. Muscles in his forearms flex like cords of thick vines as he flows through his moves.

"Stop locking your elbow," barks the other collection of muscle in the room. The scene is almost comical. The top of Jack's costume is draped over his belt, leaving him bare-chested. It flaps and billows as he pivots and lunges. His opponent wears ordinary gray sweats.

Jack repeats the same series of movements. He pants and gasps for breath but doesn't let up.

"Better, better," says the guy I assume is either Jack's trainer or the fight coordinator.

Jack downs a bottle of water. "Let's go again. Ten times in a row and then I'll own it."

My chest clenches as Jack speaks the same words I said to him that first day we met when I de-glitched his backswing and again last night at the driving range.

The trainer points his sword at Jack. "Once more will do for tonight. I'll not have you straining muscles. You've got a taxing week coming with the clan battle scene."

"Twice."

The trainer shakes his head. "Everything's a bargain with you."

So, I'm not the only one to be on the receiving end of pressure from Jack O'Leary.

Jack grins and takes his opening position. The choreography is beautiful. These two magnificent specimens of the human form spin and collide only to counter one another like reflections in a mirror. After a final series of brutal blows that creates a deafening shriek of steel, they fade into stillness.

Jack faces away from me. The muscles of his back ripple as he stretches his arms and rolls his shoulders. I want to run across the room and draw my fingers over every one of them. Touch them as steel softens back into human flesh.

"We've company." The fight coordinator winks at me. "I don't suppose I'm lucky enough to assume you'd be looking for me."

Jack glances over his shoulder, eyes widening when he sees who's come a callin'.

I'm so flustered at being caught I blurt, "I'm not looking for him." My tone is harsh, bordering on offended that I could possibly be looking for Jack O'Leary. Even though I'm trying to convince myself I can't be, I'm pissed at the absolute silence following his slumber party with Niks last night.

Instead of a smile, Jack looks pained.

"The writers sent me to get one of Donal Cam's swords." I walk across the mats, arm outstretched. "I'm Gillian, the new writer's assistant."

The man moves the sword to his left hand and wipes the right one on his sweats before taking mine. "I'm Jimmy. You're very welcome here to my training center." He gestures toward Jack. "Have you met this feller?"

Jack's face is neutral.

I smile at Jack. "Several times. Nice to run into you again, Jack. How's your golf swing coming?"

Neutral perks up. It occurs to me that my less-than-warm sign-off to our phone call last night may be the culprit of his inattention. He's probably trying to read me as hard as I'm trying to read him.

Jimmy pops his sword into a weapons rack. "Jack's the man you need to see about a Donal Cam sword. I'm off." He wipes his face with a towel and shrugs into a *Chieftain's Son* hoodie. I've got to get one of those.

"If I'm late to take the wife out tonight, I won't hear the end of it." The trainer winks and picks up his duffle bag. "Enjoy your weekend." He points a finger at Jack. "And I don't mean overdoing your workouts over the next two days. We've got a bastard of a schedule coming up."

Jack salutes him. "Aye, aye, captain."

Jimmy fans an arm across the room. "After the sword business, close down for me, will you?"

"Yep," says Jack. We both watch Jimmy walk through the door.

Heat radiates off Jack's body as he takes a step closer to me. "Hi."

I raise my eyes to his. "Hello."

He presses his lips together, causing their natural blush color to fade. "Gilly, I'm so sorry about last night."

The apology slices into me, an echo of the way Treat would approach after he'd showered attention on this female or that for the sake of the company. This is my moment to back away. Jack and I have shared nothing more than a few kisses and one or two steps toward something more. Calling a halt to the possibility of us now will prevent any emotional bruising.

I gather up my nerve and a lungful of oxygen. "Maybe last night was a sign. I get that you and Niks are on a crazy ride together and probably need each other to stay sane. Shared experience and all."

Saying the words aloud edges me closer to accepting their validity. As attracted as I am to Jack, we make much less sense than Niks and him do.

Without preamble, he lifts me off my feet and then sits me onto a stack of mats. He takes my hands in his. "I panicked. Meg's do-this and don't-do-that's are still new to me. I got boggled." He twirls fingers around his temples. "I figured dumping Niks on my couch instead of exposing her drunken stumble back to the hotel was the safest thing to do."

His expression is pathetic. He really is boggled.

Jack takes my face in those hands that feel like a blanket warmed in front of a hearth fire. "She didn't stay, Gilly. I finally got a hold of Marisa to pick her up."

"Marisa?"

A flash of panic crosses Jack's face. Over what? Does he think I don't believe him?

His skin heats up even more. "Niks's assistant. Lives at the hotel with her."

I ease his fingers from my face but keep ahold of them. Despite the self-talk I've attempted, Jack's touch begins to thaw my reservations about us. "Have you considered that Niks planned last night, Jack? Showing up at the golf course, dinner. You can't tell me you miss the fact she barely takes her eyes off you when you're in the same room."

His fingers tighten on mine, sending a thrill through me. Why is it so blasted hard to resist this man?

"She never misses an opportunity to be physical with you." A montage of Treat and the women he's wooed to be part of Lawson Graham Premier Sportswear skips through my memory. I refused to admit that touches, arms around waists, and bodies pressed close for whispers were indicators of Treat being unfaithful. He convinced me that my jealousy was misplaced, but then came Lanie. Now, when I play back Treat's interaction with all those women, I see how naïve I was. Lanie was far from the first.

Jack stills and then draws a long, deep breath. "Being an actor is to be physical. It comes with the territory."

I slide my hands free and scoot away to look him in the eye. "And that territory opens up multiple interpretations."

Jack huffs out a breath. "You expect me to keep my hands tied behind my back? That'll paint me as a standoffish prick."

"That's not what I mean."

He closes his eyes for a long moment. "If I worry I've upset you every time I toss an arm around Niks's—or any other female in the cast's—

shoulder, I'll go mad. You have to accept that a certain level of familiarity and touching is part of the world I live in."

"I do, and there's an easy fix to eliminate this issue. Friendship. You won't have to check yourself or worry about upsetting me."

His hands ball into fists. Veins stand out on his forearms. "I am fully capable of separating my private life from my professional one. You're the one that seems to have trouble handling things that are part of the game."

I spring to my feet. "Maybe I choose not to step into a situation where I'd have to constantly question that separation."

His hands dart out, catching me and spinning me back toward him. "I don't know how to say this more plainly. I have no romantic interest in Niks. Donal Cam will ache for Nieve, but Jack has nothing inside for that woman apart from whatever bond we need to play at to make the world believe we're soulmates. It's an illusion."

Our eyes remain locked as he continues. "I have no reason not to tell you the truth and every reason to be honest with you." He scratches his neck under his hair. "Since I've given you no cause not to trust me, how about taking a stab at it?"

I step out of his grip and wave my hands to encompass as much space as possible. My voice comes out breathy. "You're asking more of me than a little bit of trust."

"I know I am, but I have to. Accepting me is accepting the worlds I step into, the restrictions Meg and True Time slap on my business, and the circus that'll be likely following me for years." He crosses his arms and frowns. "I'm not going to apologize for where my life is going. I've worked for it, and I want it. If you must walk away, you must."

"And you won't try to stop me?"

One side of his mouth hitches up and his arms drop to his sides. "I didn't agree to that." A crease forms between his eyebrows. "I'm going to say something that may chase you away faster, but with you, my heart is beginning to override my head." He takes one step closer to me, then another.

Jack lays his reality at my feet. No apologies about it. "This is who and what I am, Gillian." He's an actor crossing the line to star. There are professional obligations in his life that will twist my guts. This is his admission he won't back down from the demands of his work or his image to spare my feelings.

Can I deal with that?

Self-preservation and rationality dig a finger into my shoulder and point to the exit door. Jack stands motionless, fixating on my face. When I don't retreat, his hands graze my arms.

"If what I'm saying is too much a burden for you, I'll stop. If I can. I'm a driven man, Gilly, and I see that in you as well. The first day I watched your beautiful golf swing, I wanted to fall to my knees. It was the blow of a sword, but a sword of silk, crackling and whipping in a windstorm. It was a poem, a song. The swing and you were one." He drops his hands to my hips, pulling me closer. "I wanted so badly to connect with you. God, I nearly roared your name and ran to you right there on the tee."

How can this man I've only known a handful of days make me feel more valued, more desired than Treat did in two years of intimacy? It's a feeling I'm loathe to let go of. If I don't take even a small chance to see where connecting with Jack leads, am I cheating myself out of a good thing I deserve?

For the love of God, why am I acting like this is a do-or-die decision? All those years of attempting to define the trajectory of my relationship with Treat have really screwed up my perspective on men. This gorgeous man wants to date me, and judging from the way he kisses, share some damn fine sex. Screw depravation. Taking a few steps further with Jack O'Leary doesn't seal my fate. Right now, we're nobody's business but our own.

I slide my hands slowly over his shoulders, reveling in the contour of every muscle until my hands meet behind his neck. My objections to being with him fade more and more every minute we're together.

My voice is quiet as I confess. "That night in the pub… It was so easy with you. So right. I couldn't wrap my head around how attracted I was to you so fast, then you kissed me."

"I had to." His breath is hot and moist against my neck. "Like I have to now, if you're not walking through that door."

"I don't see a door."

He threads fingers into my hair, tilting my head back so his mouth has a straight shot to mine. His lips claim me, beginning in a slow rhythm as we savor the feel of moving together. The kiss ignites a steady burn that travels down my throat to my heart, inciting it to beat faster and faster until it's racing so quickly I'm sure Jack can feel it against his rock wall of a chest.

Jack's tongue slides over mine, tasting, teasing. He takes my bottom lip in his teeth, tugging gently. I rake my fingertips through the tight auburn curls of hair on his chest until I hit a ridge that makes me pull away from him and stare. A long scar stretches diagonally from the hollow between his pecs nearly to his left hip. I trace the length of it.

"My God, Jack. Where did you get this?"

He pokes a fingernail under the rounded top of the scar and peels it away from his skin. "From Lou in makeup." In one quick motion, he yanks off the long strip that looks like a skinny worm, hissing as it tugs his chest hair. He tosses the rubbery scar over his shoulder.

I tap along the slight pink line the fake scar leaves on his skin, taking a detour to circle his nipple. It hardens beneath my touch.

Jack moans and wraps his arms around my back, sealing my body to his until I can barely breathe.

He guides me to lie on the mat. His hand works its way across my knee and up my thigh while he stretches out on his side next to me. One finger slips under the elastic of my panties, and he explores the crease between my leg and body. A noise between a rumble and purr escapes my lips.

Jack shifts to hover above me. "I believe you mentioned the need of Donal Cam's sword?" He's pressed so close, even through layers of costume, I know exactly where that sword is.

Oh, Jeez. The sword!

I pet the soft, red-gold down covering his arm, a contrast to the bristles on his chest. When I reach his hand, I reluctantly move it out from under my skirt. "They're waiting for me in the writer's room."

He drops his head against my collarbone, panting harder than when he sparred with Jimmy. "Now?"

"They need your sword."

He lifts his head, flashing me a crazy hot, Wicked Jack smile. "Are they the only ones?"

I pull him down for a lingering kiss. "Give me your silver sword."

He rolls onto his back. "Are you trying to make me burst?" His hand snakes between my back and the mat. "I'll give it to you on one condition."

"Which is?" I sit up and straighten my clothes.

He gently cups my ass. "Come home with me tonight."

My heartbeat kicks up even higher. Things with Jack are going so fast, good judgement doesn't stand a chance to catch up. "I don't know how late I'm going to be here with the writers." As the energy we stirred up with our kisses slowly dissipates, his body slumps deeper into the mat. He's exhausted. Even though Jack's clearly in enviable shape, a long day of shooting and then his workout with Jimmy takes its toll. "And you looked whipped."

He sits up beside me, kissing a path from the hollow in my throat to the top button of my blouse. "Never too whipped for—"

I reclaim the button he attempts to undo with his teeth and nudge him away. "You need to go home and collapse."

"Only if you promise to spend the day with me tomorrow. I'll take you round the Ring of Kerry."

"What if someone sees us?"

"We'll steer clear of tour buses and popular spots. I want to share places dear to my heart, so you'll know me better through them." His eyes glaze over for a moment. I know he's envisioning things I have yet to discover. "I can be careful, Gilly. So can you. As I said, we'll figure this out." He fans his finger between the two of us.

"This could be a colossal mistake."

"Could it?"

"You know it could." I brush long, honey-colored strands off his face.

He closes his eyes while I stroke. When I stop, his expression turns serious. "We're two smart people who don't back down from a challenge. Let's give us a go."

Jack speaks the language of "we", of "us"—something Treat never did. This man is not asking me to deceive or pretend not to exist. In building too high a wall to protect my emotions, I may deprive myself of potential joy with Jack. He's asking me to have a say in how we move forward. I won't let being with Jack turn into a shadow world like my life with Treat.

There's a way to be real and still be smart. Together, we'll find the right way to define "us." We have to. The more I'm with Jack, the less I can control the need to have this man in my life, not parallel to it.

I slide my thumb across his bottom lip to his chin and take him in a kiss. My "yes" to Jack. Before it escalates into something that makes my absence from the writer's room long enough to require a search party, I wiggle away from him.

He drops onto his back with an exaggerated sigh, turning his head toward me. As he watches me lift the crazy heavy Donal Cam sword he's abandoned, a smile plays across those dusty rose-colored lips.

I mimic one of the stances Jimmy demonstrated, even though I have to use two hands instead of one, and point the tip of the blade at his nose. "Okay, Jack. Let's figure us out." Before I drag the sword from the room, I turn back to him. "Happy Valentine's Day."

CHAPTER
TWELVE

The perfect place to commit death by freezing is on the shore of the Atlantic Ocean in February before dawn. My teeth chatter so hard I'm afraid I'm going to bite my lip.

Just as I find the perfect place next to the Charlie Chaplin Statue to block the wind, a single pair of headlights appears in the distance. I'm alone on this stretch of the Waterville Heritage Trail at half-six in the morning so I can safely jump into Jack's car without turning up on the front page of a tabloid.

A stab of fear makes my heart race. What if the car is Bobby coming home after an editing all-nighter? How am I going to explain lurking around Mr. Chaplin in the pre-dawn hours? I slide around to Charlie's back and catch a blast of freezing air off the water.

Thankfully, a familiar silver and blue Renault pulls up to the curb and idles. With an assist from my Atlantic tailwind, I fly to the passenger side of the car and grab the handle. The car lurches forward as my ghostly appearance nearly sends Jack into cardiac arrest.

"Mother of God, woman," he says as I surge into the passenger seat and slam the door.

It's blissfully warm inside the car. "Do you have seat warmers?"

My Celtic god punches the control to toast my ass. He envelopes me in an all-consuming hug. Hot breath flows down my neck until my lips are taken in a kiss that ignites a steady pulse between my legs.

Damp lips trap my earlobe, and a deep, rumbling voice whispers, "Good morning, love."

Love. Calling people "love" is pretty common for the Irish, but to hear the word from Jack to me, even in this casual way, is overwhelming. Deep in my gut, I wonder how it might feel if he ever used the word in a more meaningful way.

What are you doing to yourself, Gilly? Carts, horses—once again completely out of order.

When he settles back in his seat, I miss the touch of his lips on mine. "Waterville is already part way 'round the Ring of Kerry." I learn the Ring of Kerry is the road we're on and not the land. The "ring" circles the Iveragh Peninsula, the area where Jack was born and raised before he went off to Dublin and Trinity college.

"First, I'm going to take you to Portmagee, and if the Atlantic is cooperative this morning, we'll jump on a boat out to the Skelligs."

Jack is proud, showing off this land he so clearly loves. "And a Skellig is...a sea monster? A shipwreck?"

"It means rock in the sea." He squeezes the back of my neck. "You've so much to learn."

"As in island?"

"Oh, so much more than an island. It's the sanctuary in *Skies of Wind and Mist*, where one of Donal Cam's Chieftains, the King of West Munster, flees to escape the King of Cashel." The look on my face while I connect these dots makes him chuckle. "Third book down in the stack I left on your desk."

"Oh, my gosh. I've never thanked you for the books. That was so sweet of you." I lean across the car and kiss the corner of his mouth. As I hoped, it coaxes his lips into a smile I could stare at for hours, days, the rest of my life.

"I hope you don't mind secondhand. Deidre gave 'em to me when I got cast as himself."

"You gave me your books?" His generosity touches me. I don't have the heart to tell him Mom and I share our own set of well-worn *Chieftain's Son* tomes back in L.A.

"For the love of God, don't tell her. I bought the set in paperback so I can write all over them without feeling like I'm defacing relics." He looks quickly at me and then back at the road. I'm starting to notice his little quirks like the way a sidelong look precedes quick glances before he speaks. "Those stories are my world for the foreseeable future." There's another rapid-fire peek in my direction and then away. "It's a place where I want you with me."

His sincerity raises a tear in the corner of my eye. I want to tell him to sweep me off my feet and carry me into his world, but I stop myself. We have to go slowly. Our togetherness is tricky. I can't make promises that might turn out impossible to keep. Being with him is all about fun. A gift to the new Gilly.

"Losing myself in ol' Donal Cam's journey is definitely a place I'm growing very fond of."

Jack's shoulders relax. I said the right thing, confirmation I'm onboard with giving us a whirl.

He taps the top of the steering wheel with his index finger. "Speaking of Cashel, we'll have to get you some of their famous bleu cheese. Nothing like it."

Were the Kings of Cashel cheese moguls? Munster is a cheese as well. Are all Irish kings in the cheese biz? "American history" is a file drawer in my brain from years of schooling. I'm sure Jack has one for Ireland's past.

"I'd better brush up on Irish history. Any suggestions of a good read?"

"Well, I could steal one of my nieces' schoolbooks, but my big sister, Bonnie, might well beat the tar out of me for doin' it."

I'm hungry for more about Jack's real life. "Tell me about your nieces."

His face softens. "The pair of 'em are near perfect." A corner of his lip rises. "Speaking as a proud uncle, of course. Feisty and brilliant. Both gingers like me and their ma. Mary Catherine, my Cat, is ten this spring and Mary Jane, Janie, just had her eighth birthday."

"You're close to them."

"Since the day they were born. I go back and forth between wanting to eat them they're so delicious or giving them a whack on the bum for their sass." Jack takes a curve in the road so fast the seat belt nearly strangles me. He's oblivious to his speed. "Have you ever seen a Puffin?"

"Since I've never been to the Arctic, that's a firm no."

He laughs. "We've got them here abouts. When we get to shooting third season locations, you'll become acquainted. The Skellig Islands crawl with them."

I love his certainty that I'll still be part of *The Chieftain's Son* in season three.

"The feathery beasties wreak havoc when folks film on the islands. If you don't want a Puffin on screen, skip the Skelligs."

"Have you ever made it out there?"

"On a boat, weaving around the islands. There's a strict limit on how many feet they let touch the place." He takes a long, slow breath. "Shooting on a Skellig is one of the things I'm most looking forward to on this crazy *Chieftain's Son* ride."

"Not screaming crowds of women?"

Wicked Jack shoots a sideways glance in my direction. "Naw. There's just the one woman's screams I'm interested in."

I match him wicked to wicked by waving my hands in the air and wiggling my whole body. "Jack! Jack! Look over here, you hunky slice of man flesh!"

"Man flesh, is it? That's a new one." He squeezes my leg above the knee. "I like it."

The setting moon reflects off the mist blanketing the land around us, giving the whole world a silver sheen. I'm on a carriage ride with an elven prince. If I ask, he'll lift us into the sky to watch dawn break over the Ring of Kerry.

The main drag of Portmagee runs along an inlet. A bridge crosses the narrow water between boats bobbing at the dock and a strip of green that looks like an island. "Is that a Skellig?"

"Naw," says Jack. He pulls into a parking place in front of a stone building wearing a red painted sign with letters in a kicky font that read

The Port Bar. "That's Valentia Island. Best place for seeing the Skelligs if the boats aren't running." He kills the engine and taps his phone, on the hunt for something. The corners of his mouth dip into a frown. "Which they aren't. It was a long shot anyway this time of year." His hand strays to my thigh. "Any time of year, really. Sorry, love."

"Guess I'll have to wait for season three. Where to next?" I chirp, not entirely disappointed to avoid a boat in the sloshing waves of the Atlantic even with the reward of puffins.

"We're here. Our first coffee stop." He roars in character as Donal Cam. "And food."

If there is anything I'm more enamored with than Jack O'Leary, it's Irish butter and brown bread. The pile of potatoes and ham we polish off for breakfast come in a close second. With my belly full, I'm tempted to recline my seat and snooze while my tour guide winds through this gorgeous countryside. Awe beats nap as I take in endless fields of waving green grasses and their tiny yellow wildflowers vying for my attention.

Jack slows for a moment, which doesn't matter since there aren't any other cars behind us. "Look at that majestic fellow."

Near the road, poised on a small patch of green amid white-spotted granite slabs, is a ram. He's as still as the rocks surrounding him, chin slightly tilted up to give him a regal air. A single line of blue spray paint runs down his shaggy back. "Behold the king of sheep," I say, sweeping a hand in his direction. I steal a picture before the fine fellow decides to take off. Mom and Dad will love this one.

Jack lets out a low grunt. "I'd say he's more the emperor type." He nods to my phone. "Haven't filled your quota of sheep shots yet?"

I tuck the cell back in my pocket. "I promised my parents one sheep picture a day for as long as I'm here."

Jack lead-foots the gas. "And how long do you see that being?"

I feel his eyes on me as I shrug. "There are plenty of sheep waiting for their close-up."

We're both quiet as we float through the landscape.

Jack screeches off the road into a miniscule stretch of gravel and jumps out of the car. "I want to show you *Caiseal Leaca na Buaile,* a ring

fort." We trudge up a path under the watchful eyes of many sheep. I'm
going to have to get in better shape if I'm going to keep up with Jack and
his insane fitness. He waxes historic over the ring of stones up ahead,
homestead of wealthy landowners from days gone by. "Entrances face
east to avoid prevailing winds." Who needs a book on Irish history when
I've got my own personal docent?

A cow peers at us over a wooden fence. "Hello cow." My words must
translate to threats of death or dismemberment in cow language because
it turns and trots away at the sound of my voice.

"You spooked the poor lady," says Jack.

The cow stops to look back at us over its shoulder. *"Maidin mhaith,
bó,"* says Jack with an adorable Irish lilt. Not so cute to our bovine
friend, who lows what is clearly a cow insult at him and disappears
around a small hill.

"Now who scared her?" I thread an arm through his. "What did you
say?"

"Good morning, cow."

"Ah, that explains it. Terrifying."

He jerks his chin at the animal. "The name of this ring fort means
'summer cow pasture' in honor of her kind. You'd think she'd be a more
gracious hostess."

We stroll up the hill, soaking in the day. "Will you teach me Irish?"

His face is aglow. "Aye, lass." I see why they cast Jack as Donal Cam.
In the diffuse light, with his sculpted features and shining flaxen hair, he
is a man from another time. He pulls me against him, hands clasped
behind my back. "Here's your first word, *'Póg'.*" His lips meet mine, and
the kiss is as sweet as the fragrance of the fresh grasses covering the
hills around us.

"*Póg*," I whisper afterwards, running my thumbs along the creases on
either side of his lips.

"Come on. We've a lot to see." He takes my hand and drags me up to
the circle of stones where we climb and chase each other, laughing like
kids on a schoolyard.

Each place we go is more enchanting that the last. Peeking through a
tangle of ferns at the Glenbeigh overlook, we see a gray-blue curve of

ocean caressing the shore. Jack gestures toward a distant stretch of green. "When we get time away, I'll bring you back here to play Dooks Golf Links."

Further down the road, my eyes fix on the landscape as Jack's narrative fills me with a peace I haven't felt in a very long time. "Over there is where folks claim the gates of Tir na nÓg lay."

"Nieve's hometown."

"The same." The mention of Nieve brings Niks to mind, and my peace frays around the edges.

He gazes over the palette of green, chewing his lip. "I imagine Deidre's Sidhe Otherworld Tribunal lurks there as well."

"You mean the good ol' boy network who dumps poor Donal Cam in whatever time tortures him the most?"

He grunts. "I suspect Deidre sits at the head of their table."

The city of Killarney is as charming as I'm beginning to suspect all Irish cities are. Still full from breakfast, we can't tackle a meal, but we both need a caffeine fix. Killarney is too crowded a place to risk being seen with Jack. He suits up in a baseball cap and sunglasses before pulling into a car park at the edge of town. I pop out to get us coffee.

We sit in the car and watch a line of horse-drawn carriages clip clop down the street. I understand why Deidre set her stories in Ireland. There is a strong overlay of the past even here in what passes as a city. Mist and stretches of land cover more ground than houses and towns.

"I do love it here, Jack. Everywhere we go is so beautiful." I'm tempted to admit I'm also more drawn to him with each passing hour. He's charming without trying and so down to earth it's incomprehensible I've known him such a short length of time. He could be someone I went to school or grew up with.

He leans over to bump my shoulder. "I told you this could work, you and me." I try to ignore the niggling of pressure behind his words. This man wants what he wants and isn't afraid to push his agenda.

I'm not sure hiding in a car qualifies as working, but I won't be the storm cloud to ruin our day. "I have to admit Mr. O'Leary, today ranks as the best first date I've ever had."

"Fourth date. Pub is one. I count the stables and the car ride home as two. I did give you a gourmet energy bar for dinner." Jack throws back the rest of his coffee. "Add in the driving range as a third." He starts the car. "Which brings us to today and number four, which we're not half done with."

I'm suddenly blindsided with the thought that I never want to go on another first date. I can't imagine anyone fitting their puzzle piece to mine as perfectly as Jack. The sensation is so overpowering it brings tears to my eyes. I pretend to be transfixed with the view out my window.

I don't have to pretend for long, as we leave the city of Killarney and enter Killarney National Park. How could anyone not believe in ancient magic and faeries while driving through a forest so lush that water clings to the leaves like frozen waterfalls of diamonds? We climb, passing meadows and stretches of trees so tightly packed I'd have no trouble believing we've strayed off the main road into another realm. Fantasy overshadows reality. The beauty surrounding us permeates my soul. I'm afraid to speak and shatter the otherworldly vibe.

Jack's screech-to-a-halt parking style is not for the faint of heart. I'm going to insist on at least a thirty-second warning in the future so my stomach can prepare.

He's around to my side of the car, opening my door. Abandoned sunglasses sit on the dash. After a check of the immediate area, which appears to be empty, he flings the baseball cap into the back seat and holds out a hand to me. The look of anticipation on his face is so alluring, it makes me want to jump him right there in the car park.

"I've something to show you."

I take his hand. He yanks me across the street so fast I almost trip. We pass weather-worn boulders higher than my head and step out onto an overlook.

"Oh, Jack." Through the cool and mysterious late Irish afternoon, a landscape, the stuff of love songs, unfolds before me.

"This place is called Ladies View. Named for the delight it gave Queen Victoria's ladies in waiting. Do you love it?"

I wrap my arms around his waist, but I can't take my eyes off the view. A dozen different shades of green from hunter to mint roll down hillsides. Caps of granite covered in mosses of orange and tan dot the countryside. White lichen on the rocks read like delicate lace. At the bottom of the slope are lakes as dove gray as Jack's eyes in low light.

"It's a poem."

He wraps his arms around me and we hold each other, drinking in the glorious scene before us.

"Will you come home with me now, beautiful girl?"

I turn in his arms and slide my thumbs along his cheeks. Bringing his face down to mine, I brush my lips against his in a dozen tiny kisses. He snatches me off my feet and into his arms. I wrap my legs around his waist, as light kisses shift into an insane longing for one another.

A car grumbles to a stop in the car park beyond the trees, preventing me from giving myself to Jack under the shadows of the yew at the edge of the overlook. He sets me down. I slide my hands under his coat and down the back of his jeans, exploring the taut muscles of his backside. "God, I hope it's not far."

CHAPTER

THIRTEEN

J ack takes the mountain roads to the tiny town of Sneem at
breakneck speed. I can't keep my fingers away from his lips. He
kisses and bites. When his hand strays under my thigh, it's all I
can do to keep from guiding it the rest of the way to a destination
too distracting for someone already struggling to keep a car on the
highway.

We cross a stone bridge over the river and into the center of town. I
swear the car tips onto two wheels when Jack tears up a small side road.

"Are we going to a hotel?"

He honks as we pass a yellow house surrounded by a low stone
fence. "I'm taking you home. I'm just telling Tim and Imelda it's me."

"Tim and Imelda?"

"Neighbors. They keep my roommates in check when I'm down in
Waterville."

"Whoa. You have roommates?"

He favors me with a sly grin that's swiftly becoming my favorite.
"Tom and Max. They'll be glad to meet you."

"You live with two guys?"

I feel the blush rise from my chest up to my forehead. When I imagine what Jack and I are about to do, a couple of dudes listening on the other side of the wall is far from a turn-on.

"Two ladies. Tomasina and Maxine."

"And you never thought to mention you don't live alone?" Oh, God, two women eavesdropping is worse. When Jack sets his mind to something, he develops tunnel vision, ignoring any obstacles that keep him from getting what he wants.

We pull up to a one-story cottage made of stone and brightly painted red wood. "You're very welcome to my home, Gillian Bettencourt."

The place is small. The obvious lack of privacy we'll have inside douses my plan to shove Jack through the door and rip his clothes off. I can't deal with an audience on the other side of his bedroom wall. I'll meet his "ladies" and then convince him to find a discreet B and B.

He's already up the path, unlocking the door and eagerly waving me on. Flower beds brimming with winter Irises stretch under windows from the door to the corners of his house.

I start toward Jack. What is he planning to tell the two women he cohabitates with? Can he trust them enough not to blab about us? How close are the three of them? Oh, Lord, what if he used to date one or both of them? Jack is totally the type that would stay friends with exes.

As soon as the front door swings open, a pair of gray tabby cats wind around Jack's legs. He scoops one up in each hand. "I'd like you to meet Tom and Max."

"Your roommates are cats?"

When he chortles at his joke, the cats rub their heads against him. "Worried the piss out of you, didn't I?" Jack dumps the girls onto the path. They approach to give me the once-over. Definitely the jealous types.

I slap his shoulder. "Stinker." Now that we're on the threshold of the actual place Jack calls home, I feel a little jittery. Once through that door, a significant point of no return will be crossed.

Sensing my hesitation, Jack strokes my hair. "You know I burn for you."

I rest my hands on his hips. My eyes are riveted on his as the dusk rolls over the hillside.

Jack sighs. "I know I can be a pushy bastard." Tapping a finger against my temple, his voice turns serious. "If this has decided you're not ready, I'll honor that." He drops his head back, watching the sky. "But you'll have to excuse me while I pour a bucket of ice cubes down my jeans." Gently, my Celtic warrior raises my chin. "You are too important for me to pressure."

My fingers slowly stroke the side of his face. Jack is pushy, but everything with him has felt mutual. Mutual attraction. Mutual connection. Mutual burning. I trust him and want to be vulnerable with him, open up and begin to purge the damage Treat did. This isn't a life commitment; it's giving myself permission to try something new that I have a say in.

"You're very welcome to take me into your home."

I'm off my feet in an instant and in Jack's arms. His mouth finds mine. Our kissing is a scrumptious frenzy of lust. He carries me into his living room and kicks the door closed behind us, leaving his roommates to fend for themselves.

My hands tangle in the soft waves of his hair as I capture his lips, refusing to set them free. We fall onto the couch. His body presses mine deep into the cushions. Hands travel up and down my sides until they make their way to my breasts. I clutch his back and arch up against him.

He rises on elbows to catch his breath.

I grasp his shoulders. "Get back down here."

In one swift motion, he pulls me up onto his lap to nuzzle and nip at my neck. "My body is screaming for me to take you straight away."

I shift so I'm straddling him. Good God, he's not kidding. I feel waves of heat pulsing out of the precise portion of his body doing the screaming. To my surprise, he lifts me to my feet.

"But I want to give you firelight and romance, not a quick pounding."

I burst into laughter. "A quick pounding?"

He wraps his arms around me to grab my ass and crushes me against the proof he's fully prepared to deliver the aforementioned pounding. When he steps back, my eyes drop to the gift I'm about to unwrap. *Holy Jeez.* I fear for the seams on the front of his jeans.

Jack stumbles to the fireplace, not entirely in control of his movements. Thank goodness he's got ceramic logs and a gas fire that ignites instantly. He guides me to stand in front of the flames, shedding his own jacket before peeling mine off. Hands slip under my sweater, lifting the fabric an inch at a time until it joins my jacket on the floor. I flick the clasp on the front of my bra and shrug out of it.

"My God," says Jack as he cups my breasts. He runs thumbs over my nipples, and they rise to his touch.

"Don't move," I say and raise his sweater to expose his flat stomach. I bend to kiss the half circle of skin above his navel and work my way up the center of his body, exposing his chest inch by inch until he's shirtless. Tiny pebbles that I'm sure have nothing to do with the chill in the room rise along his skin. While I flick my tongue across his nipples, my hands slide inside the front of his jeans, exploring the glorious length of him.

Variations of, "My God" and "good Christ" rumble from his lips. By the time we've both stripped out of our jeans, he's unsteady on his feet. His completely naked body is more beautiful than the sum of its parts that I've already seen. He's as sleek and muscled as a mountain lion. The light from the hearth turns the red hair on his arms and legs into tiny licks of flame. I turn him sideways so the ruddy thatch between his legs glows in firelight.

His eyes are as wide and bright as the whole of a summer sky as we stand naked before one another. Jack takes one step closer to me so he can cup the back of my neck. His voice is thick and husky. "And in the moonlight, the evening breeze swept away her petals one by one until only the sweet core of her desire created for him alone glistened beneath the stars."

I recognize the words from *The Chieftain's Son*. The words of joining from Donal Cam to Nieve on their first night together. Lovers blessed by the heavens to follow each other through eternity. Words with the weight of lifetimes.

The rug before the fireplace is soft and thick. Jack eases me down and kisses his way up the inside of my thigh, slowing at my core to taste and tease with his tongue before finally sliding the length of his body against mine.

This darling man is sculpted to near perfection. My hands flow across every inch of his skin, learning, discovering. When I guide him inside me, light flickers around the room faster and faster. He's careful at first, as he disappears deeper into my flesh, but then neither of us has any restraint left. My legs wrap around his body, and we rock together as one, riding wild Atlantic waves.

With a fierce call to the night, Jack plunges past the last of my petals. I arch up to bring him to a place inside me that's never before been breached. It's more than a mere joining; all our lines and curves perfectly compliment one another's. Together, we form a magnificent sculpture. This is more than physical. My heart and spirit give over completely to this person as if they've been searching for him. Their quest ends in blinding success.

My own cry answers his, and we grip one another with bone cracking force. Our bodies refuse to separate. Jack's mouth consumes mine with a fury I return as his tongue sweeps round and round with mine in a whirlwind.

It takes a long time before we loosen our grip on one another. Jack reaches up to pull a quilt off the back of the couch but stops. He flips me over his body so I land on the rug closer to the fire. When I try to turn onto my side, he presses his hand to my stomach so I'm on my back. Rising up on an elbow, he stares at me.

"What are you doing?"

"Shh," he says and begins to draw circles around my breasts. "You're a she dragon, glowing red in the embers."

His fingers circle lower and lower until they find their target. *Circles.* More circles, until I moan so loudly no one in all of Sneem will have to guess what's happening in the little red house.

"Oh, God. Jack. How long until you can—"

Instead of answering, his mouth closes over my breast, sucking gently. I can't wait. I have to have him again or I'll lose my mind. I slide my hand down his chest and don't have to go very far before discovering no waiting is required.

He takes me more slowly this time, bringing me to madness in several creative ways before he finally embraces insanity with me.

My fingers dig into the muscles of his back as he collapses on top of me. I turn his face toward mine and drop light kisses across his cheek all the way to the shell of his ear so I can whisper. "Jack?"

"Mmm?"

"I never knew being with someone could be this intense, this..." I search for the right word to describe pulling my soul from my body and turning it to star fire. "Consuming."

He kisses the tip of my nose. "A very wise woman once told me you've got to do something right ten times before you own it."

When I curl his auburn chest hair around my pinkie, he spreads a hand across my ass.

"Well sir, then we've got work to do."

CHAPTER
FOURTEEN

T he bubbles in Jack's spa tub do wonders for the over-exercised places in my body. "This tub is enormous."

"A big man needs a big tub." He flashes me a naughty smile. "And I'm a big man." Jack arches up just enough out of the water to prove his point. He's already halfway to more than his smile being naughty.

"What are you, eighteen?"

"Haven't you heard? Thirty is the new eighteen." He flicks a small stream of water at me. "I didn't take advantage of my sexual prime. I'd best make up for it."

I yelp when his toes stray into forbidden territory and yank his foot up so fast he slides into the water up to his nose. "This is supposed to be a recovery soak."

He scoots back up, swiping water off his face. Stubble of reddish beard and mustache give me a glimpse of what a full-facial-hair version of Jack would look like. Toes caress my leg, steering clear of off-limit zones.

Jack's half-closed eyes give him the contented look of a big cat lazing on a tree branch. Watching him, my body hums at a low but constant frequency, savoring the pleasures from last night and this morning.

"Jack."

"Yes, love?"

"I meant what I said last night. What happened between us was on a whole new level than anything I ever felt with—"

His arm crooks around my middle, gliding me onto his lap so fast a wave sloshes over the edge of the spa. A warm, drippy hand covers my mouth. "Don't bring that man into my bed." I give his fingers a little nip and he moves his hand to settle on my breast. "Or my tub."

I lean back against his chest, the perfect combination of solid and soft. "The truth is that it's been a very long time since Treat has been anywhere near my heart." I play with a wet strand of buttery hair draped over Jack's shoulder. "I guess the time I'd already invested in him made me believe I should try to stick it out."

Quiet grunts and huffs escape from Jack like a volcano gassing off energy before it blows. "Did you love him?"

I rest a hand on Jack's knee. "For a time, I thought I was on the way there, but being his secret instead of a real part of his life kept me from taking that risk."

The timbre of Jack's voice darkens. "And I'm asking you to be the same."

I shift so I can tilt his chin and look directly into his eyes. "Will you be dictating everything we do, or will we navigate this as equal partners?"

"Partners." He nods. "You have my word."

I press the button to start up the jets and settle back against him. I haven't blissed out like this in a long time. As the bubbles rise and pop around me, so do lingering niggles of concern. I vowed to never again fall into the role of secret lover, but this does have potential to be a total rewrite of my toxic Treat situation. I trust Jack. If he promises we'll be partners in the way our romance will play out, I want to believe him.

Jack fidgets behind me. "If I ever meet the bastard, I hope I have a sword in my hand."

"Take it down a notch, Chieftain's Son." Reaching behind me, I stroke the side of his face. I stretch up to kiss the three tiny brown moles on his jawline.

He taps them one at a time. "My mother called these the belt of Orion." He lets out a long, slow breath. "She said the row of them popped up because I spent so much time looking at the stars."

I want more about Jack, his childhood, his past, but he's gone silent and rigid. It's like leaning against a rock. I never should have mentioned Treat. "Jack, neither of us needs to pretend there haven't been others."

He rests his chin on the top of my head. "None of the others matter anywhere close to this." Jack raises me onto one of his sturdy thighs so we can look into each other's eyes. "At least not for me."

My wet cheek slides against his whiskers. "I'd never write this because it sounds too corny, and don't you dare laugh, but I think you're a dream I've been afraid to dream." He holds me captive with the intensity of his gaze. I kiss the dimple in his chin and slide up to his lips. We kiss for a long time before I settle my head in the hollow of his shoulder. "Tell me about your befores."

He fits me closer against him and blows a breath that ripples across the top of the water. "One serious relationship for two years at Trinity." A pinch on my nipple makes me squeak. I slap his hand, and he snickers. "She's the one who stole my virtue."

"And…" My fingers explore the corded muscles on his arms.

"After that, only one who qualifies as a girlfriend, but that's been finished for nearly three years. As a rule, I don't attach easily." He rubs his lips back and forth across my shoulder. "So much for rules."

We shift so he's in front, leaning back on me. He guides my hands to his shoulders and encourages me to work out the stress kinks that I probably put there by bringing up Treat and prompting Jack to talk about his past. I shouldn't ask my next question, but for my sanity, I have to. "What about Niks?"

Jack stiffens. I prepare for a scolding since he's already sworn he has no feelings for her, but his voice is low and quiet. "When they first cast us, we were thrown together constantly. Irish classes, horse training, publicity, location shoots for the opening."

The jets time out, and I'm suddenly aware how cool the water has become.

"We got tight."

"Tight?"

He spins so we're face-to-face. "No, Gilly. I did not sleep with her." His lips press together until they're white. "I'm only telling you this next bit because she'll be in our lives, and I want nothing between you and me that isn't the whole truth."

"I don't think I want to hear this." I try to slide away from him, but he grabs my wrists so I'm held captive.

"I did kiss her once." He bobs his head to the side. "Off camera. It was my doing. I learned real quick that was a mistake. So, there you have it." I close my eyes, and he releases me.

"Did you ever bring her here?"

He slaps the water, spraying it all over the floor. "Why in the name of sanity would I do that?" Fingers tighten around my upper arms. "Do you hear me? There's nothing there for me with Niks. Absolutely nothing."

I work my way back to my end of the tub. "Does she know that?"

Jack pulls his knees up and drops his head onto them. "I feel responsible for taking care of Niks. Don't ask me to say any more about it, okay? There are things that aren't mine to share."

I bristle at the sting of his secret. The burn inside me from the image of Jack kissing Niks in any way close to the way he's been kissing me is so hot I'm afraid the water in the tub will start boiling. I study the condensation on the ceiling and decide to honor his request not to press. That doesn't mean I'll allow my self-preservation to go offline. "Okay."

Jack lies back, extending his body across the tub. His big hands glide me through the water until I'm stretched out on top of him. Both our chins dip below the surface, and we're nose to nose. His hands lay claim to every inch of my body, showing me who does matter to him.

"Gillian, you're the one who's brought starlight into my life. All I see and want to see is you. Do you hear me? There's no sun that can rise to make your starlight fade."

Any protest or further discussion is cut off with a kiss so possessive it turns my body to sea foam. If we go for all ten times today, it just might kill me. The water churns and splashes around us as Jack splits my legs, sliding them to either side of his hips. There's nothing sweet or careful as I grip the sides of the tub and we join with a ferocity to keep that sun from rising.

It's like a scene in a spy movie, me hiding in Jack's car and waiting for an all-clear text to join him in the River View Bistro on Sneem's main street. I'm so hungry I may start gnawing on his headrest. The only edible things besides cat food in his pantry were a bag of pretzels and peanut butter. We polished those off hours ago.

He didn't want to sneak into town until after the supper rush. I wonder what constitutes a rush in the tiny town of Sneem, a party of five? Jack's biggest concern is that a tour bus might pull in for a coffee stop to end their Ring of Kerry day.

The text finally comes.

Walk straight through to the kitchen.

I scan the street, checking for an ambush before bailing out of the car and through the front door of the bistro. The bell on the door is still tinkling when I'm swallowed by a chubby, gray-haired woman a few years older than my mom.

She holds me at arm's length. "Aren't you as precious as advertised." Threading an arm around my back, she shuttles me past a counter to a small table in the corner of the kitchen.

Jack already has a cup of hot tea in front of him. "I see you've met Imelda." He stands and lifts the woman up off the floor. "She's my second mum."

Imelda swats his arm, and Jack sets her back on her feet. "Have a seat over there with this darlin' brute, and I'll fetch you some tea and pie."

She waddles over to a counter and fiddles with a teapot.

Jack slides his cup my way so I don't have to wait. "Bewley's ginger and lemongrass, my favorite."

The tea is delicious and does a perfect job of erasing the chill from my vigil in the car. I'd really prefer a dinner before diving straight into pie. Although Lord knows my activities in the past twenty-four hours have burned off all the calories I could possibly gobble down for days.

"Wait until you taste Imelda's cheese and onion pie." He smacks his lips. The affection between Jack and Imelda is another layer of proof that Jack O'Leary may be as wonderful as my besotted brain suspects.

Imelda leans her back against the counter, hands flying through the air as she speaks. "I make my pie with filo dough. Picked that bit up when Tim and I traveled to Greece. Makes the crust so light it doesn't sit like a knot in your belly later." An old-fashioned dial egg timer dings. "Here we are."

Imelda plops two plates of fluffy cheese and onion pie in front of us and then scurries back into the restaurant. Jack cuts a corner of my pastry with his fork and feeds it to me.

"This is incredible," I say, still chewing. "I may never eat anything else as long as I'm in Ireland."

He digs into his pie. "I plan to make sure you're addicted so you've no choice but to stay put beyond the first season."

"Mission accomplished." Cheese oozes from the crust. I capture it before it falls to the plate. Jack stops eating to stare at me. "What?"

"I'm serious, Gilly. I want you here with me. The thought of you going back to L.A. is a fist to my gut."

I rub his knee. Touching him sends a sizzle of energy up my arm. I want to make promises to those eyes, but for now, honesty is what I've got. "Being with you, Jack, is a brand of happy I didn't know existed." I nearly add, *and too damn perfect to be true,* but the expression of pure joy on his face shuts me up.

He lays his hand on mine. "Does that happy include having to sneak into kitchens with me for dinner?"

I turn my hand over to twine my fingers through his. "For now."

There's a commotion near the doorway to the restaurant. Imelda shoos a delivery guy toward the front door.

"Imelda's one you don't want to cross," says Jack with a wink.

I pick up a stray blob of cheese and pop it into my mouth. "I see that."

He gestures toward the street. "On that bridge into town, Imelda faced down a Guinness truck." His smile widens. "It's a one-at-a-time bridge, so the feller waved her back. Imelda did the same to him. The two of them sat there for five minutes or so before Imelda stopped her car, left it on the road, and came in here for a cup of tea."

Besides being a kick-ass cook, Imelda is one plucky dame. "What happened?"

He slaps his knee. "The Guinness driver had to wave back the line of cars behind him so he could back off the bridge and let her by."

After Bobby's story and now this one, I hope to never meet a Guinness truck in the wild. If I do, I'll call Imelda for backup.

Jack's face shifts into a serious expression. "There's something I need to ask of you."

Here comes the fist to my gut. Dread squeezes my heart. I know what's coming, and it will involve words like sneaking, hiding, and deceiving.

"How fast can you finish reading all *The Chieftain's Son* books?"

Surprise makes me choke on my bite of pie.

Jack commandeers a pitcher of water from the counter behind us and pours me a glass. "Are you alright, love?"

I down the water and flap a hand to signal I'm going to survive. After a few gulps, I'm able to speak. "Rereading. I've been through the series a few times already. Why?"

He runs a hand through his hair. "I need you to help me dig deeper into Donal Cam. The bugger is giving me belly wibbles."

I bark out a laugh. "Belly wibbles?"

Jack's ears redden. "It's what we used to call being afraid with my nieces. Fear can have fangs and hide in the dark. Belly wibbles can be swallowed down quick to make them go away."

"How can I help your wibbles?"

He leans closer, tracing a line up and down my arm with his finger. "You see the layers in a story, in the characters. I know that from reading your lovely manuscript. I've got to keep Donal Cam from turning into a two-dimensional cutout."

I trap his finger and bring it to my lips. "What? You think ol' D.C. is more than a Celtic battle stud by day and lovesick puppy by night?"

Jack frees his finger and wags it at me. "Hold on, you know he's got a bit more than"—he swings an imaginary sword through the air—"and" —his lips graze mine. I taste lemongrass tea and cheese. "Help me find all his layers, keep the man interesting for ten seasons."

"I'm sure Deidre would love to help you dissect her boy."

A strong hand cups the side of my face. "I want to share this discovery process with you. I trust you to help me find all the feelings I'll have to pull up to do Donal Cam justice."

I close my eyes and let the warmth of his hand flow across my skin.

"It's a vulnerable place sometimes, being an actor. I need to feel safe with someone when I let them inside my process."

It's not a stray bit of pie keeping me from speaking now. Jack is inviting me into his art, the way he inhabits a character. This is what I've dreamed of, having a partner to share a creative life. I'd begun to believe it was impossible to find what my parents have but sitting across from me in this tiny Irish town is the man who could bring that hope back into my life.

"Mr. O'Leary, I'd be honored."

Jack raises my hands to his lips. "I'm afraid to go back to Waterville. What we've created on this beautiful weekend feels as fragile as a soap bubble." Worry lines flare from the corners of his eyes.

I squeeze his hands. "Then we'll have to be damn careful to keep that bubble afloat." As I fall into those Atlantic blue eyes, it hits me what a significant detour I've taken from any rational and logical plan I'd laid out. Somewhere between correcting the glitch in his swing and eating cheese and onion pie, I'm falling damn hard for Jack O'Leary.

CHAPTER
FIFTEEN

E ven though I've only woken up in bed with Jack once, it already feels wrong to open my eyes and not see him beside me. We're so easy together, it's as if we started in the middle of a relationship.

"What do you think, Gillian?" Bobby taps his script. "Cut or keep?"

We're on set during rehearsal. Bobby's stressing about the scene being too long. I'd like to cut the whole damn scene since it's Donal Cam and Nieve's profession of love and their first stolen kiss in a secluded corridor of the castle.

I force myself not to make eye contact with Jack He keeps shooting me apologetic looks. I'm scared shitless someone is going to pick up on them.

"I don't mean to criticize your choices here," I say to Bobby. "But I think you can lose one of the love metaphors."

He aims his pen at my nose. "I didn't hire you to hold back when I ask your opinion, so please don't." Bobby slashes a few lines of his script. "And you're right. Love comes across fine with one metaphor. We need to get to lust faster."

There's an "L" word I'm not enthused to hear when it concerns Jack and Niks. I need to program my brain to think of them as Donal Cam and Nieve on set. The man Alan Rafier pushes to salivate more over the fair lady is not my lover. Not here. Not in this reality. *God, I hope this gets easier.*

I tap on the cut line in Bobby's script. "That'll get them to Deidre's uncontrollable passion much faster."

Bobby laughs. "My pragmatist has become a romantic."

If you only knew, Mr. Provost. When he moves in for a confab with Jack, Niks, Alan, and the intimacy coordinator, I hang back. They chat about the changes and mark the new blocking.

Bobby is all smiles when he returns. He slings a lazy arm around my shoulders like we're sporty teammates. "Good call. I'd rather spend airtime on the carnal rather than the verbal in this scene."

"Give the people what they want." I applaud myself for keeping the sour taste in my mouth out of my tone.

His arm is still around me. From the corner of my eye, I see Jack frown. "We've got about half an hour before we go to camera," Bobby says as he guides me over toward the craft service table. "Read through the scene with me. I need to hear the flow with the cut and maybe find a few more darlings to kill."

With fresh coffee, we put our heads together.

Bobby reads the line as clinically as a scientist in a safe room. "My dearest heart, I'm a man of blood and death, but in you, I've the grace to love."

"This maid does not deserve such faith from one who commands clouds to fly across morning skies."

"With one touch of your lips to mine, clouds will fall to earth and require a master no longer." Bobby jots a note in his script. "I'm feeling a heavenly light moment here. Shaft through the window, Donal Cam on his knees." He snags Alan. They gesture the director of photography and the intimacy coordinator to join the convo.

I scan the pages, my dagger at the ready to kill any superfluous love lines. "Objectivity," I whisper to myself. Just because I don't want Niks and Jack gushing at each other doesn't mean Donal Cam and Nieve should be shortchanged in the love department.

A shadow falls over my script. "How late is Bobby keeping you tonight?" Jack's voice is one click above silent, but it thunders so loudly in my ear I'm sure everyone on stage heard it.

I grab his script. "Yes, these three lines are cut." He leans down, playing along so our heads nearly touch over the script. "Stop looking at me."

"Jack," calls Alan. "Once more before I lose you to wardrobe."

"On my way." He lifts a water bottle from the craft service table with one hand and scribbles something in his script with the other, holding it open so I can see it.

Stables three o'clock?

"Let me run that change by Bobby," I say. Jack, ever the actor, nods as if we've just uncovered a nugget of paramount importance in the script.

It's not even eight-thirty, or as everyone here says, half-eight, yet. They still need to run the scene at least once with the changes. After that, Niks and Jack will slip out to finish their transformation into Donal Cam and Nieve while electricians adjust lighting for the scene to capture the addition of Bobby's heavenly moment. The actors started their day in hair and makeup. Costumes won't take long. If Bobby is pleased with the way the scene's going, he'll want to bop off to editing, leaving me free for a session with the ponies.

"Stop distracting my assistant, J. If you need help with your golf swing, get in line."

I didn't see Bobby closing in on us. Did he see Jack's note?

"About time you admit that swing of yours is ragged," says Jack over his shoulder as he heads back to set.

Jack needs to grasp the fact we've officially stepped onto a knife's edge. One of us has to be in charge of not screwing up at work, and I have the feeling it's going to be me.

Bobby pats my arm. "I'm sorry I abandoned you this weekend. The fires of editing hell held me prisoner. I hope you found something to entertain yourself in good ol' Waterville."

I nod. "Curled up with a book and wrapped my head around the time shift."

"Spent the weekend in bed, then?"

I nearly do a cliché choke-take but manage to swallow it down. "Something like that."

"As soon as my schedule eases, we're hitting the golf course again. It'll give us a nice slice of alone time for me to catch you up on my vision for the transition from season one into two."

The opening is so wide I could drive a Guinness delivery truck through it. "I know there's a lot of action on horseback in the last quarter of the book. When do I get that hands-on horsey research you threatened?"

He glances over at the rehearsal. "We're good here, head on over now. Track down Moose. He's the horse wrangler. His rules."

I bite my tongue to keep from telling Bobby I've already had the pleasure of Moose's company in the shadows of the stable.

"I'd like to finish my crash course on production here first. Feel the vibe of the actual filming."

Bobby runs a hand down my arm and takes my hand. "Of course." He's awfully touchy today. *God.* I hope that's his personality, and the dinner and golf invites are only trivial. I make a mental note to observe how much he touches other people on staff.

I pull my hand away a bit too quickly. Bobby gives me a strange look. "Sorry, I had an awkward workplace situation back at Lawson Graham. Excuse the knee-jerk reaction."

His eyes widen. "You've got me curious."

"Maybe I'll regale you with the tale over a pint after our round of golf."

He tilts his head, studying me. "Woman with a past?"

One I don't intend to share with Bobby since he's haggling with Treat over the fashion shoot. Too few degrees of separation there. "Not that interesting. I'm trying to sound intriguing and mysterious."

"Speaking of Lawson Graham, I signed on the dotted line for Treat Graham to use *The Chieftain's Son* property for his shoot."

Oh, shit. Zero degrees of separation.

"Niks is in as the spokesmodel for his clothing line. Great publicity for the show. I'm angling for Jack to replace the bugger they hired for Irish County Lad. Cross promotion at its finest."

So Lanie Blesch's sexual bartering fell flat. My satisfaction is short lived when the shock wave hits. Treat will be coming to Ireland. Not just Ireland—he'll be here. I've got to keep him away from Jack and lock up the swords.

How many goddamn angles do they need of a kiss? I die a little bit more every time Jack's mouth slides over Niks's.

"Hungrier," Alan calls from behind the camera.

This is a thousand times harder than I thought it would be. I have to sit here with either an analytic or passive look on my face while my lover drips passion all over someone else. If I avert my eyes, someone will notice. I've got to play it cool since I'm the idiot who told Bobby I wanted to taste production.

It doesn't matter that I know Jack's intention is make-believe. Those kisses are real.

When Alan calls, "Cut," Jack's hand taps his swollen lips. We make eye contact for the first time since filming began. Without warning, my eyes fill with tears. My attempt at a no-big-deal smile falls apart when I catch sight of Niks. *Oh, holy hell.* From the look on her face, there's no doubt she's seen this entire exchange between Jack and me.

Should I leave? That would probably make things worse. I opt for grabbing a tissue and doing my own role-playing with a fake sneeze and nose blowing. Fanning the air in front of me, I sidle up to Jack's makeup woman, Lou. "Something is really bugging my nose."

"It's the dust. I told Bobby we need better HVAC in here. We're in the middle of a sheep pasture for Christ's sake."

I do my best impression of casual and hang out with the crew. On the next take, I can clearly see Niks's tongue lead the way into the kiss. What is she thinking? It's totally out of character for Nieve to stick her tongue down Donal Cam's throat on their first kiss. Is this her way of pissing on territory she feels should be hers? *Oh, crap.* She did see the silence exchange between Jack and me. Was her real-as-it-gets kiss for my benefit? Acid reflux indicates she hit her mark.

While Lou freshens Jack's makeup, Alan Rafier and Niks have their heads together. *Please don't let him demand another ramp-up of lust.* I bury my head in the script and write nonsense in the margins, attempting to get ahold of myself. My hands shake, and I drop the pen. Flashes of Lanie Blesch shoved up against a tree while Treat works her over wipe away any chance I have at composure. Not even an ocean between us and Jack have healed that bloody gash of rejection. My rational mind knows this situation with Niks is one thousand percent not the same, but witnessing kiss after kiss rips me open all over again. I press thumbs into the corners of my eyes to dam up tears before I lose it completely and make an ass of myself. Is it my fucking role in life to be mired in shadow while I watch men I care about slop affection over other women?

The next take is the last. *Thank God.* Equipment and people disappear as fast as stars at dawn.

I'm careful not to make eye contact with Jack. It's not fair for him to feel guilty. He's doing his job. I'm the one who needs to get my shit together.

Lights snap on as a commotion rises at the far end of the studio. Meg calls Jack and Niks over to where a sweeping curtain of silver fabric hangs behind a forest green couch. A sea of light stands and giant reflectors are poised at the ready. A few feet from the couch, the logo of *Entertainment For You* magazine hovers above a trio of seats in place for an interview.

After makeup artists and hair swoop in, the photographer poses Jack and Niks in more and more suggestive positions on the couch.

I stand like a freaking deer in the headlights and grit my teeth. "You can do this."

"What's that?" asks one of the crew guys as he peels off leather gloves.

Since I'm staring at Jack and Niks, I'll look like a lunatic if I comment on anything else. "They look good together."

He jerks his thumb at the shoot. "I've seen it before. That's a pair that keeps things sizzling after the camera stops."

CHAPTER
SIXTEEN

Owing to a few happy bruises from the weekend on the inside of my thighs nearly down to my knees, I wore golf slacks to work today instead of a skirt. The bulky sweater my mom gave me as a *you're going to need this in Ireland* gift and the loan of Maureen's running shoes compile an acceptable ensemble for horseback riding.

"Moose?" I call into the dim stable for the third or fourth time. He's not an easy man to find. When I catch sight of his bulk through the wide-open door of the stable office, I get an inkling he may be ignoring me. Why shouldn't he? It's late in the afternoon, and I'm not one of the essential people like actors who he has to train to be one hundred percent horse competent. I'm probably one of many pains in his ass.

I could leave and ignore Jack's request to meet here. A sour grumble in my stomach nearly turns me around. Doesn't his slobbering all over Niks for hours provide me with sufficient justification for some "me" time?

A chestnut horse bobs its head in my direction. I rub its nose. "I know." I confide in the beauty. "It's his job."

His job. His responsibility. I distracted him today. Even after our amazing weekend, prickles of doubt over the wisdom of what we're doing run up and down my spine.

Jack knows watching the kissing scene made this a bitch of a day for me. Otherwise, I wouldn't have been the recipient of a dozen or more quick eye darts and head twitches from him. Anyone paying attention could figure out something is up between us.

Niks was paying attention.

"Shit." It comes out much louder than I intend. I'm scolded by more than one horse for raising my voice during their hour of equine introspection.

Moose's bulk fills the doorway to the office. "Who's there?" So, the key to Moose's acknowledgement is to curse at his charges.

"Hi. Do you remember me? I'm Gillian. Bobby was supposed to call to let you know I was coming to ride this afternoon." I swing the pearl blue riding helmet in an arc at my side. "I've got a helmet." Nodding to the closest horse, I add, "I'm not a newbie. I have riding experience, even jumps."

Moose's eyes narrow to slits during my soliloquy. His looming countenance makes me nervous, and I babble on. "You don't have to start with bare basics. I'm guessing you want to see me up on a horse."

"Are you finished with your life story?"

"Pretty much."

He flaps his hand for me to follow as he heads into one of the stalls. I'm tightening the strap on my helmet when Moose walks my intended mount into the aisle. The bones in my knees dissolve, and I clutch the nearest post to keep from ass planting in the hay. It's Streaker, Jack's—well, Donal Cam's—horse, saddled up and ready to go.

"Am I allowed to ride this horse?"

Moose grunts. "Come on," he says, either to me or Streaker or both of us.

Riding Jack's horse feels like an infringement on his territory, but I'm too intimidated by Moose to ask for a different animal. I follow man and beast out to the arena. Moose walks to the far curve of the oval track by a door open wide to green fields. Streaker tosses her head and busts out a very loud whinny. Before I realize what's happening, large hands I'm very familiar with lift me onto her saddle.

Jack swings onto Streaker's back behind me, pressing in so our thighs snug up together as he takes the reins from Moose.

"Don't you dare ride her past dark," warns Moose, aiming a thick finger at Jack. "You walk her back here, or I'll roast your balls to feed my dogs."

"Yes, sir," says Jack. With a click of his tongue, he digs heels into Streaker, and we clear the open stable doors.

Frantically searching the fields, I shout, "Have you completely lost your mind? Someone is going to see—" Words catch in my throat as I twist in the saddle, getting a full view of Jack. The man behind me has stepped through the curtain of time. A wide silver band circles his brow. Wind and dying sun transform Jack's flowing hair into gossamer wings. His leather tunic hugs his chest in a perfect echo of the magnificent body underneath. I catch a glimpse of my own hair as it spills across the taut muscles of the arm guiding our steed into dusk. Shining red-gold, it echoes the fiery stripes that color the sky above us.

We are the stuff of myths, a pair of lovers riding a white horse across verdant fields to catch the sun before it abandons the land to night.

His lips tickle my ear. "We're out the back way, no one'll look."

The full scope of *The Chieftain's Son* property reveals itself. Beyond sheep pastures, land stretches far into the distance, sloping up to higher ground covered with trees. The same kind of peace I feel on a lush, beautiful golf course settles over me. As far as I can see, there are no signs of anyone else. Jack and I ride alone through this vast expanse of countryside.

Costume layers of tunic and other draped fabrics bunch between us. Jack flares his cloak so it settles around us. In the welcome pocket of heat inside the thick navy fabric, my body molds to his. Our close contact coupled with the rhythm of the gallop inspires a rising interest behind me. My chieftain's son is ready for the sort of ride that does not require Streaker.

"Will you please slow down? You're going to dump me off this horse."

Jack keeps a hand on Streaker's reins and tightens his grip around me with the other, pressing a forearm against my breasts. "We're fine." Behind me, Jack's definition of "fine" presses hard against my ass.

Without asking permission, my body begins to respond to Jack's arousal. At this rate, neither of us is will be in a rational state for a frank discussion about our situation. I vow to keep my legs together until we can talk about how to deal with the unwelcome slice of reality we both endured during the shoot today.

We approach a small copse of trees on the crest of a hill. Jack slows the horse to a walk as we slip around to the far side of the rise away from The Clan. It's a quick climb up the short slope to the top. In a single, fluid motion, he's off the horse and reaching for me. I swing one leg over the saddle to face him. Jack's large and talented hands seize my ass and guide my body tantalizingly down the length of his. Our contact speaks to one another at a frequency beyond the range of hearing. I'm simultaneously overwhelmed by my desire for him and frustrated that I've lost my reason.

Jack's panting sends a curl of mist across the hilltop. Still holding reins with one hand, he bends me backwards, swooping in for a kiss that just might kill me with its intensity. A rumble from his chest escapes in a muffled growl as he captures my bottom lip in his teeth. Hips bore into mine as he works his hand between us to unfasten the buttons of my slacks. They slip to my ankles like a raindrop down a windowpane.

"Horse," I gasp as Streaker stamps uncomfortably close to my foot.

Jack's eyes are as wild as the animal's. He twists the reins around a low branch. Spinning back to me like a cyclone, his cloak falls to the ground. He sheds his own britches and snatches me up into his arms. I lock my legs around his waist, hands roaming his body as if it's the first time I've been allowed to touch.

Murmurs, husky and raw, surround me like warm wind. Jack wedges me between his body and a blanket of velvety moss covering the slope of a massive boulder under the trees. Hands slide under my sweater, stroking my breasts.

I press against him. When I try to say his name, it comes out as a long, low moan.

"I must have you, Gilly."

Digging my fingers into the broad muscles of his shoulders to encourage him, I press my face into the side of Jack's neck as he thrusts with a savage cadence in time with the low thunder echoing across the fields. He takes me with passion far surpassing the graceful lovemaking he's shown before, and I'm mad for it. When our mutual storm collides in a burst of frantic energy, I sink my teeth into the leather tunic covering his shoulder. He roars loud enough to chase the sun below the horizon. We frighten the horse into a loud whinny.

He lifts me off my rocky backboard, and we collapse onto his fallen cloak, legs tangled, both taking hungry gulps of air.

I want to clutch Jack to me, succumb completely to the joy of his body wrapped around mine, but the intensity of our savage lust reduces me to emotion laid bare under the darkening sky. Open and vulnerable, the enormity of the changes in my life slam into me. I begin to shake. Rolling onto my side, I curl into myself.

Why has fate brought me to this man, this force of kindness and passion, only to drive us into the shadows?

Jack pulls me into the shelter of his body and strokes my hair. "Gilly, I'm so sorry. Are you hurt?" Fingers probe the skin of my back. "Forgive me"—he leans over to kiss me gently on the corner of my lips—"for using you like a madman blinded by his cock."

I pull his arm tighter around me and snuggle against him. "Don't you dare apologize. You weren't the only one blinded." My lips graze the back of his hand. "I was desperate for you too."

His chin nestles into the space between my neck and shoulder. "Oh, love. *Mo chroí.*" He drops sweet, little kisses across my throat, the tip of his tongue tasting with each contact. "I've wanted you this way since that first night in the pub." Gently, he takes my earlobe in his teeth. "Once more will be ten, and then we'll own this."

Ten times and you own it. My own words come back to bite. The intensity in Jack's tone shakes me. I've fallen into a dimension created by Deidre LaRochelle. Jack and I are characters in a fantasy. How can I possibly fit into his world? He's bound for fame and dazzle, a life so much bigger than we exist in right now. I sit up and hug my knees.

"Everything is happening so fast. All of it. Being part of the show. Us."

"I told you before. It's been a longer time coming for me. Since the day I read *Traipse of Moonlight*, I imagined you to be the woman, Cally." He lets out a soft snort. "Without the useless husband and ailing infant." His fingers play in my hair. "A woman of courage and conviction and such a beautiful sense of herself that she defies anyone to knock her down." He flips me so I'm facing him. "Then this feisty girl attacked my golf swing, drank me pint for pint, and made me laugh hard enough to soften my bones." His lips part mine for a kiss so deep and unrelenting my own bones turn to gravy. Then he simply looks at me with a gaze so completely smitten, little shocks of warning fire across my body.

Christ, have I taken advantage of Jack's interest in me? Is he my romantic reboot, my desperate grab to feel desirable after my debacle with Treat? When I saw him kissing Niks, the gut-burning agony from catching Treat and Lanie on the golf course boiled up as fresh at the day it happened.

"A week, Jack. We've known each other a week. An eyeblink. It's only enough time to know what we want to know about each other. Not to understand who we really are."

Jack sits up next to me. "Gilly, you must know, during this week with you, my heart's opened up like never before. If you don't think that scares the piss out of me, too, you're mad." He pulls the circlet off his head and frisbees it across the hilltop. "I've done my best to show you who I am. Are you honestly telling me you haven't done the same for me?"

"But the hiding. Are we kidding ourselves this has any chance of working? I can't do it again—lie about what is important in my life and pretend it isn't happening."

A fist lands on the ground next to me. "For fuck sake. This is about the scene with Niks today, isn't it?"

A blast of cold air knocks against my side when Jack leaps to his feet. He pulls on his britches and starts to pace, arms flailing. I dress as well. In our short time together, I've seen quite a few sides of Jack, but not this one. He is furious.

"Do you not know how miserable I was today with you so close while I pretended to be loving on Niks?"

I stare up into the boughs of the tree behind him. For the first time, I notice ribbons, swatches of fabric, and even a tiny silver cup hanging from the branches. It's a faerie tree, a hawthorn like the tree in my story, *Traipse of Moonlight*. Irish folklore says these trees mark the entrance to the faerie realm. This is a wishing tree where lovers, or those in desperate need of something, hang tokens or pieces of fabric on branches as requests for aid from the good people, the faeries. If I had something to tie onto a branch, I'd wish for the image of Jack kissing Niks to be wiped from my memory.

"Probably as miserable as I was watching."

He swipes a loose strand of hair out of his eyes. "You know every move is planned, choreographed. Not a single spontaneous second."

On his part. Niks slithered around Jack like a serpent coiled for any spontaneous second she could get away with. I think of my parents' stories about on-set affairs and destroyed relationships because of love scenes between actors. Choreography doesn't erase naked.

"Like Niks sticking her tongue down your throat."

Jack strangles a low hanging branch, causing the decorations to dance. "My God, tell me you don't think I reciprocated." There is a fair amount of huffing and half-snarls. He yanks a leaf off the tree and rips it to bits. "It's her first love scene. She was caught up. Alan kept barking at us to increase the heat, so she did. That's the whole of it." He shakes off a leaf that's sticking to his palm, then catches me in those sea blue eyes. "You've got to trust me when I tell you there's nothing behind it for her. Can you do that?"

"How can you be sure?"

Jack's hands tighten into fists, and he doesn't look at me. Here it is again, the traces of a secret between Niks and him. Why can't he open up about it? He's been transparent about everything else.

When he whips back to face me, the moonlight catching his hair is a flash in the darkness. "I'm made promises to Niks that I can't share, even with you. I keep my promises, Gilly."

So, there is something between them that is off-limits to me. As much as I want Jack to come clean, I'll respect his integrity to keep his promise. Still, there will be seasons of intimacy between Jack and Niks. Every take today was a knife in my flesh, and it was just a first kiss scene. In the course of the series, Donal Cam takes Nieve to bed, and to bed, and to bed.

"You've got to understand, Jack. I've spent the last two years of my life getting stung by things that can't be shared."

His voice cracks the sky open like a thunderclap. "I'd never lie to you the way that bastard did."

As awful as I feel knowing there's secret-keeping between Jack and Niks, I do want to believe in him. In us.

He drops down beside me. "I'm drawing a line to fix this. You can't be there if it's a physical scene between me and Niks. At one point, my stomach was churning so badly knowing you were ten feet from us I nearly had my breakfast come back up. I kept imagining myself driving a fist into Bobby's face for making you be there." Jack squeezes my shoulder. "Make whatever excuses necessary but stay away from now on."

When Jack gets in this pushy mode, he doesn't see past the way he's decided things should be. Screw anyone else's point of view. "What if I can't? Being on set is part of my job."

He frowns. "Let me think on it."

"It's not your problem to solve." Here it is. One of a million obstacles that will rise between us because of our dynamic. One we have zero control over.

The silence between us is not peaceful. We both jump when the headlights from an equipment truck on the road below sweep over the hilltop. It's too far off to see us through the trees, but the blaring reminder we tread on forbidden ground shreds the last of my patience with myself and this whole unfair situation.

As if sensing my growing reticence, Jack presses lips to my forehead. "You've got the right of it. It's ours to solve. I'll be gone the rest of the week on location up north. Will you join me outside of Dublin on Saturday for a golf tournament?" He leans back against the hawthorn's trunk. "It's for a charity dear to me and my whole family. We raise money to let underprivileged kids get involved in golf and other sports. It raises their self-worth. Gives them a language to connect with others." His hands spin through the air. "We're working on creating scholarships as well. When I can, I help coach a junior golf team hereabouts."

I nudge him. "God, I hope they all don't have a glitch at the top of their backswing." Coaching kids, another layer of good guy. Have I lost my mind not to shout how much I care about Jack to the sky and just say "What the hell, we're doing this."? I watch the line of clouds heading our way. "I don't know if meeting up is a good idea."

"It's a chance to spend time in the open without anyone thinking a thing about it." He waves his hands in bigger circles as his enthusiasm gains steam. "We'll walk the course together, no carts. That'll give us time to figure out our issues if you must be on set for"—he clears his throat—"those personal scenes. We'll make a plan."

Truth turns my body to lead. I want to picture any version of a plan that makes this relationship work and allows me to keep a sense of self-respect. I'm falling down an all-too-familiar rabbit hole. As glorious as our beginning has been, if we're forced to hide, I'm scared it might mortally wound the value of us.

I rise and wander over to the faerie tree, gathering nerve to say what should be said. Don't I owe it to Jack to use my experience to protect him from the blowback our relationship may cause? We jumped off a cliff onto unforgiving ground. No one will celebrate us being together. Meg and True Time will freak if we spoil their meticulous publicity path. I'm in danger of losing Bobby's respect by sneaking around. God knows how Niks fits into this.

I pinch a pearl-colored ribbon between my fingers. "You going on location gives us a chance for perspective."

He moves incredibly fast for a hulk. "I've got all the perspective I need." Jack traps me in his arms. "We've got my home in Sneem as an oasis."

"It's reckless to believe that's safe. Eventually, someone will show up with a camera." I squeeze his arm. "Niks didn t miss any of the looks you gave me today, and what about Moose?" I push against his chest so there's enough distance to look him in the eye. "He's not stupid."

Jack paws the ground with his foot. "Moose knows you're with me."

"You told him?"

He nods. "It's the only way he'd let me steal you away on Streaker."

"Oh my God. He'll talk to Bobby, and all hell will break loose."

Jack holds my shoulders. "He won't say a word. Trust me."

Thoughts crash through my head like a rockslide. *Who knows? Who doesn't know? Who can we trust?* I can't think. I've been here before. I need to be alone and sort this out in my head. With Jack, it'll be Treat all over again. I'll be adored and not loved, because Jack can't love me. Not out loud. Every kiss will be a risk. Our time together taboo. I won't survive because every moment with him brings us closer. I refuse to sublimate something so precious to the spaces between words. If we can't put a public face on the way we feel about one another, it will wither.

"I've got to go." I hold up a hand to stop him when he tries to follow me. "Take Streaker back."

"Don't pull away from me, Gilly. I'm sorry I told Moose. I won't open my mouth to anyone else."

"It's not about Moose. I'm messed up, Jack. Confused. Scared. Please. I just need to…" Words catch in my throat and all I can do is point toward the studio in the distance.

Despite my warning to stay back, he takes both my hands in his. "Please don't give us a beginning and then take it away from me."

I drop my head against his chest. "You're wonderful." I meet his eyes. "How can I endure not shouting to the skies that I've found someone who makes me see colors in the world I didn't know existed?"

Those arms of pure muscle wrap around me. "Then let's shout it. Bugger the scenario Meg and her bosses at True Time want to strap on my back. We won't hide our relationship, and damn the fallout."

His words set my insides aflame. This lovely person is willing to tell the world he's mine. That means more to me than a thousand kisses.

I draw him down until our lips barely touch. "You know we can't do that." He slumps against me. "Think of what this looks like to them. At best, mutual infatuation. At worst, me being starstruck and you taking advantage."

He tenses. "We'll set them straight."

I shake my head. "No, we won't. Meg will go ballistic, and she'd have every right to." My face heats. "If I wreck your perfectly planned image, Bobby could regret he took a risk on me."

At the mention of Bobby's name, Jack's eyes narrow and darken. He's jealous. Well, there's another layer of crap to coat this whole awful situation.

"Jack, you said it yourself that first day in the stable. *The Chieftain's Son* is what you've been working for. You can't jeopardize it. We'd have no choice but to steal time together." His faces coils, objections ready to spring, but I touch his lips with my fingertip. "The stress, the pressure of lying, will eventually ruin this." I run my hands up his chest. "Please don't fight me. I know what I'm talking about. We can still step back before sweet turns sour."

Laying one hand on his chest, I stare up at him, waiting for him to agree. He closes his eyes for a long time. When he opens them, dull resignation clouds their brightness.

"If this is what you want."

I gently grab two fistfuls of his shining hair and pull his face to mine. "Never think it's what I want. It's what's has to be." I kiss him quickly before I turn my back and make my way down the slope.

I am surprised he doesn't follow. He's all about getting what he wants, but it doesn't matter if I'm what he wants. This show is the threshold to his future. Despite his proclamation to tell the world about us, he can't. Every step rips me apart more than the last. Did I lose my mind to believe Jack O'Leary dropped from the sky to possibly be the love of my life?

I kick a rock that proves to be bigger than I thought and stub my toe through Maureen's shoe. Toe, heart, mind...everything hurts. I glance back at the hill, but the angle prevents me from being able to see if Jack's still there.

I take a stuttering breath. He's not like anyone I've ever known before, with his love of books, family, and even golf. He could have been the creative partner I've always yearned for. The few facets and nuances I've learned about him only make me want to discover more, but the price is too high. The demands of being Donal Cam, the Chieftain's Son, are inhuman. Not just the professional aspect, but Meg will parade him around until she's built a stack of swooning females that reaches the clouds.

I can't stand the thought of Jack being less to me than he has already become. I have to do more than take a step back to prevent these golden memories from tarnishing. I have to leave him.

Navigating the rocky caps that seem to grow from the land gets trickier as I pick my way down toward the front doors of The Clan. I'll go to my office and call Patrick to take me to Waterville. I need tea and bed.

A week without Jack will allow me to get my head on straight. It's better to end on a high note, before we're discovered and suffer God knows what kind of fallout. God may not know, but I do. It'll be my head on the platter. My new life wiped away before it has a chance to begin.

I reach down the front of my sweater for the lanyard that holds my key fob to get into the studio. It comes out in one long cord, the buckle undone.

"Are you kidding me?"

There's no mystery how it came unfastened. I'm forced to retrace every hard-earned step. I trudge across rocky ground and back up the slope, grateful angry-looking clouds keep their distance while the moon brightens the night.

The figure next to the faerie tree stops me. He's a vision as grand as any brushstroke by a master. Long bright hair dances in the breeze, shining like moon glow. The body is all warrior, Celtic royalty, untouchable by any, save a god. It's the sadness, the pain in his voice that drives a blade through my heart.

He faces the faerie tree, oblivious he's no longer alone. Streaker doesn't give me away as she munches on a patch of grass. A strip of golden fabric catches the light as Jack raises it to a branch. My heart nearly bursts when I see it's threaded through my key fob. As solemnly as if he's performing a ritual, Jack ties my fob to the hawthorn tree. He touches it with one finger.

"God, help me, this woman has gone straight to my heart. I know our timing is damned. I respect my duty to the show. It's not fair of me to expect Gilly to put her dreams on the line just because the wish in my soul is to be with her."

Jack gives the tree a shake. "We've only met the morning once in each other's arms, but it's single moments that change a person's life forever. And, oh God, mine is changed."

He drops his head. When he speaks again, his voice is strained and so full of sorrow it takes crazy self-control not to run into his arms and comfort him.

"Why did you bring her now when it can't be? What can I do not to lose her?" He raises his eyes to the moon. "Just tell me, and I'll do it."

Jack's sincerity, his longing, drives cracks through my resolve. Every word he speaks finds an echo in my heart. He's not blowing past our duty to the show or what being together might cost us. Even though he understands why we shouldn't be, he still doesn't want to lose me. My chest aches from holding in breath. I release it in a gust and press a hand to my heart.

Perspective I planned to find while Jack was away hits me with blunt force, and tears splatter down my cheeks. I do want a life waking up next to him in the morning. Yes, the show and our careers matter, but Jack matters more. He's right. The challenge of being together is ours to solve, together. Damn Treat and his emotional wrecking ball for making me believe running is the right choice. Happiness is the right choice. Jack is the right choice.

I move so lightly up the hill, it's as if I'm floating. Call it faerie wishes or fate that brought me back up this hill, it doesn't matter. My decision is made. Not vetted, over analyzed, or dissected, simply made. I wrap my arms around Jack from behind and lay my head against his fortress of a back. He doesn't speak. His heartbeats reverberate through his body into mine. Neither of us moves. We become part of night's stillness.

If I leave Jack now, he will forever be a beautiful place I lingered in for a moment, the beginning of potential love never to be visited again. Here on the hilltop, I return to paradise. If I stay, there is no going back to a life free of secrets. This time, I'm not being forced into a secret alone. We will be the secret together.

I breathe out a single phrase. "Ten and we'll own this."

With painstaking slowness, Jack swivels within my arms as if he's afraid any rapid movement will send me running. He grasps my hands and traps them against his chest. "Swear to me you aren't faerie magic come to break my heart." The words are barely out of his mouth when thunder rolls over the line of nearby hills. His eyes dart toward the sound and then back to me.

"I swear."

"Last night, I dreamed I was pulled underwater. My arms and legs were bound so I couldn't swim." The breath he takes is powerful enough to push against me. "Looking up, I saw you above the water." He stretches a strand of my hair. "Your hair shone like rubies. You called to me, but I fell farther away." He leans in so our foreheads touch. "I couldn't bear the agony of not touching you. I welcomed the drowning, but it didn't come. Only the falling." His grip tightens. "You walking down that hill away from me was that dream come to be."

Bringing our joined hands to my lips, I whisper against his skin. "I'll play in your tournament, and we'll try to figure out this mess we've gotten ourselves into.

He adds a kiss on top of mine and whispers. *"Mo chroí."*

I press against him. "You said that before. What does it mean?"

The moon's brightness reflects off tears welling in Jack's eyes. He truly looks like a being not quite of this earth. "My heart."

I lay a hand over his heart, feeling its strong beat under my touch. *"Mo chroí."*

Icy wind slices across the hilltop, and Jack cocoons us inside his cloak. We hold tight to one another as rain begins to fall.

CHAPTER
SEVENTEEN

Paranoia is an effective motivator. I skitter around the writer's room like a chipmunk on stimulants, doing my damnedest to anticipate everyone's needs. Despite Jack's assurances that Moose is trustworthy, my eyes flick toward the door with every movement, expecting the stable master to barge in and expose me.

"For God sakes, Gillian," says Maureen, throwing a pencil at me, "if you don't stop spinning around the room, I'm going to need Dramamine."

I stoop to pick up the pencil. "Sorry. Can I get you some coffee?"

She throws her arms wide to block me. "Step away from the coffeemaker." Maureen kicks out a chair and nods to it. "Sit. Bobby forbade us from asking you to fetch coffee.

I roll the pencil back to her. "I go a little crazy when I don't have something to do."

A script comes sailing through the air and lands with a smack on the table in front of me. "Let's read. I need to hear it." Maureen turns her chair backwards to straddle it. "You're Donal Cam."

As I read Jack's lines, an ache for him tolls inside me like a bell. He's been gone for three days on night shoots up in Northern Ireland. The vampire schedule he keeps is in direct opposition to my days here at The

Clan, so we've only texted. I erase them immediately, certain I'll do something idiotic like leave my phone out on the big table in the writer's room for everyone to see Jack's messages. I added another layer of security by changing his contact name to *Cheese and Onion Pie*.

"Nice accent," says Maureen. "You've nailed Jack's speech pattern."

Heat rolls across my face as I focus on the words *you've nailed Jack*. "It's pretty distinct."

Maureen laughs. "It's just plain pretty, like the rest of him. Damn fine casting."

"Was the Donal Cam in your head from the books anything like Jack?"

Maureen straightens her arms and arches back as if she's in the throes of the best sex ever. "So-oh-oh-oh much better." She snaps to attention. "And if you ever tell him I said that, I will have to kill you."

Even though Maureen is clowning around, I sense she's as smitten with Jack as every other female on the planet aged fourteen to four hundred. The pulsing waves of lust crashing over Jack from every direction knock my spine out of alignment. If only I had the freedom to snarl "Stay away from my man" to the feminine collective.

Jack's ringtone chimes from the pocket of my jeans. "Excuse me, Maureen. I'm expecting a call from L.A." I quickly do the math in my head to make sure the time differential makes sense. Check.

She waves me off.

I try to be cool as I answer *Cheese and Onion Pie* on the way into my office niche. To my horror, I accidentally hit speaker for a split second before I tap it back off. Thank goodness I have impeccable reflexes. Turning my back to the writer's room, I cradle the phone against my ear.

"Hi."

"Hi, yourself."

"Shouldn't you be asleep?"

"Shouldn't you be in my bed for number ten?"

The need I feel for Jack drops from my heart to lower regions. I speak as quietly as I can without looking suspicious. "I'm not alone, Mom." Benj and Benny emerge from their office to confer loudly with Maureen over some point of historical accuracy. "My *not alone* just tripled."

"I'm near to dying for you sitting in this wild and brilliant place."

"Where are you?"

"Carrick-a-Rede Island. Birds are going mad in the sky while the sea throws a fit down below me."

"Pictures please."

"Naw. I'm going to bring you here. I want to carry you across the rope bridge, lie you back in the grasses, and kiss you 'til you cry for mercy."

Benj pokes his head into my cave. "Gillian, we need a referee with a viable I.Q."

"Be right there."

Jack's voice is low and throaty. "You're leaving me alone with the wind and the sea?"

"And the birds."

He groans in my ear. "Truth is, I'd like to drink in a little more peace, but I'm on my way to a radio interview in Belfast."

"With Niks?" He doesn't answer. I wish I'd kept my mouth shut. "Sorry, that wasn't fair. I'll stop being a pain in the ass about her."

I hear him release the breath he'd been holding. "Fair enough. I'll call you tonight."

"Wait, don't go. I really am sorry." He's still on the line. "Tell me more about the interview."

A breathy inhale precedes a few more beats of silence. "I'm to answer for our shoot of episode 101 up here."

"Answer for what?"

"We might have started a bitty fire filming the opening battle sequence. Bobby had to do class A persuading and a fair amount of replanting before we got the go to use this location again."

Sweet relief sweeps over me, hearing Jack's more casual tone. Why did I have to go to the petty place so quickly with Niks and the interview? Jack doesn't deserve that.

"I miss you, Cheese and Onion Pie." My reward is a quick chuckle.

"It's the same for me." Someone calls for him. I'm ashamed of myself when I revel in the fact it's a male's voice. "I'm off for now, love." He ends the call.

I set the phone down and then pick it up to call back and apologize one more time. My finger hovers above the phone screen, but I don't follow through. *Let it go for now.* We'll work this kink out with the rest of them on Saturday at the tournament and, hopefully, in his giant spa tub afterward. I vow to keep a lockdown on my insecurity over whatever that something is between Jack and Niks that's none of my business. I can't torture Jack when he's thrown together for publicity with Niks. He can't control that.

This goddamned wariness is Treat's fault, that son of a bitch. I tap my index finger on the top of my desk. No, it's my fault for giving him all the power in our relationship and being grateful for whatever affection he chose to toss my way. Jack and I are not like that. We've started the beginning of a true partnership.

I stare at the new lock screen on my phone, the portrait from the lobby of Donal Cam and Nieve. It's the only way to have Jack on my phone that won't look like I'm fangirling.

"Appreciate him, Gilly." I promise myself not to go home and stress over Niks and him on location. I'll use our time apart to curl up in my window seat and reread the rest of *The Chieftain's Son* series. I'm beginning to play more and more with taking a literary beat and condensing it into a series of images. The challenge stokes my creative engine.

After researching Benj's historical snafu, I busy myself for a couple of hours, refining the spreadsheet I'm playing with for an episodic breakdown of book two. Donal Cam has it rough. Nieve is betrothed and refuses to give the poor bastard a second look.

I suppose my dabbles into season two are a step closer to buying this reality as a viable future.

When Danna calls my name, I return from the twelfth century. "Join us, Gillian. Bobby's on his way." The entire team congregates in the writer's room. "He wants to discuss 113." She looks directly at me as if translating. "The season finale."

I grab my laptop and take a seat in one of the green mesh chairs.

Collin fans his arm across the huge white board covered in scene cards labeled *Episode 113.* "Tell me we're not going to throw those up in the air again to see if they land any differently from the last ten dissections."

Danna purses her lips.

Collin presses the heels of his hands to his forehead. "We've beat it to death. Literally."

Bobby crashes into the writer's room like the Atlantic at high tide. I know he's been at the location for night shoots all week. Jack spilled details about the ongoing artistic skirmish between Bobby and Alan Rafier over crucial scenes.

Bobby slaps both hands on the table and drops his head. "I'm fried." Judging from the bags and dark smudges under his eyes, fried is sugarcoating it. "My draft for the finale is flat. Pacing is sluggish, and I'm floundering to hit the perfect tone." His face tenses with the battle still going on inside him. With an impressively loud exhale, he declares the victor. "I've decided to hand it off."

Eye contact sizzles and sparks between the writers like a downed electrical wire. The season finale has just gone up for grabs. How does this work? Do they bid like an auction? Pitch insights? Duke it out? Does Bobby close his eyes and point? Is Deidre in the running? Every person on this writing staff is amazing. Anyone in this room will write a masterpiece.

Bobby runs a hand through his hair. "I don't have to tell you that we've got to have the audience screaming 'No. You can't leave me hanging like this until season two!'"

I understand a finale needs to leave viewers ravenous for more, but it's not like the books haven't been around for a decade.

He raises both arms. "There must be emotional resonance that transcends what people know from the books."

That's the answer. It doesn't matter that the ending is already out there. The people who love this series have yet to experience it as a multi-dimensional entity. In that one sentence, I understand why Bobby Provost is the right man to bring *The Chieftain's Son* to life. The depth of his investment to the heart's blood of the work is staggering. Legions of fans trust his creative mastery to elevate this saga that is so vital and precious to them into tangible reality.

I am no longer outside looking in.

"I'd like you all to take a shot at it. I'll know what I'm looking for when I read it." He turns to me. "All of you."

I'm flabbergasted. "Me?"

My squeaking disbelief breaks the tension in the room, and there's laughter all around.

Maureen throws an arm around me. "Hey, *Traipse of Moonlight*, there's a reason he doesn't let us ask you to get coffee."

Bobby shakes his head. "It's time you take your talent out for a spin, Gillian." He raps a knuckle on the table. "Consider it your foray into joining the writing staff for the long run."

There's a general buzz as discussions erupt over the finale. Before Bobby gets subsumed by Danna, I lay a hand on his shoulder. "Can I talk to you?"

He scratches the stubble on his chin. "Sure."

I nod toward my niche. "In private."

Once inside, he perches on the edge of my desk. "What's up?"

I wish I had a door. "I'm so grateful you're giving me a chance to do this, but I don't think I'm ready."

Bobby ages a few decades as he takes a long, slow breath. "Okay, look. I'd like to be more encouraging and mentor-esque, but I'm too fucking exhausted. Sit down."

Sweat breaks out under my bangs. Bobby's never spoken to me in such a curt tone.

"Bottom line, you're a damn good writer. It's no secret we all hold *Traipse of Moonlight* up on a pedestal." He barks out a laugh. "Your pieces in the Lawson Graham catalogues convinced me slacks and a chambray button down are portals to adventure."

I'm sure my face is as red as my hair.

"You've been here a minute and a half and have already contributed nuances and story points that shake things up." He pulls my rolling chair forward until we are practically nose to nose. "You're equal parts intelligence and wit. In other words—you fit in." He gestures to the throng of writers. "We like you. Deidre's smitten with you. She wants to work with you to break down the other books so we can map out the seasons." He shoves my chair with his foot so I roll backward and points a finger between my eyes. "Man up, Bettencourt, and write me a script."

His avalanche of praise and expectation leaves me speechless. I manage a drunken nod, which earns me a grin and click of the tongue before he hails Danna. I'm left to process the pile of *what just happened* sitting in my lap.

Warring factions of thrill and panic buzz through my head. Bobby Provost, wunderkind showrunner, has just invited me to write my version of the season finale for *The Chieftain's Son* as my first ever script. I squeeze my fists until my fingers are numb. This is my crossroads, my shot to prove myself and dig into the creative future I've hungered for. One so much more appealing than writing about waterproof hiking shoes.

A blur of color smears across the writer's room. Meg. She grips Bobby's arm.

"Raise a shield, my friend. A PR shitestorm is heading straight for us."

Bobby looks a hundred years old. The rest of the writing staff tactfully fades into their offices.

Meg retrieves the remote off the table and turns on the flatscreen, clicking until she lands on a mob scene outside a Belfast studio. Jack and Niks, surrounded by security, thread their way through the crowd. The screen switches to a shot of the pair in headphones, sharing a mic in the radio studio. "This just went live," she says. "Damn it, I never authorized cameras in the interview."

The host reminds me of one of the smug, middle-management jerks at Lawson Graham Premier Sportswear. The type that are so spoiled and entitled their mommies probably wiped their asses until they graduated high school. He leans forward, targeting Jack. "So, are you ready to fill us in on the mystery girl you're hiding in Sneem?"

Holy freaking hell.

"Look at Jack's face," snaps Meg. "He's as red as a sunburned ass."

Bobby squints at the screen. "Is it true?" He looks genuinely bewildered. "Jack hasn't said anything to me about being involved with someone."

"Have you ever seen a more blatant admission of guilt?" Meg flicks a hand at the screen. "True or not, all those women who want their hand under his tunic are going to take it as a betrayal. It might start folks sniffing around too close to his house as well."

My phone buzzes.

Cheese and Onion Pie

I slink down the hall away from Meg and Bobby. The call goes to message before I'm far enough out of earshot to answer it safely. It's probably for the best. I, unlike Jack, am not an actor, nor do I have any semblance of a poker face.

The mastodon sitting on my chest gains another ton while I wait for the voicemail to come in. The second the alert pings I hit the blue play arrow.

"Gilly, it's me. Something's happened. I just got off the phone with Imelda. She's a mess, blaming herself. It seems her delivery guy saw us in Sneem and recognized me. He's running off at the mouth about it. The fool on the radio brought it up as well. Listen to me, love, I don't want you falling to pieces over this. There aren't any pictures. It's just the idiot's word against mine. We are fine, and we're going to be fine. Trust me, love. Talk later."

My sweet, optimistic Jack. I want so badly to believe we can blink our eyes and make this go away. Every step back to the writer's room feels like I'm lugging a fifty-pound weight strapped to my ankle. I play dumb and ignore Bobby and Meg. I pour a cup of coffee and vanish into my office.

Meg's volume has doubled. "If this screws up any leverage at San Diego Cali Con one iota, True Time will have my head on a platter. They want women camping out for his panels and swooning once they're inside."

Bobby paces. "Just have him say it's not true."

She replays the clip and pauses on Jack's flashing billboard of guilt face. "Deny that reaction? He'll look like a liar." She presses fingers into her temples. "Women hate liars."

Bobby captures her hands in his. "We say his reaction isn't about guilt. He's flustered, still not used to probes into his personal life." He nods furiously. "That'll work. Jack does genuine better than anyone because he's the real thing."

Meg slaps her palms on the table. The smack ricochets around the room. "If it's true, hiding it is the only way to keep to the network's PR game plan. We need his single-guy romantic traction to keep building the buzz for season one."

I pretend to be engrossed in work while taking in everything they say so I can tell Jack later.

She lays a fist against Bobby's chest. "This is on me. I should have pressed harder for more specific public image clauses in his contract. Made sure he wasn't seen out and about with any woman we didn't set up."

Bobby's face reddens. "You can't orchestrate the man's whole life. This isn't Hollywood in the 1940's."

I could kiss him dead on the lips for sticking up for Jack, and without knowing it, me.

The two of them face off for a tense moment, then Bobby drops into a chair. He taps his finger a hundred times on the tabletop, eyes wobbling. As quickly as his drum solo began, it ends. He grabs the edge of the table and leans back, triumph brightening the exhaustion in his eyes. "J's got a sister. She's a Kerry local. We'll point that out and say that's who he had dinner with. That keeps his Sneem address quiet." Using the table to push up, he's on his feet and heading toward the door.

A ball of disgust hardens in my stomach. I hate the way they talk about Jack like he's a commodity. Now, they're bringing his family into the charade. Neither one of them picks up a phone to ask Jack what his take on all this might be.

Meg pinches his sleeve and shakes. "I'm afraid that will sound like a cover-up." She bites on her lip in a series of furious nips that by all rights should draw blood. "True Time will want us to get out in front of this. Spin the game plan of Jack and Niks together. We'll move up the reveal timeline. There's our fix."

Bobby holds up his hands. "I don't think—"

"Let me paint the scenario." She wags a finger. "Fans have a hard-on for Donal Cam and Nieve to be together. They'll accept that. Hell, they'll swoon with gratification." She flings her arms wide. "Jack O'Leary and Niks Tellefson are the real thing. True love mirrors the story of true love. We redirect fan disappointment from Jack being unavailable into every woman dreaming a love like the one we present to the world is possible. Bam! We're back in the lust business."

Bobby's shoulders droop. "Schedule a meeting with Jack and Niks. It's their lives we're messing with. They have to be on board."

I bite my tongue to keep from screaming.

Meg's expression dares him to argue any further. "If True Time tells them to be on board, they will be on board."

I have an unhealthy urge to push Meg off a cliff. Niks thrown together with Jack even more is my Lanie Blesch nightmare all over again.

I press my phone to my heart as if I'm clinging to the last remnants of Jack. His nightmare of being pulled underwater flashes through my mind. Is this how the damn faeries answer the wish he made at the hawthorn? Did they not understand it's me he was talking about, not goddamned Niks? Or do they know, and they're having a rip-roaring belly laugh at we mortals' expense? The good people, my ass. If I ever catch a faerie near that tree, I'll have Streaker stomp it into the ground.

A sinking feeling in my gut warns that maybe the faeries aren't mistaken after all. This might be the fair folk's way of saving me from a relationship that can only exist on the dark side of the moon.

CHAPTER
EIGHTEEN

S aturday is gloomy. Gray clouds with full bellies hang low in the sky above the Irish Sea, waiting for just the right moment to drench the golf course in a sheet of rain. My mood isn't any brighter. Jack and I are not in the same foursome He's in the group ahead of me with a pair of chat show hosts and the president of the charity.

His brutal schedule hasn't given us a chance to do more than promise to talk about our situation. Which we are supposed to be doing right now.

Thanks to Meg's campaign of hints about a possible Jack/Niks relationship splattered across every platform in the known universe, the press has closed in. Jack won't be caught with any more mystery women on Meg's watch.

The throng of reporters, photographers, and spectators crowding around him is so thick I haven't had more than a glimpse of him for the last fifteen holes.

"You're away, Gillian," calls one of the three octogenarians in my foursome from across the green. They're cheery enough to me but bicker among themselves at every opportunity, constantly complaining about their various parts replacements. I'm rapidly becoming an expert on the best minerals to take for joint pain.

"Represent the show," I hiss at myself through clenched teeth.

I nearly miss my birdie putt on the sixteenth hole as the gag-inducing TV3 interview from last night takes over my conscious thought. Jack and Niks, sitting on a white furry couch, holding hands and gazing at one another. Every answer was coy but tantalizingly noncommittal. Niks with her overly precious Norwegian accent blathering about Jack being as sweet as a *chokladbiskvier* made me want to vomit.

Meg and the True Time Network are teasing the fans with a Jack and Niks coupling but haven't come out with a blatant announcement yet. I imagine a fat playbook on her desk with every step of the romantic reveal.

I hold the flag at the edge of the green, pretending interest as my trio of great-grandpas finish out the hole. My eyes stray to the next tee box where I have my first clear view of Jack. He bends down to stab his tee into the sod, that magnificent ass pointed directly at me. His swing is the marriage of strong and smooth. I take credit for his glitch-free flow, especially at the top of his backswing, but the grace is all his.

My heart pounds with such powerful beats as I watch him, I expect to be shushed for being too noisy on the green. As if I'm speaking to him on some primal level, he snaps his head around to find me. It's only a fleeting look. There are too many eyes on him. He's got to be careful. But it's enough to make tears sting my eyes because of the horrible situation I've landed in with him. Shadow Gilly rides again. I'm so goddamned sick of being a dirty little secret.

He strolls back to the cart path, and I watch him pull his phone from a pocket.

Panic grips my chest. *No, don't call me, Jack.* Too many eyes. Someone is bound to catch him.

To my relief, he throws an arm around one of his teammates and takes a selfie. Crisis averted. The pic will be up on social media any second, immediately garnering thousands of likes.

"Nicely done," I say to my teammates, complimenting their putts as we head back to our carts.

"Well, aren't you just a darlin' for sayin' so," says the wobbliest of my ancient crew.

Before I make it to the next tee box, I hear my phone buzz. I hang back to check it. My heart races when there's a text from Jack less than five minutes old. The man is going to give me a coronary.

Give me an hour after tournament awards are handed out, then meet me in Howth at Lobster Lee's. For the love of God, have a bowl of chowder and whiskey waiting for me.

Jack promised to take me to Howth, the kicky, little fishing village north of Dublin where lots of famous people live. Is that why he picked it? Does Howth protect VIPs from press invasion?

I text him back.

Kind of public, don't you think?

His answer is quick.

Get a table in the side room. Not much traffic. It'll be grand.

Before I have a chance for any more protest, another message follows.

I miss you to bursting.

The seagulls in Howth are the size of pterodactyls. A troupe of the screeching beasties perch atop multi-colored boxes as tall as my shoulder near the dock. With night falling, their white feathers reflect the streetlights in an eerily over-bright glow.

The smell of fish permeates every air molecule surrounding the piles of green netting and massive coils of rope lining the sidewalk. I make the mistake of peering through the slats on one of the boxes.

"Ugh." I jump back after practically coming nose to nose with a pile of unidentifiable fish parts. The king of gulls lands right in front of me, flapping its wings to drive me away from his dragon's hoard of nasty.

On one side of the street, rows of fishing boats rock on the evening tide. Across from the docks are a line of buildings made of stone, or whitewashed fronts with blue trim and awnings. The theme is definitely nautical. Like everywhere I've been in Ireland so far, Howth is postcard perfect.

Lobster Lee's is hard to miss. A giant, red wooden lobster sits in the center of a big blue circle. A sign underneath the smug crustacean reads: *If it swims, we'll catch it.*

I've got a good hour and a half to kill. I wish I'd snuck my clubs into Jack's Renault since he's driving me back to Waterville. Would sneaking have been necessary? Is there such a thing as too careful? We do both work on the show. Carpooling makes sense. I hoist the bag over my shoulder and stroll down the West Pier.

I'm alone when I reach the end. Mist swirls in a yellowish curtain around the lights. Across a small expanse of water, the Howth lighthouse's beacon cuts through the thickening night. I whisper to the slender finger reaching to the sky. "Keep me from crashing onto the rocks."

I raise my face to the wind. It's crisp and clean, vanquishing the reek of fish from the dock. There's texture to the air that slides across my skin with a refreshing caress. My heart, heavy with disappointment from being robbed of walking the golf course with Jack, lightens from this kiss of Irish breeze. A sense of renewal bubbles up inside, and with it, a flicker of hope.

"I want to find a way, Jack. I really do."

An idea pops into my head. Maybe watching past interviews with Niks and Jack will desensitize me to the pretense of their couple act. Any hint at romance is a construct, a publicity check mark. I'll flood my system with the sham to help me separate image from reality. Dropping onto a bench, I pull out my cell and Google them.

The first few interviews before the show premiered are banal. It's all chit chat about the upcoming season. Niks and Jack come off like buddies heading off on an adventure, but nothing more. I'm not sure when the tone shifts, but it does. An intimacy of knowledge springs up between them.

One interview in particular uses the format of a contest for the two *Chieftain's Son* stars to answer personal questions about the other. It's exquisite torture to watch. I know in my bones this happened after their initial flirtation. There's a bond between them surrounding a secret.

The question about Jack's middle name makes my stomach flip. I don't even know his middle name.

On camera, Niks grins before she answers, giving Jack a poke in the ribs. "Dawson. Jack Dawson O'Leary. His mom had a sweet, little Titanic obsession."

Jack turns as red as the lobster on the Lobster Lee's sign. "Not correct. That movie came into the world long after I did."

Niks scoots closer, gazing into his eyes. "Jack and Rose have nothing on Donal Cam and Nieve's love story, do they?"

So much for desensitizing. Now, I'm just plain pissed off. Early or not, I head for Lobster Lee's.

It's easy to score a table in the narrow side room through an arch off the main dining area. The row of cramped booths designed to accommodate overflow are empty, plus there's a convenient corner to stash my clubs.

"You look like you could use a hot whiskey there," says my waiter.

I shouldn't start drinking until Jack shows up. We've got important ground to cover, and I need to be clearheaded. The lure of whiskey, sugar, and lemon wins out. As I take the first sip, my phone buzzes.

Fifteen minutes out. Order up.

I order matching bowls of chowder and a Jameson neat for Jack. A thrill races up my body. Fifteen minutes until I feel those big warm hands on mine and lose myself in eyes as blue as the Irish Sea on a sunny day.

A thump on my table makes me look up with a start. "Well, look who busted out of Waterville." Meg slides into the seat opposite me.

Oh, shit.

She's working on a very full glass of red wine. Not her first of the evening, I'm guessing.

"Hey, Meg. This is a surprise."

She waves me off. "I just finished interviewing a new assistant."

New assistant? I never noticed an old assistant. I assumed Meg was a one-woman PR machine. "Promising?"

She raises her glass to me. "Very. True Time is always trying to ship one of their people out here, but I prefer to run my own show with my own team."

I think of the splash *The Chieftain's Son* has already made on the entertainment scene. I raise my whiskey in return. "So far, so good." We drink. "What happened to the old assistant?" The thought of leaving a show destined for greatness doesn't make sense to me.

Meg shrugs. "We didn't mesh. I can be a bit of a task master." She tries to laugh it off, but I can see there's a sting there. She points to my clubs in the corner. "I heard after the fact you played in the charity tournament today at Portmarnock. I would have arranged some pictures. We like to toot *The Chieftain's Son* family's philanthropic horn whenever possible."

My throat tightens. God, what if Jack and I had been together, walking the course? Meg would flip if those pictures got out. I take a calming breath. I'm freaking out over nothing. So what if Jack and the writing assistant were golfing together in a charity tournament? No scandal there.

"You got yourself up to Howth. It's lovely, eh?"

"It was recommended, so I thought I'd take a peek before I head back to Waterville."

"It's fine luck I've run into you. Bobby and I started hatching an idea. He thinks very highly of you, you know."

I search for a casual position, but I feel myself squirming like a preschooler who needs a bathroom break. "That's nice to hear."

"We'd like to start a companion podcast to the show. It'll be a touchpoint for fans between seasons. The plan is to throw in a bit of the history, behind the scenes business, and of course, guests, cast, writers, design team, and the like." She polishes off half her glass of wine in a long slow draw.

"Sounds interesting."

She sets the glass on the table a little too firmly and a splash of wine escapes. "Maureen's salivating to take point, and she asked for you to work with her. What do you think about giving it a go?"

"A go?"

Meg leans on one elbow and points at me with her free hand. "Be Maureen's right hand. Help her shape the identity of the podcast."

I've started glancing over her shoulder, expecting Jack to show any second. What will I say? Acting surprised may be my only option. Meg's offer takes a moment to sink in. I gape at her. "What me?"

She laughs. "Have you not figured out that Bobby's got a mind to make you more than a single season fixture on the show?" Leaning in closer, she whispers conspiratorially. "If you ask me, I think there may be a bit of an interest there as well. You know what they say about men falling for women who nurse their wounds."

"I don't think that theory holds water if the nurse is the one who inflicted the wound." An image of concussed Bobby under quilts in my bed flashes through my mind. His subtle excuses to touch me, dinner invitations, hints at a future with the show—all those things I wish I hadn't noticed start to add up.

I take a gulp of hot whiskey. "Your offer is flattering."

Meg leans back. "It'll be work, but True Time is keen on the idea. We wouldn't launch until after season one is put to bed." She pats my hand. "Mull it over. We're doing the same. It's all in the planning stage. Can't spread key people too thin."

"I get the impression from Bobby that there won't be much down time between season one and two, especially for the writers."

Her head bobs. "True. We might need a whole different team, but core folks would give the podcast a tidy verisimilitude." Meg flicks her wrist, tabling the issue. "We'll bat it around back at The Clan."

Good, it sounds like she's winding down. I've got to get out of here before Jack shows up. I'll lurk out in front and catch him before he gets inside. "I'd love to be in on the discussion." I throw back the rest of my hot whiskey as if fortifying myself for a duel. It burns something fierce down my throat all the way to my chest. Liquid scorch rather than liquid courage. What I'd give for an icy diet Dr. Pepper chaser. "Well, I think it's about time I head out."

She glances at the clubs and gives me an odd look. "How are you getting back to Waterville?"

Double shit. Jack is my ride. Do I tell her the train? Or a taxi? Uber?

What is the least ridiculous answer? Before I blather something, bad goes to worse. The waiter sidles over to set two bowls of steaming seafood chowder in front of us.

"I'll be back in a pop with your Jameson, love."

One of Meg's eyebrows disappears under her bangs. "Didn't realize you weren't here solo."

To my horror, Meg turns to scan the restaurant for my invisible companion just as Jack steps through the arch. His eyes sparkle like candlelight on crystal when they find me. He breaks into the sort of smile that fails to mask his pleasure. A split second too late, he registers Meg.

Fury ripples across her face. She shoots to her feet. In one quick swipe, she thrusts Jack into the booth so his back is to the main room. I'm tempted to crawl under the table and cover my head the way I learned in the California earthquake drills we practiced in school.

Meg pounces onto the seat next to Jack. "What in the holy hell is this?"

God bless him, Jack recovers in a flash. "I asked Gillian up here as a thank you for playing in the charity tournament."

Meg's lips twist. "Come on, Jack. Where's your head at meeting her alone in public after the cock up with the woman in Sneem?" As she glares at him, realization dawns. Her head whips between us. An accusing finger comes at me like a sword. "You *are* the woman from Sneem."

Blood stops flowing through my body. I don't dare look at Jack. Do I deny it? Do I let him deny it? My mouth opens and closes.

Megs drops her head in her hands.

Jack breaks the silence. "Yes, Gilly and I were together in Sneem." He reaches across the table as if to take my hands.

I sit back, attempting to casually move out of his reach. We tread dangerous ground here. One of us has to be sensible. "Jack offered to give me a tour of the Ring of Kerry, and I took him up on it. A day of sightseeing, that's all."

Meg's eyes narrow to slits. "Gilly, is it?"

Oh, crap.

Jack waves her off. "Where's the harm in helping a friend know a bit more about the land she'll be writing about?"

"The same harm we dealt with when you got caught taking Niks on that private tour of New York during the press junket."

Private tour of New York? Unwelcome imaginings of Jack walking hand in hand with Niks through snow-covered Central Park invade my brain.

"Photos, explanations, disclaimers, speculation." Meg presses fingers to her eyelids. "I know your heart is in the right place, Jack, but it isn't your responsibility to play big brother to every female who joins the team."

I like the sound of "big brother," especially in regards to Jack and Niks. It adds an unlooked-for corroboration to his denial of any romantic feelings between *The Chieftain's Son* stars. Still, there is some mystery between the two that I wish he'd just come clean about. I'm trying hard not to let the slobbering green-eyed monster dig its fangs into me, but a dangling secret poses a real challenge to keep the beast at bay.

Meg's voice is a dagger of ice as her hard expression targets Jack and then pans over to me. "Both of you, listen very carefully. I can't shake the feeling this meet up is a little too cozy. Whatever you are not telling me"—Jack tries to speak, but Meg slashes the air with a long, deadly looking French-tipped fingernail—"puts us all on dangerous footing with True Time."

Jack presses his leg against mine. My eyes are glued to a soup spoon.

Meg taps her finger hard on the tabletop in front of Jack. "They insist on orchestrating your image, Jack." She searches the restaurant, undoubtedly on the hunt for raised cell phone cameras. "I'm afraid the best way to diffuse mystery girl rumors is to escalate the buzz over an off-screen relationship with Niks."

He attempts to break in again. "I don't think—"

Meg cuts him off. "Getting caught with anyone but Niks"—Meg jerks her chin at me—"could sabotage our entire media strategy." She lets out a gust of air that ruffles her bangs. "We are only three aired episodes in. The momentum on popularity for both you and the show, Jack, has meteoric potential. Deidre LaRochelle's books hold scores of hearts and groins in the palm of their hands. We *will* cash in on that." She pounds a fist on the table.

Jack's voice is preternaturally calm. "I feel this conversation is turning into a manifesto."

"Gillian isn't blind to the effect of Donal Cam and Nieve's story on women." Meg's eyes beseech me to agree. "Are you willing to dilute that lure by killing Jack's mystique?"

"I'd never—" My eyes shift to Jack. He gives a curt shake of the head for me not to finish my sentence, but I can't stop. "Compromise Jack's image."

Meg huffs. "Bless me with simple victories." Her expression shifts from steel to a softer metal. "Please understand the position this puts me in with True Time. If I can't sell Jack as unattached, then the next best move is to offer up Niks and him as the real deal. I fail to pull that off and my association with *The Chieftain's Son* will be as short-lived as an Irish heat wave."

I bite my lip to keep from bursting into tears. Sticking with this show is the future I didn't see coming until it fell into my lap. I can't go back to who I was, what I was. I have a shot at a creative life. Bobby believes in me and can guide me into a career that I was made for. If I burn that bridge before the paint dries, I suspect it might not just be Meg's future with the show that's screwed.

Jack's foot exerts a gentle pressure on mine, urging me to hit the brakes on my mouth. He leans an elbow on the table to speak softly to Meg.

"You're jumping to doomsday prophecies."

Jack is an eternal optimist. Meg's worries about the scope of this mess feels closer to the mark. If what she says about Bobby possibly having a thing for me has even a grain of truth, I'll lose his trust for good when he finds out I've hooked up with Jack. I'll be branded a traitor. A traitor to his signals, traitor to Meg and True Time's public vision for the show and its people, and traitor to the opportunity Bobby Provost, the golden boy showrunner, laid at my feet.

I ignored the voices in my head and fell for Jack. How many times do

I have to get kicked in the teeth before I accept that hush-hush relationships are toxic? I took my first steps down a pretty path of independence, and then let a blinding burst of desire derail me. I'm repeating the same god-damned pattern. Treat kept us behind a curtain, and Jack has no choice but to do the same. If a relationship can't catch the sunlight, it isn't capable of shining.

Every doubt simmering in my head and heart about a relationship with Jack erupts. Despite a savage pain to my heart I'm struck with an urge to run as far and fast as possible.

Meg grabs my hand. "Gillian, I am thinking of you as well. Do you have any concept of the avalanche of hate you'll find yourself buried under if his fans find out about you? It's a no-win. You've either killed their dreams of being Jack's great love or come between the budding romance between Niks and him." She lays her free hand over Jack's. "Do you wish that on her?"

He looks wretched.

Meg pulls her hands away and drains the rest of her wine before zeroing in on us again. "Do I have your word that this goes no farther?"

Jack runs a finger down the side of his whiskey glass. "There's playing the game, and playing with people's lives, Meg."

I can't look at either one of them when I pipe up. "I'm sorry I put both of you in this position. I got carried away. It's all my fault."

It appears I said the right thing, because a few layers of pissed off and stress slough off Meg. She gives me a percussive nod. "Get your clubs and meet me out front. I think it's best you ride back to Waterville with me."

Jack's voice is low, and a little scary. "There's no harm in me taking Gilly home."

I want to tell Jack this is not the time for him to press for getting his way. We're all upset. Meg is doing her damnedest to steer her PR ship in the right direction. We need to give her this one.

My future on the show feels as fragile robin's egg in the palm of True Time's hand. If I'm the one to blow their fantasy about Jack and Niks out of the water, I may find myself back to writing about silk thermal underwear in five pastel options.

I crook my leg around Jack's under the table. It's the closest I can get at the moment to taking him in my arms. "I should go with Meg. It's okay." She's trying to protect me, to protect Jack the way she did that first night in Blennerville where we shared a spontaneous kiss in the shadows of a pub.

He squeezes my leg between his knees, our silent agreement we will let Meg have this one.

She lingers to whisper to Jack while I retrieve my clubs and cross under the arch into the main dining room. My fatal error is looking back. The despair I find on his face condenses the flame for him that burns in my heart into a small black stone.

NINETEEN

This week has been equal parts hope and hell. Hope that I'll be able to pull off a version of the season finale to validate Bobby's offer of a more permanent position on *The Chieftain's Son* writing staff. Hell being away from Jack.

The ride from Howth to Waterville with Meg was its own special brand of torture. She painted one of her extended scenarios as we drove through several counties, illustrating every ugly ripple a fling between Jack and me would cause. Every time she said "fling," I bit my lip to keep from insisting we were so much more than that.

The angry tears at her intrusion into my private life came first, followed by a well of frustration as I painfully came to grips with Meg's outside-looking-in perspective. To her, Jack and I had *temporary* written all over us. I wasn't about to share real details of our relationship to set her straight. What good would it do? The outcome of Jack and I going public would have the same negative effects, no matter our truth.

Guilt gnawed a hole in my gut as Meg continued to pepper me with how blowback from our pairing would also ruin her best laid PR blueprint to cash in on Jack's popularity. *The Chieftain's Son* is her first gig as a major player. I'd learned from my parents' experiences that studio executives can be unforgiving masters when plans go off the rails. True

Time Network's potential displeasure at Jack, Meg, and the show could escalate ripples into damaging waves.

Even though it's unfair, our situation is bigger than Jack and me. A sadness as dark and thick as the Irish country night seeped into my heart. The selfish, defiant side of me wanted to take Jack's *fuck all* attitude and see where we could take this relationship. The truth I know Jack and I share at a gut level is that neither of us want fallout from our actions to hurt any of the people who make up *The Chieftain's Son* family. He tried to brush off the obstacles, but I can't allow our being together to negatively affect his career. That's not something I could live with.

To Meg's credit, she warned rather than scolded. Her intention was to help, and there was compassion in her arguments. I began to understand a bigger picture than the one Jack and I chose to acknowledge. When she finally said, *"I'm going to be the one to say what neither you nor Jack want to hear. It's going to hurt you some now to step away, but waiting until you're any further down the lane will cut you to pieces,"* I felt her metaphorical blade.

The restless pre-dawn Atlantic I watched after Meg dropped me off mirrored my own turmoil. Doubts that I'd been trying so hard to shake about the odds of Jack and I having a real future fused with Meg's brutal honesty to create certainty. I should call Jack to share the only decision I felt I could make to serve everyone's best interest, not just mine. That was the brave move, but I knew the moment I heard his sweet, cheery voice, I'd crumble. A single, cowardly text was all I could manage.

Meg is right. Being together could hurt both of us and maybe even the show. Please understand that being apart is best for everyone. I'm so sorry.

And then, even with Jack's words at the hawthorn tree that broke my heart and drove me to give him false hope lingering in my mind, I shut him out. The potentially disastrous consequences for all involved, directly or tangentially, make me feel I have no other choice.

This morning, copies of the magazine with pictures from the photo shoot of Donal Cam and Nieve's wedding grace the conference table in the writer's room. It is a lovely spread. The dewy-eyed couple decked out in gilded finery is justification I've made the right choice. This is the couple the fandom wants. This pairing is best for the show. For Jack.

I tuck one of the magazines in my desk drawer. It'll be there for me in moments of weakness. When I ache for Jack, I'll open to the pages of Donal Cam and Nieve to remind me why I walked away. For him. For me. For the show. When the nuptials episode airs, I vow to be at a pub worshipping the great god Guinness to avoid watching.

My cell rings. Bobby.

"G, I need your notes from editing."

It was cool to sit in on the editing session with him yesterday. "Hard copy?"

"Email is fine."

"On it."

He ends the call without a goodbye. I'm thrilled that Bobby includes me more and more to discuss scripts and pitch solutions to problems. He's threatened to ask me to dinner, but thankfully, his schedule derails any solid plans. If he does get around to it, I can't say no again. It would be weird and seem damn ungrateful.

Despite loving this job, there's a gaping hole in my existence.

"Jack."

I close my eyes and picture him riding across fields on Streaker or drinking clansmen under the table in the banquet scene they shot yesterday. He's become a spirit, occupying the same space as me, but never truly with me.

I retrieve the magazine and run my finger down the length of Jack's body, remembering every stretch of muscle, the hollow behind his knee. "I miss you."

With a sigh, I swivel my chair to face the whiteboard in my slit of an office. Scene and beat cards for my stab at the season finale blossom across it like the window boxes full of geraniums on Jack's house in Sneem. Working on this script is the only thing keeping me from flinging myself into the Atlantic during the soul-stripping nights in my apartment. I ache to the point of pain, longing to wake up with my body pressed against the warm skin of Jack's chest, stomach, thighs…

My cinematic vision for the last beat of Deidre's first book is nearly in focus.

"Then sit down and write it, you coward."

Hell of a time for writer's block, when I've only got a few days left before Bobby's deadline. Ideas and words swirl within a structure my fingers refuse to build on a keyboard.

"Don't piss this away."

I should be able to compartmentalize my life. The stone-cold realist inhabiting my body needs to force the emotional mess into action. Even after a week apart from Jack, I'm too raw to write about the great love between Donal Cam and Nieve when I know my words will be spoken by soft, sumptuous lips that once belonged to me.

A commanding figure wrapped in a white terrycloth robe with a long braid of dandelion-colored hair trailing down his back crosses the writer's room.

Jack.

It's the first time I've seen him this close since the night in Howth.

He glances toward my office. The writer's room isn't empty, so there's no chance he'll try to talk to me here. Benj and Benny, bless their souls, are volleying ideas back and forth over the conference table. Jack won't risk being caught with me when Meg could waltz in any second.

"No donuts today. Maureen's had a falling out with her chef. We're all buggered," moans Benj.

My heart aches for Maureen. I wonder if it's just a fight or if her engagement is off. I'd reach out, but we haven't forged that kind of closeness yet. If I want to travel through time and ten books with the writing staff, I should invest some effort to become better acquainted with them instead of indulging in a pity party over Jack.

"The coffee's a mite better in here as well," says Jack, stealing one of Danna's mugs and helping himself.

He must have just escaped makeup and hair since he isn't in costume yet. It's painful to have him near and not be able to throw my arms around him, bury my face in his broad chest. I'm not having a pity party. It's bigger than that. So much bigger. This is mourning for the loss of what might have been, a love that I forfeited.

Benny fakes a bow. "Our coffee is honored to serve you, my liege."

"Enough of that business," says Jack. As he heads for the door, he shoots me a look and then glances down at his robe pocket. He lifts his cell, shakes it in my direction, then is gone.

I feel like a class A shit ghosting him. He's been texting me or trying to call all week. I haven't listened to the messages or read the texts. I can't. Nothing he can say changes our situation. I don't want to know if he's making promises that, through no fault of his own, he can't keep.

I suddenly feel faint. Jack O'Leary is not one to take no for an answer. If he pushes too hard, could Jack's stint as Donal Cam be cut short? The True Time Network might pull a *Doctor Who* and reincarnate the chieftain's son in a completely different body. I can't believe Bobby would allow that to happen, but if it did, Jack's career suicide would be my fault. I'd never risk doing that to him.

I let B and B's chatter morph into white noise as I open my laptop.

"Opening image?" I click my mechanical pencil until a tiny piece of lead falls onto my desk. Closing my eyes, I summon the opening shot of my script. I see fog. Smallish, rolling hills undulate between me and a low mountain in the distance. Hoofbeats are faint at first but get louder and louder until Donal Cam and Streaker burst through the wall of mist, a splash of gold and white against the emerald ground. I'm Nieve. I raise my arms and Donal Cam whisks me off my feet onto the horse. He wraps his body around me, hot breath and kisses climbing up my neck until he yanks my hair just enough to bring his mouth down to mine with a hunger that shuts out the world. Lips, hot breath. Jack. *Jack.*

My eyes snap open.

"Donal Cam. Nieve. Nieve. Nieve." Not me.

I stare at my screen.

EXT. MORNING – Mist rises above

Forcing my fingers to the keys, I attempt to break into the scene.

"Gillian," calls Benj, tapping at the scene cards on the Episode 113 board. "Are you opening the episode at the campsite or castle?"

I roll back from my laptop as if it just stung me. Forcing myself to appear calm and introspective, I stroll into the room. "Outside, definitely. I'm going for the-world-is-ours vibes before I toss Donal Cam and Nieve into the fiery pits of hell."

We spend the next hour debating which tortures from the end of book one the characters should endure and which are superfluous or redundant. I'm about to convince Benj to drive into Waterville for fish and chips when Beth, one of the production assistants, pokes her head in the door.

"Gillian, Bobby wants you on set."

"Now?" I'm rattled. Bobby hasn't called me on set at all this week, thank goodness. He said he's giving me space to write the finale.

"As I said. Main stage in five. I'll take you."

I dart into my office to get my laptop and the shooting script for this week. We scurry through the complex toward the cavernous sound stage that houses several of the reoccurring sets.

"Did Bobby say why he wants me?"

Beth flicks her wrist. "Niks wants a woman's perspective on the goings on. I think it was her that asked for you and Deidre, and Bobby sent me runnin'."

In a corner of the sound stage under rafters crowded with massive lights, a line of hardwall flats blocks the live set. I stumble when it hits me where they're filming—the hot set I saw my first day here, Donal Cam's bedchamber. Luckily, my script, not the laptop, falls from my hands to the floor.

This is not happening. I am not about to walk into the consummation scene between Donal Cam and Nieve.

CHAPTER
TWENTY

Beth retrieves my script and whispers in my ear. "Go on in. It's a closed set, so I'm to stay out here."

I feel as if I'm walking through a wall of molasses, every limb straining to move through viscous resistance. I slip around the wall of flats and stop dead. There's Jack, naked as he was before the firelight on the first night we made love, on top of Niks. He groans and seems to thrust into her with a rhythm so familiar, I nearly scream. Beneath him, Niks arches. Her cry is an elongated wail of pleasure that curls through the air to punch me straight in the gut.

I know it's not real. Every move has been directed by Alan Rafier. Jack is not fucking Niks.

But he is. Everyone that sees this scene yearns for Donal Cam to make love to Nieve with passion the viewer can enjoy vicariously while they watch.

"And cut," says Alan.

Jack practically leaps off Niks. Bath robes sweep in like a pair of huge white birds to cover the actors. Beth was right, only essential production people are on this side of the barrier. I hang back in the shadows, away from Donal Cam's candlelit love nest. Alan, Niks, Jack, and the intimacy coordinator cluster on the edge of the bed, deep in discussion.

I shake all over, biting back tears and doing my damnedest not to vomit. Seeing my Jack giving Niks what he can't give me is agony.

"There you are," says Bobby, invading my pocket of misery. "Niks has a bee up her ass about this scene being too objectifying. She wants Nieve to be simultaneously virginal and a ball-busting goddess."

I swallow hard and will my voice not to shake. "Is she asking for more dialogue?"

"For starters. I think she also wants to ride Donal Cam like a rodeo cowboy, but here's what I'm thinking..."

I barely hear him through the fog of disgust rolling through my head. Niks might as well jam the flag of Norway up Jack's ass and claim him as her own. I nurse fleeting hope the intimacy coordinator will throw ice water on Niks's intentions.

Bobby quotes a line of Nieve's from the book that didn't make it into the script.

"No," I say. "Not the best." I know the words that will give Nieve some serious power. "You should use her internal monologue at the end of the chapter, '*As you take my body, I claim your soul, Donal Cam. 'Tis I that holds the greater gift.*'"

"Yes," says Bobby. "That packs a helluva punch." He acts out a light knuckle bump on my shoulder to illustrate his point before flitting over to feed Niks the new line.

I fade as far from them as possible, using cameras and booms as a wall of protection. As soon as Bobby returns, I'll ask to leave before I'm forced to watch another second of skin on skin between Jack and Niks.

They reset the scene with a burning golden light bearing down on the couple. To my horror, the next beat will be the mutual climax of the happy pair.

Alan calls out a series of moves and actions. The intimacy coordinator doesn't raise any objections. There's no romance in the technicality of the rehearsal, but naked rubbing naked is more than I can take.

"I want no doubt that Donal Cam and Nieve are bound forever," says Alan. "Take the audience with you into your moment of supreme abandon."

They rehearse. Every kiss, every stroke of a hand over flesh, knocks me sideways. I'm hyperaware of my own breathing, the way I'm standing, my racing heart. Pulling off casual and disinterested is less attainable by the second.

Cameras roll. I'm forced to watch the man I yearn for disappear into a haze of ecstasy with Niks Tellefson.

Why does Jack have to be so convincing? I drop my eyes to the floor, hoping it looks like I'm being discreet instead of pixilating into a million tiny pieces. When a hand grips my arm, I nearly cry out.

Deidre LaRochelle leans in to whisper. "You've gone a lovely shade of ivory."

"I don't want to stare." Or see what's happening on the furs a stone's throw in front of me.

Deidre buzzes in my ear. "Brilliant call on the line. And I say that because it's exactly what I would have suggested. They called me in, but you'd already handled it."

Shoot. Did I step on Deidre LaRochelle's toes? "Oh my gosh, I didn't mean to butt in."

She waves a dismissive hand. "Honey, you get me. You get my characters. I can't wait to see your take on the season finale." She slides an arm around my back to get closer. "When the season one dust settles, I'd love to have a tête-à-tête with you about the state of our book two breakdown."

Cameras roll. I'm forced to watch Jack pretend to turn to goo inside Niks Tellefson.

Deidre gives me a quick hug. "It's their job, sweetheart. Nothing more."

I stiffen so quickly there's no way she's missed it. "Uh huh." Does she know about Jack and me? Did Meg tell her? We haven't admitted anything. Plausible deniability.

To my surprise, Deidre pulls my head to her shoulder and kisses my hair in a move so like my mother's, it shatters me. "You'll get through it."

Somehow, Deidre knows what this is doing to me. I manage a smile. "Thanks."

She pats my back and saunters off in Alan's direction.

I trace the lines of cables on the floor with my eyes, trying to shut out the moans and sighs of pleasure coming from the bed. I hear Niks deliver the line about owning Donal Cam's soul.

"And cut," says Alan.

Bobby zips to my side, chatting me up like he's just birdied a hole.

"Perfect. Niks nailed it, don't you think?" All I'm capable of producing is a nod. "Let's finally have that dinner I've been asking for since you arrived." Another nod. "Great. Give me a couple of hours."

"May I be excused?" My voice resembles a robotic eight-year-old's, asking parental permission to leave the dinner table.

Bobby gives me an odd look.

The damage control switch in my brain flips on. "Actually, I was planning on working on the finale script tonight. I'm on a roll."

He relaxes. "I don't want to screw with your momentum. Dinner can wait."

I open my mouth to answer when the sight over his shoulder strangles me. Swathed in their robes, Niks and Jack are off in a corner of the set, arms around each other, foreheads touching while they whisper. He reaches up to stroke her hair, and she lays her head on his shoulder. The intimacy of that moment is more devasting than their naked bodies sliding together.

"Thanks for understanding."

"Of course. But soon, okay?" he says. My smile is so stiff, lips press against my teeth. Bobby takes it as a "yes" and pops back over to Alan.

There's a clatter as people and equipment move out. Theatrical lights snap off and work lights take over. My shadowy nook is suddenly as bright as the rest of the set. I've got to get out of here before Jack sees me.

The way I came in is clogged with the exodus. I wish I could just hurdle the flats to escape the sight of Jack and Niks cooing over one another. I'm close to losing it. I need to get the hell out of here.

I swing around one of the cameras to get free of this place. Before I make it to the edge of the last flat, I hear Jack curse. A quick glance confirms I'm the source of his expletive.

A roar screams inside my head. He can't come after me. Not here. Not in front of all these people. I want to run like the devil is on my tail, but I force myself to walk with purpose across the sound stage toward the sanctuary of the writer's room where Jack won't dare confront me.

I'm so flustered, I zip through the wrong pair of double doors and find myself in the design wing. Passing the costume shop that's abuzz with activity, I head toward the end of corridor. There's a way to cut back over to the wing with the writer's room without having to backtrack through the sound stage.

I make it as far as the armory before a rock-solid arm wraps around my waist and lifts me off the ground. I clamp onto Jack's forearm through the sleeve of his white robe and shove. "Put me down!"

He kicks the door of the armory open and propels us through as I break his hold. We both stumble forward, but before I gain any distance on him, he clutches my hand in a death grip.

"You either talk to me now, or I swear I'll toss you in a sack, stuff you in the boot of my car, and drive out to the middle of a pasture so you can't get away."

I frantically search the darkened room. We're alone. No weapons from the bedroom set to put away.

Without warning, he pulls me against him. The tie of his robe has come undone, and I'm crushed against a sweaty, very naked Jack, who reeks of Niks's perfume. It turns my stomach.

"Jesus," I say, flattening my palms against his chest to push him back. I can't help but look down at the part of him that's been very busy this afternoon. Instead of Jack's beautiful anatomy, a flesh-colored sock masks the details of what I know lies underneath. A weird relief comes over me that at least Niks didn't have access to the real thing.

He seems to read my mind. "Good lord, Gilly. Did you really think I'd be all free and clear in there?"

"I... I didn't know what to expect."

He runs a hand through his hair, which is so stiff with spray it sticks up like a line of weeds. "I thought I made it clear I didn't want you on set for love scenes."

Anger pops like a firecracker in my chest. "Not my call."

He slaps a hand on one of the weapon racks, knocking swords together in an ear-splitting clang of metal. "For fuck sake, none of it's real." He's on me in a flash, catching my head in lion-paw-sized hands. Thumbs press into my temples. "Clear out the mess in your head about Niks and me, will you?"

I break his hold. "And how am I supposed to do that when, by your own admission, there's a secret between you two that I'm denied access to?" Before he can interject, I stab a finger in the air to stop him. "It's not just the scene. I saw you two cuddling up and whispering afterward."

Jack lowers his lids. I can't tell if calm or fury will be in those wild Atlantic irises when he opens them. I seize the opportunity to put a few more steps between us in case it's the latter.

He speaks with eyes still shut. "I don't know how to explain things so I'm not the bastard here." Then he's looking at me with that straightforward honesty that dumps my heart into his hands. "It was Niks's first ever intimate scene with her own body, not a double. It shook her up. It's goddamn embarrassing when you come right down to it, but there's nothing for it. We do it because it serves the story." He closes his robe and ties the sash. "You, being a writer, should appreciate that and not crush my balls over it."

It's next to impossible for me to believe Niks wasn't all-in for a few hours in bed with Jack, choreographed or not. "I'm sorry. It's just that you two looked pretty tight after Alan called 'Cut'."

"I was being kind, not loving on her." He moves in very slowly as if I'm a horse about to rear. "Do you believe me?" I don't back away. I want him near. I want to be in his arms.

Jack lays his hands on my shoulders. "Gilly, I've been trying to get to you all week. Why are you locking me out? It's got my insides in a snarl."

I lay my hands on his. "Mine, too, but we don't have a choice anymore. Meg painted a pretty damn clear scenario."

And then I am in his arms. Jack's touch flattens all my best intentions at resistance. He rests his cheek against the top of my head. "There's got to be a way 'round her doomsday predictions."

If only I could believe him. Stay here in the dark where no one can intrude on what we've found in one another. The stink of Nik's perfume on Jack's skin snaps me back to reality.

The dark.

The lies.

The secrets.

The snuffing out of what should be celebrated.

I reach behind my back where his hands are clasped and twine my fingers through his. Gently laying them on the lovely bed of springy hair covering his chest, I shake my head. "I can't do this again—be with someone and *not* be with them. I won't be an object to be valued in the dark and then denied in the light of day."

"I'm not him, Gilly."

"No, but this situation makes you have to act like him."

I hear the rumble of Jack's anger rise in his chest like a curtain of steam. "How can you compare me in any way to that bastard? Have you no trust in me at all? In what I feel for you? Where's the faith?"

"I can't have faith in something that will ruin me."

I might as well have clouted him on the head with one of the maces hanging against the wall. His look of absolute devastation is unbearable. I turn away.

"Ruin you. That's how it is then?" His breath comes in short huffs.

"You heard Meg. Your future is bruised, but mine is finished if we're together. There's no way around it. I'm making the same mistake I made before with Treat. I'm sublimating myself for an 'us' that is impossible."

"Stop throwing that man in my face. I am not him and won't ever be." Jack moves close to take my cheeks in his fingers. "'Us' is a beautiful thing to me."

Tears roll down my face. "To me too. I wish there was a way, but there isn't. If you care for me, please let this go." I pull his face to mine and lay a soft kiss on his lips. "Let our beautiful thing stay beautiful before it blows up in our faces."

Jack walks backward away from me. "You're the one kicking it to shit."

"That's not what I'm doing. Please try and understand how huge the stakes are for me, for my future."

The overhead lights cast dark shadows beneath his eyes. "Gilly, can't you see how invested I am in us?"

Jack O'Leary believes if he pushes hard enough, the world will tilt the way he wills it. When he's made up his mind, there's no reasoning with him.

I dig the heels of my hands into my eyes before I look at him. "The situation has gone beyond what you and I want. It's going to damage both of us, and possibly even Meg and the show, in a huge way if we don't end it now. Please accept that."

He paces back and forth in front of me. How I love his adorable skinny legs with huge bare feet that have a slight turn out like a dancer. The stance he takes before me is far from a graceful pirouette. It's no-nonsense battle ready. "You could stand not talking to me for nearly a week when I was going mad with missing you." Weariness softens the angles of his face. "That tells me our being together means more to me than to you because I'm in fecking misery and you've chosen to move on."

Frustration with this whole damn situation raises my body temperature a thousand degrees. I stamp my foot hard to keep from blasting apart. "This is killing me, Jack. Absolutely killing me." A flicker of hope lights his eyes. I can't let it get any brighter. "If word of our relationship ever got out, you could recover. I won't."

"You're givin' too much power over to Meg and True Time."

"It's not just them." I scrape my foot across a seam in the floor tiles. "It's fans who drive the success of this show. I mess with that, and it could piss Bobby off enough to get rid of me."

"Bobby and I are tight. I'll come clean about how much I adore you, and he'll have to be on our side."

Adore.

Fucking *adore*.

Not love.

This is Treat all over again. Gilly Bettencourt is worth adoring but not loving. A rush of anger heats my face.

What is so lacking in who I am that the men I let into my heart can't say they love me? I won't lay my future on the line only to be adored. Not this time. *Adored* has an end date. A drop of sweat slides down my temple. I will walk away. "This is as far as we can go."

He turns his back on me to grip the top bar of the weapons rack. His robe falls off his shoulders, and I see the muscles of his back ripple. "So, you're writing us off as a mistake." His knuckles are so white I'm afraid the bar is going to bend. "You've decided I'm nothing more than the next in a line of unattainable men you've welcomed into your bed."

Air rushes out of my lungs so fast he might as well have punched me. I clutch my chest and try to take a breath.

His fists drop to his side. "Where's the Jack O'Leary in that?"

First *adored* and then this. After what we've shared, how can Jack reduce my affection to a mistake, to a list? Does he truly believe I don't know him for the wonderful man he is? Can't he see it's our situation and not me that's crushing what might have been?

I double over, clutching my stomach, and stagger out the door.

Jack's panting and grumbling masks my exit. He apparently doesn't realize I've left the room until the door almost swings shut.

"Gilly, oh Jesus God. I went too far. I didn't mean it. Come back." His feet slap on the floor, coming closer, so I speed up. He only voiced what must have been festering in his mind.

And maybe there's truth in it. I knew Treat was off limits, but I let us happen anyway. Now I've done it with Jack. From our first rendezvous in the stables, he laid out the obstacles. What did I do? Play the game again. Attach myself to the impossible. If I want to be loved, why do I keep accepting inevitabilities that, by their very nature, can't go beyond *adored*?

Tearing down the corridor, I shut out the sound of my name being called as he tries to follow. When I reach the crossover to the other wing, I slam the door behind me and lock it with Jack O'Leary on the other side.

TWENTY-ONE

I stumble down the hallway like I've downed five pints. I feel like the puppet I had as a kid, the type where you push up on its base and all the strings holding it together go slack.

Forget the writer's room. Too many people will be nearby pounding keyboards to finish their version of the last episode.

And Jack might come looking for me there.

I hurt him, and he hit back.

Leaving Treat felt nothing like this. Walls collapse, trapping me under wreckage. My spirit is crushed into smaller and smaller pieces.

Doolin's language classroom is dark. I duck inside and slam down the switch before the automatic lights go on to reveal my hiding place. I skirt the table to the farthest corner of the room and slide down the wall. Hugging my knees, I rock back and forth, wailing inside while trying to keep quiet on the outside.

"Jack. Oh, Jack."

I want him here beside me, wrapping those warrior arms around me until all my sadness evaporates into his warmth.

"Why did you have to say 'adore'? Anything but 'adore.'"

I drop my head to my knees. Tears blind me. I'm granted less than five minutes of solitude before I hear voices on the other side of the door. *Shit.* Do I stand up or just hope they don't come in?

Doolin and Deidre enter, laughing like loons.

"I thought they had a mind to boot us off the range this morning when you let your club go flying after the ball," says Doolin.

"That's what you get for trying to convince me it's fun to whack a ball with a metal stick."

Doolin falls onto a chair and slaps the table. "The face on the whole line of 'em on the driving range frozen in backswings when you marched out in front of them to pick up your club."

"I only asked them to hold up for a minute."

"It's just not done that way, love."

When Doolin pulls Deidre onto his lap for a kiss, I figure that's my cue to make myself known. I clear my throat.

Deidre spies me over Doolin's shoulder. "What in the name of Saint Patrick on a biscuit happened to you, girl?"

Doolin sets her on her feet as he rises. "Are you all right, Gillian?"

Deidre fans an arm over me. "This is no portrait of 'all right'." She approaches and holds out a hand.

I take it and wobble to standing.

She narrows her eyes and stares into mine. Pressing lips together, she gives a curt nod to the chair at the end of the table, and I sit. Treating Doolin to a sunbeam of a smile, she waves him to the door. "Give us the room, darling."

Doolin asks Deidre a question in Irish that I don't understand. Judging from his reaction, I must look like I was the sole survivor of a plane crash.

"Nothing like that," she says, patting my hand. "Why don't you go make a nice cup of honey and lemongrass tea for our girl?"

"As you say. Right. I'll be doin' just that." Doolin bustles out, clearly relieved to be given a task that doesn't involve talking to the sodden wad of misery slumped in his classroom.

As soon as the door closes, Deidre sits next to me. She twists me to face her so our knees touch. "Our man came after you, didn't he?"

I swallow five or six times before I'm able to speak. "I don't know what you're talking about."

She frowns. "Darling, my life is all about the tangled mess of romance. I know it as clear as a patch of blue through an Irish rainstorm when I see it in the wild."

A sob busts out. If only I could confess my broken heart to the person who has splattered heartache across thousands of pages.

"Look, if I was forced to watch Doolin rub nasties with another woman, I'd spit nails at the both of them." She wipes my tears. "Dissolving into a puddle is the high road."

Alarms go off in my head like air raid sirens from a World War II movie. I can't talk about Jack. About us. The repercussions may oust me from *The Chieftain's Son* for good. No matter how much I want to confide in Deidre, my secret has to stay a secret.

"Thanks for picking me off the floor." I nod to the corner. "Literally. You don't know how much I appreciate it, but I've got to get to work."

When I try to stand, she pushes me back into the seat. "If you won't spill, allow me."

I feel raw and exposed. There's fear deep in my gut that Deidre knows the truth about Jack and me.

"You'd have to be dead not to give Jack O'Leary a second look. So, we'll start there."

"Deidre, please." If she knows, who else has guessed? The knot in my stomach jumps into my throat, and I can't swallow.

She holds up a hand. "Attraction. Definitely mutual. He meant to be subtle and, to most eyes, he was." Tapping the corner of her own eye, she laughs. "These see all, dearie."

"We shouldn't talk about this."

Deidre pats my knee. "Let me ease your mind straight off. I haven't said anything about the two of you, and I don't intend to. You can relax." Her full lips stretch into a smile. "And for the record, I think you're grand together."

It's useless to deny my connection to Jack in front of Deidre anymore. I do believe she's trying to help, not out us. I need a mom right now, and she's the closest thing around. I decide to trust her. "Okay."

She settles back in her seat. "You both tested the waters and liked the way it felt. Dove in pretty deep, from what I saw run across your face on set today."

I stare at my lap. "Yep."

She raises my chin with a finger. "And all the while you were held prisoner on that set, you had a dark, little song playing in your head with all the reasons you can't be involved with Jack O'Leary."

I nod.

"I've been called a human can opener when it comes to digging down to the core of a person, and I know Jack. He's as real as they come. If he was swimming in the deep water with you, he meant to."

"It was a huge mistake. Too fast. Too intense."

Deidre lays a finger on my lips to quiet me. "Only a fool overanalyzes such a gift."

I search her eyes for any intention other than brutal honesty. I'm met with a direct, calm insistence that she believes every word she says.

"Darling, it doesn't take much to sense an unhealed gouge inside you that I'm guessing wasn't put there by Jack. Don't you see it's that war wound trying to convince your brain you're stepping in a pile of something best avoided, not truth?"

I try to hold back, but the damn bursts. Freeing a handful of tissues from the box on the table, I mop up the worst of the damage. "Meg found out about us."

"Ahh," says Deidre, her lips twisting in an unattractive way. "And the witch hopped on her broomstick, heaving fireballs at the two of you."

"She's not a witch for doing her job. Everything she said against us makes perfect sense for the good of the show." I blow my nose and breathe in long and slow to reset. "Jack is supposed to be a super magnet to attract fans, this uber available god walking the Earth."

She hands me another tissue and points to the pool on my chin. "Trust me, seeing the way Jack O'Leary looks at you, he's anything but available."

I dab at the puddle in the groove beneath my bottom lip. "That doesn't matter anymore. We sneaked around and got caught." I stare out the glass wall. "I want to belong here. I can't get fired."

Deidre closes her eyes and shakes her head. "You've broken up with him. I suspected this might be fresh wound licking." She squeezes my shoulders. "Listen to me, Gillian. You don't take risks or get into this state over someone who isn't worth it." Shaking me none too gently, she raises her voice. "You are in love, my dear."

I pull away. "I can't be."

A smug look crosses her face. "Ah, denial. I love torturing characters until they drown in what you're feeling right now. It's all part of the process of earning the love."

I preferred her sympathy. "Well, it's a shitty part of the process."

"Maybe, but when destiny finally grants that happy ending, it's all the sweeter."

"Destiny is crapping all over me. I have a script to write, and I'm a wreck. Every creative bone in my body is shattered and useless. How am I supposed to write a script when I can't put a cohesive sentence together in my head?" Oh, my God, what if I can't write the script? Is *Traipse of Moonlight* my swan song? I *am* a one hit wonder.

"Oh, honey. Do not let your creative juices freeze over troubles with a man, even one as lovely as Jack."

I sniff and dab. "That statement doesn't exactly match up with your dedication to love and happy endings."

She laughs. "In my books, loving a man makes my women have more confidence in themselves. You won't catch me writing a woman giving up who she is for romance. That is not love. Love strengthens who you are. It doesn't diminish the fire in a woman's soul. It ignites a blaze."

Deidre squeezes my upper arms so tightly I nearly cry out. "Use this misery. Use the passion that's raging through you. Dump it all into Donal Cam and Nieve's despair over losing each other."

I blink until my eyes clear. She's right. I'll channel every negative morsel to feed my creativity, not squelch it. The roiling soup of awful rising up around me is exactly the right tone for the season finale.

"Go bring my people off the page, Gillian. Give me grit and pain and sorrow so thick there's no getting through it."

I throw my arms around Deidre's neck. "You may have just rescued me."

"For now, my dear girl." She holds me at arm's length. "Promise me, when you finish this script, you'll heal that gouge inside and claim the blue sky you deserve."

I kiss her cheek. Before leaving, I turn back. "I know you think my blue sky is Jack, but what we had was a fantasy, not a romance. Different set of rules."

"Blast that. Joy is not just about the kissing. It's also the blissful comfort that comes after."

"Maybe for you and Doolin, but showing up in Ireland to meet my dream man is too good to be true."

Deidre's features melt into a knowing look. "Maybe 'too good to be true' is just another way of saying 'what's supposed to be'."

It's a lovely thought. One that drives her stories, but not real life. As I walk toward my office and the script waiting to be written, Jack's shining blue eyes fill my mind. I hold on to the vision long enough to say goodbye.

CHAPTER

TWENTY-TWO

B obby sits at the head of the conference in the writer's room. The rest of the writing staff, including me, stand in a line, each with pristine, bound copies of our own versions of the finale. It won't be long until they wear Bobby's red slashes and margin notes.

"What I'm hunting for here is a strong base. You know I'll cannibalize pages from all of you to build the final script." He leans back, gifting each of us with an appreciative smile. "I do cherish this team." Bobby knocks on the table in front of him. "Now gimme."

It's strange being back in "the room." We've all scattered, writing our opuses in private. With a script in my hands, I feel more a part of things than ever before.

I tucked into my Waterville nest, only emerging to buy more tea or walk along the shoreline to feel the bite of wind against my skin. I'm exhausted from the emotional bloodletting it took to produce this script. Donal Cam and Nieve are not on my pages. Every embrace, kiss, and whisper are between Jack and me. As the hearts of the lovers ripped and tore, so did mine. All I want now is to sleep for a week until I can emerge from my chrysalis as an emotionally battered but serviceable butterfly.

Our procession laden with offerings marches toward the

showrunner. Benny and Benj go first, placing their version on the table with such reverence I expect them to bow and back away. Danna follows, two crisscrossed pencils barely holding her bun together as she drops her script on top of B and B's. A little attitude there, I think. She is Bobby's second in command and probably expected to inherit the episode outright when he gave it up.

Collin gives his script a playful toss like he's playing horseshoes. "Enjoy," he says and heads for coffee.

Maureen dances up in mauve ballet flats, her footwear of choice, and a matching sweater. After adding her script to the pile, she slaps a twenty Euro bill on the top. Her wink at Bobby breaks the tension. Everyone laughs and then slaps their own bills on top of Maureen's, trying to outbid one another.

Bobby gathers the cash and faces all the bills in the same direction. "This'll stand a few rounds at the pub."

I hold my position at the end of the line. Half of me wants to clutch the script to my chest and run out the door. What an idiot to think I can compete with the pros in this room. Maybe in a round of golf, but writing the finale of the world's new favorite soul-rending, heart-thumping television show—not so much.

The room stills. Eyes lock on me.

"Do I have to pry that script from your cold dead hands?" asks Bobby.

I have an image of Jack wrapped around me from behind, guiding my hands to add this script to the pile. Emptiness throbs inside me with every heartbeat.

Bobby walks over to ease the script out of my hands. "Got it." Everyone applauds when he holds it aloft.

The team, my team, surrounds me with congratulations and hugs for finishing my first script. I accept it for the tiny victory it is. Scant embers of happiness begin to warm my hollow places. Staying with *The Chieftain's Son* will set me on my path to artistic fulfillment. Of course, my script has no chance against the brilliance in this room, but just maybe it'll earn me a shot at staying here to learn and grow. Tragically, committing to this vision cements the certainty that Jack can never be the partner to share my dreams of a creative life.

Our shared dreams have ended.

"Okay, I'll get through these right away. I've scheduled an informal table read tomorrow morning to listen to whatever I come up with tonight." He drums the table. "No studio people, but Alan, Jack, Niks, and the regulars have agreed to come in. Call it a bit of workshopping so we get this right."

Bobby stuffs the scripts in his messenger bag. "Danna, I need you to finish up for me on set." He turns to me. "Gillian, grab your coat and come with me."

So much for my dream of disappearing under my new goose down comforter. I'm back on the job as Bobby Provost's writing assistant.

We burst out the front door of the studio to face the cobalt sky of a crisp, late afternoon. "Where we off to, boss?" I'm going to bug out if he has any notion of including me in reading these scripts. I can handle rejection, but not in real time. The thought of watching his face screw up with disappointment as he reads my version of the finale makes my belly churn.

Bobby zips to the car in full hummingbird mode. "You'll see."

I barely have time to hop into the passenger seat before he's swinging the car around onto one of the dirt roads leading away from the complex. It only takes a few minutes for me to figure out our destination. I grip the armrest as we off-road over fields to the base of the hill with the fairy tree where Jack tied my key fob and wished me into his life.

There's a crowd on top, but not a film crew. It's a photo shoot. Clothing racks line the edge of the hill and giant reflectors cast a dreamy haze over the tree and moss-covered rock where Jack and I made savage love under the moon.

With every step up the hill, my heart beats become heavier. I haven't seen Jack since I left him in the armory, and now I'm going to have to face a romantic publicity shoot with Niks and him at the very spot that should belong only to Jack and me.

I turn to Bobby. "What's happening?"

"You don't recognize the Irish Country Lass Collection?"

An all too familiar voice rings out over the hilltop. "Sweetheart!"

Equally familiar arms squeeze me against a lithe chest. I'm immediately struck by the contrast of Treat Graham's flimsy hug compared to Jack's all-consuming embrace.

I escape Treat as Bobby claps him on the shoulder. "Did you get what you need up here?"

Treat holds my gaze for a moment before turning to Bobby. "Yes, perfect. Tomorrow, I'd like to set up in the fields over there with the sheep."

Anger starts as a bubble in my gut but quickly escalates to a writhing ball of snakes. I hate the fact that Treat Graham's feet are planted on this hill that holds treasured moments with Jack. I want to shove him off the edge into the heather.

"I'll let you two catch up," says Bobby. "I'm off to digest these scripts." He points a finger at Treat. "Late dinner tonight? I'll need the break."

Treat, the louse, nods in my direction. "The three of us, I hope."

"I've been trying to get this woman across a dinner table from me since she got here," says Bobby.

Treat flushes, pressing his lips together. The goddamn nerve of this guy, acting jealous.

"I'd like to add a round of golf in Waterville with the three of us before you head back to L.A.," says Bobby. He snaps his fingers. "I'll get Jack in our game as well."

And I'm going to wade into the Atlantic naked to join a troupe of mermaids. "I've got to get back to the writer's room. I promised to help Maureen with research before she leaves."

Bobby doesn't pick up on my attempt at avoidance. "She'll live without you until tomorrow. Go, go. I'll see you both at dinner." Bobby darts down the hill but stops halfway. "Hotel, half-nine. Gillian knows the one." He's gone before I can argue.

Treat brushes a hand down my arm. "I'll be right back," he says and pops over to his model. There's some gratification that the Irish Country Lass for Lawson Graham Premier Sportswear is Niks, not Lanie.

She waves at me and blows a kiss. I offer a weak smile in return as any good colleague would.

Jack. Oh, shit. What if Jack sees me with Treat? Worse, if Jack realizes who Treat is, he may be inclined to flatten him. I've got to get Treat out of here to somewhere we won't run into Jack. Thank God, they're filming interiors all day on the castle set. I saw Hot Set signs festooned like banners across it on my way in this morning.

Treat gives his leading lady a peck on the cheek, and I can't help but wonder if that's the only place his lips have been on Niks.

Better idea, I'll get away from Treat. I seize the opening and scrabble down the hillside. Below are boulders I can duck behind, and Treat won't have a clue where I've gone. The ass can chalk up my disappearance to a bit of faerie mischief.

I've barely started down the path when Treat takes me by the arm.

"Gilly, wait."

I round on him. "Please don't touch me."

"What?" The look on my face makes him back off. "Your silent treatment these past few weeks tells me I fucked up big time, so I gave you space for your vacay writing fun since I knew I'd see you here. I'm fully prepared to grovel."

"Not necessary." I dig fingernails into my palm. How dare he belittle my place with the show? I could be petty and point out there haven't been any messages or emails from him either since I flew over here. My fault, in a way. I was always the one in charge of communication between us.

Treat shakes his head. "You didn't call."

"I had nothing to say."

He steps closer. "After two years of being happy together, you have nothing to say?"

My laugh is not what he expects. "I'm sure you were happy. Why wouldn't you be? I was the perfect little bed warmer."

"You know damn well that's not all you are to me. We're a helluva team. Tell me how to fix whatever I did. Your work at Lawson Graham is a cornerstone of my success."

His success, not our success.

He rubs a hand across his chin, eyes searching the far-off hills. "Hey, when you've done your time here, we'll cash in on your connection with the show."

Good *God.* Treat Graham is deaf to the fact I walked out of his life. I'm standing right in front of him, and he still doesn't see me. What misfired in my brain to believe this man ever valued me at all? "Let me be clear. I'm never coming back to you or Lawson Graham Premier Sportswear."

Treat gawks at me. "What? Isn't this Irish thing temporary?"

"Even if that were true, our arrangement is finished." I should have said these words to him the day I knocked Bobby cold back in L.A.

"'Arrangement?' That's what you're calling us? I took you to meet my mother and stepdad. That's more than an 'arrangement'."

I flash back on our trip to Oregon. I really thought we were about to turn a corner and be a real couple, shouting our togetherness to the world. But then he said he adored me, not loved me. How naïve I was to have fallen so completely for his con. I step back. "I saw how important our arrangement really was to you when you dry humped Lanie Blesch against a tree. Did you take her to meet Mom after I left?"

His face goes as gray as the dusky clouds gathering overhead. He moves in so quickly I don't have time to counter. Hands grasp my hips. "I am so sorry. That was me being an idiot. Don't you know I've adored you since the first time I met you?"

And there it is. Adored. The ugliest possible word he could have chosen.

"Gillian, I want to be with you. It's been hell for me since you left."

To the casual observer, Treat is his dapper self, but I see smudges beneath his eyes and a slump to his shoulders. Neither of which moves me at all. "Since I left you, Treat. Do you get that? I left you." I peel his hands from my body. "But why would you? According to you, we didn't exist, so I didn't think I needed to spell it out."

He attempts to approach, but I hold him off.

Frustration shades his voice. "You agreed with me to keep things quiet. My father would go nuts if he knew about us."

"I agreed at first."

Treat looks baffled.

"You promised we'd move past the secrecy. Promises, Treat. Have you conveniently erased any memory of your promises to stop hiding our relationship?" I let out a laugh. "Of course, you have because you didn't mean them."

"For Heaven's sake, Gilly."

"Real relationships don't come with an escape hatch. You were always ready to chase after someone brighter or shinier than me. I just didn't want to see it."

The crew streams down the hill. Treat throws a flustered glance over his shoulder. "Come back to my hotel room. We'll discuss this in private."

I look deeply into the eyes of the man I tried to convince myself I loved and admit I never did get past only wanting to love him. There can't be love where there is no trust. I never loved Treat Graham. My spirit lightens as the emotional burden of Treat floats away.

There is someone I do love and trust and value and believe in. Jack O'Leary. The short time we've known one another does not matter. Jack showed me who he truly is without reservation. He gave me honesty and love. I'm the one who kept holding back. Looking at the man in front of me and feeling nothing heals the gouge that Deidre saw in my soul. She was right. Jack is my blue sky. Love for him fills me like the richest honey.

"Will you come with me, Gilly?"

I give a tiny start of surprise. My heart has traveled so far from Treat that it seems ludicrous he's still standing here.

"Why?"

"Because I want to be with you. Go back to the way things were."

I've been such a fool. Being with Jack O'Leary is not a mistake. What we have is the way love is supposed to be—genuine and full of light.

I lay a hand on the shoulder of my past. "Oh, Treat. Never settle for what we were. There's so much more to wish for." I kiss the cheek of this sad, sorry bastard. "Goodbye." A few steps down the path, I turn back. "Say hi to your dad for me."

TWENTY-THREE

I have to find Jack. Please, God, don't let me have ruined things with him because I convinced myself I was repeating the same mistake. Jack and I are nothing like the sham I had with Treat. I have to tell him how much I love him. Screw Meg, True Time, and their scenarios. We'll outplay them all. I choose to be secret with Jack because the decision belongs to both of us. Our reasons are sound, not a manipulation spawned from either one of us, the way Treat forced secrecy on me with no choice.

In Jack's eyes, our togetherness is something delicate and precious, not a selfish omission of the truth. If I let him, he'd skywrite the way he feels about me over the Ring of Kerry. I will partner with him and find a way to make us work because we are love, and love deserves whatever sacrifices honor it.

"Please still be here, Jack."

Picking along the hillside, I pull out my phone to text Bobby. *Can't make dinner. Not feeling well.* I start a message to Jack but stop. What I have to say to him will not happen in a text. I need to touch him. Feel those strong hands pulling me home against him.

The anger and hurt from those last awful moments in the armory slow my steps. What's been going through his mind during these days apart? For me, I've been with him as I wrote of the desperate love between Donal Cam and Nieve. He's been alone.

For our fictional counterparts, fate opens wounds that need a new lifetime to heal. We are not them. Jack and Gilly can be together, stay together.

As I approach the main road to The Clan, I hear a low rumble in the distance. From my vantage point on high ground, I see the crowd gathered near Dev's little shack. Now there are also Garda cars near the entrance to prevent fans from streaming onto company lands. *The Chieftain's Son* has hit the world like an atomic blast. Meg's mirrored love story of Jack and Niks add to the frenzy for people first enchanted by Deidre's books and now the show.

Doubt claws at my chest. Life isn't what it was on that first weekend when Jack gave me the Ring of Kerry and welcomed me into his home. Infinite complications have risen like hidden spikes from the ground to stand between us.

Finally freeing myself from Treat opens my eyes to the gift I have in Jack. Do I still have it? Did I forfeit our future when I chose my position on the show over him?

Murph, the guard in the foyer of the studio, is his cheery self. "Made it in before the rain, I see."

I smile back. "Have I been here long enough to claim luck of the Irish?"

He chuckles.

I nod toward the crowd at the gate. "Getting crazy out there?"

"Mad as a box of frogs." Murph gestures across the sheep pasture. "Poor buggers haven't found our canny back way yet."

The back way. The road to Jack's little house. The one I haven't seen but Niks has. I shake off the pang of jealousy. God, I hope Jack hasn't left The Clan.

"Are they still filming?"

Murph looks at his watch. "Supposed to be done." I use my fob to open the studio door.

Each heartbeat is stronger than the last as I approach the sound stages. The red light outside the double doors is off. Are they done filming or just between takes? I ease open the door and my hopes sink. Only a few stray crew members remain near the massive castle interior. They tidy up and wind cables into neat piles. A single wardrobe assistant wheels a rack of costumes toward the design hub. I don't see Alan Rafier, Danna, or any P.A.s. No hairy clansmen either.

Is Jack still in his dressing room? I should text, but I can't risk it. I don't know who he might be with. Does he have me coded on his phone like he's *Cheese and Onion Pie* in my contacts? It doesn't matter. I want to stand in front of him and tell him I've finished being stupid.

Steeling myself, I head toward the dressing rooms. I can say I'm looking for Danna or Bobby if anyone catches me with Jack. That's plausible. At the last minute, I choose the corridor to the writer's room. I'll head all the way down and approach the dressing rooms from the far end. Coming from the less traveled direction will give me a chance to see what's up ahead before I step in it.

Doolin's classroom is empty. No one graces the hallways. The writer's domain is a ghost town. I'm probably missing a pub call and the round paid for by the writers' bribes to Bobby.

I swing around the connecting hallway to the dressing rooms. Crap, it looks like everyone has gone home for the night. There's only one thing left to do, go find Jack's house.

Two figures approach at the far end of the hall from the direction of the sound stages. My heart sings when I see one of them is Jack. A second later, the song comes to an end when he draws Niks into a tight embrace. They stand together a beat too long while his nose disappears into her hair to whisper in her ear. It's too dim to tell if his lips make contact, but it's enough to send me back the way I came.

"Too late." I clap a hand over my mouth, praying they didn't hear me. Neither spares a glance my way.

The closeness I just witnessed is no publicity driven intimacy for the media. Jack and Niks are having a moment alone in a dark hallway. Probably planning their evening. After I turned my back on what we had, he's accepted life will be easier with Niks. They can be together on and off screen without any flak from Meg or the fans. She has her warrior and he, his lady.

The high that fueled me from my realization on the hilltop about how deeply I love Jack dies. I had my chance at love, and I didn't trust it. I'm no better than Treat, who devalued our relationship.

My legs hold me long enough to reach my office. I drop my head onto my hands while the world spins.

"Gillian?"

I tilt my face just enough to see the doorway. Niks leans against the frame. Can fate bitch slap me any harder? She's the last person in the universe I have any desire to see.

"I need to ask a favor." She flows into my office. My eyes flick to my computer. Jeez, I've been slumped at my desk for nearly an hour.

"I'm not comfortable with my dialogue for tomorrow. It's harsh. Danna is brilliant, but she sharpens my edges too much. Nieve is strong, but not brutal."

I have to take a few deep breaths before answering so I don't snap at her. "You really should talk to Danna, it's her script."

"Oh, ya, I will. But I thought if you work out some ideas with me tonight, I'll know better what to say to her tomorrow." She pulls me into a side hug. "Please, please?"

There's no way I'm going to weasel my way out of this, so I open my laptop and click on the file for the shooting script. "Which scene?"

"Oh, shoots and pickles," she says. "My script is on set. I want to write our notes in it." Niks tugs at my sleeve. "Let's work out there. Easier for me to become Nieve." She must sense my reluctance but doesn't back down. "Come on. They've all gone. No one is here to bother us."

"*They've all gone*" must include Jack.

Niks chatters and complains about everything from costumes to her call time in the morning on our way to the sound stage. Just before we enter the dark cavern where the world of *The Chieftain's Son* comes alive, Niks squeezes my arm. "Stop here, my lovely." She checks the hallway to make sure we are alone.

"What's up, Niks?"

She takes a deep breath. "I have caused you pain, and I am sorry for it."

Oh, God. This is about Jack. I do not want to hear apologies or confessions of feelings for the man I love. "You're mistaken. Let's go get your script."

Niks shakes her head. "Jack is my person here on this show and in this new crazy world that is so strange to me. I feel so many times like a fool not knowing about what is the right way to act and be professional. Jack explains these things. He protects me in every way."

I want to shut her out before my worst fears about her feelings for Jack are proven true. I strain to paste a neutral expression on my face. When Niks cups my cheek and gives me a gentle look, I know I didn't pull it off.

"You understand because you protect Jack by keeping the secret of you two the way he protects my secret. We both love him. It's not an easy thing to find such loyalty these days."

We both love him. She might as well have knocked me to the ground and started kicking. I pull away from her. "Please, talk to Danna about the script. I need to go."

She captures my arm. "Jack says I can trust you."

As much as I'm dying to run away from this conversation, the sudden worry lines on Niks's gorgeous face keep me rooted in the hallway. She takes a series of quick breaths as she prepares to lay the secret between Jack and her at my feet.

"I am in love, like you."

Hearing her admit it is worse than my most painful imaginings. I stare at the carpet to avoid seeing the look in her eyes for Jack that also lives in mine.

"She is my world, but—"

She? At first, I assume Niks is faulty with her pronouns, but when my head snaps up, I find a beautiful, dreamy look on her face. "With the show so new, Marisa and I agreed it is not the time or anyone's business to share our relationship. We keep it in the family for now." She takes both my hands. "You and Jack are family, yes?"

Wow. I will never underestimate Niks's acting. I try to wrap my head around the promise Jack made to keep her truth safe from those who might use it against her. Niks is in love, but not with Jack, with Marisa, her so-called assistant that keeps an extremely low profile. Marisa, who picked tipsy Niks up from Jack's house the night of the driving range. Instead of punching my heart from my chest, the secret between Jack and Niks makes me feel protective of her, and to love him even more.

"Now that True Time and Meg want Jack and I to play at being lovers, it is best Marisa and I stay quiet for a while longer. It's not a game I agree with, but I chose this business of games. Playing it is right for my career today, yes?"

A flood of compassion nearly chokes me, not only for Niks, but also for Marisa. What has Niks's significant other been going through, having to watch the woman she loves plastered all over Jack O'Leary this whole time?

"I am sorry to put this burden on you like I have on Jack, but he says okay. Is it okay, Gillian?"

I pull Niks into a hug. "Of course, it's okay. You and Marisa can trust me."

Niks wipes a tear of relief. "It is painful to lie about the person who fills you with joy."

"Believe me, I completely understand." I never dreamed Niks Tellefson and I would have so much in common. "I would really love to meet Marisa."

She opens the door to the sound stages. "Yes, yes very soon." It's so quiet, I hear the horses blow and stamp from the distant stables.

Every thought in my head screams *Jack*, and it takes Herculean restraint not to call out his name until we find each other in the dark studio, if he's still here. "Niks, I really need to see Jack. Can we meet in the morning to talk about the lines?" There is no way I will put together a cohesive thought about anything but Jack.

"I will be quick." Niks leads us toward the Donal Cam bedroom set. This woman has just let me into her truth. She called me family. I'll at least hear her out about this script dilemma before bolting to find Jack.

My heart races. How will I find Jack? Niks! She knows where his company house is. The line of flats wearing a string of hot set banners block the scenery. Even after this revelation of Niks's life, I'm not eager to sit on the bed where Jack pretends to make love to her.

"We can't go on set," I say, pointing to the nearest large yellow hot set sign with its red block letters.

"Not we. You." Niks kisses both my cheeks. She swivels and flits toward the double doors to the lobby. "I'll say I'm last out and every lock will go *click click click*." She nods to the set. "Go, sweet thing. Step onto the page of your own story."

Niks pauses briefly to shut off the last bank of overhead work lights before she disappears through the doors. In the dark, my eyes are drawn to the buttery glow on the opposite side of flats blocking Donal Cam's bedchamber.

I stand motionless, waiting for something to happen, but nothing does. Heartbeats roar in my ears as I take a step toward the set and then another. I duck under the rope holding the hot set signs. When I round the end of the last flat, every breath is stolen from my chest.

The room glimmers from the light of a hundred candles. Standing before an arch on set is a figure from an illuminated manuscript or a stained-glass window. Jack's already impressive height is enhanced by an ornate clan headdress. His body is swathed in layers of silvery fabric, a jewel-tone blue tunic, deep brown leather, and bands of silver over his arms. Candles turn his hair into rivers of molten gold, flowing across chieftain shoulders. He is magnificent.

Speechless in the presence of this glorious vision I'm frozen in time with him.

Slowly, he glides over to take my hands. One step at a time, he brings me through the frame into his world. Words still inside me. It is not my place to speak in his kingdom.

Jack drops to a knee before me, my hands in his. Flickers of candlelight reflect off the silver in his headdress. The features of his beautiful face soften in the radiant shimmer. The eyes are far from soft; they burn with the intensity of sapphires reflecting the sun itself.

"You are my heart, my breath, the very blood that flows through my body. Without you, I am as weak as a breeze that dies before it makes a single leaf dance on the rowan tree."

I recognize the words from the love song Donal Cam sings to Nieve on the night they pledge themselves to one another for eternity because I have used some of these very words in my telling of their story.

Jack releases my hands to slowly lift his headdress and set it down beside him before he twines his fingers through mine. He drops his forehead to touch our joined hands. "I pledge myself to you through every phase of the moon. I promise you my loyalty in the blessing of every sunrise and the peace of every sunset."

He raises his eyes to mine. "Will you take me as I am, daughter of the stars, to fill your spirit with light and love?" Strong arms wrap around me. "I do adore you..."

I tense within his touch. How can he use that word, that horrible, awful word that's poison to me?

Jack gives me a gentle shake. "It's true I adore you more than reason, but beyond that, I love you, Gillian Bettencourt—with all that I am and all that I will ever be. I love you. I love you, and nothing or no one has the power to change that. I will do anything you ask of me to honor and protect that love. I'm asking you to believe this of me."

Essence of myth and magic surrounds us. Nothing but truths dare enter this sacred realm. With the strength of my own truth beating in my breast, I fall to my knees and take his lovely face in my hands. "I love you, Jack O'Leary."

For a long moment, we revel in each other's eyes, and then he draws me closer, lightly brushing his lips against mine. Ever so slowly, he parts my mouth with his, taking me into a kiss that begins as a caress then goes deeper, burning with an intensity that melts my bones until his arms are the only things keeping me from falling.

Jack runs a hand up the back of my neck into my hair, pulling gently until my throat is exposed to his lips. He kisses in time with the pulse beneath my skin and whispers over and over, "I love you. I love you."

Not so gently, I pull his mouth back to mine and take him in a kiss, leaving no doubt any barrier between us has risen into the sky like dawn mist over a loch.

He lifts me into his arms without a break in the kiss, increasing the already scorching heat between us. I feel as if we fly across the room to the massive fur-covered bed. There he lays me, standing above me with an expression equal parts love and lust. I'm dizzy with wanting him. I gasp as he backs away.

When I try to rise onto my elbows, he lays a palm between my breasts and eases me back down. His fingers dance along my body, slowly peeling off clothes until I'm naked before him.

Standing at the end of the bed, he stares down at me. "You glow like starlight."

And I do. The gentle luminescence of candles kisses my skin with ribbons of light.

I raise myself, sliding closer to where he stands and lift his tunic. To my delight, he is naked beneath and fully ready for what I need from him.

He untangles himself from my grasp, kissing my hands as he places them at my sides and once again has me on my back. "Tonight, I'm going to give myself to you as an honorable chieftain's son worships his love."

My body pulses, and I'm ready to scream if he doesn't get down to the business of giving himself to me.

His touch is silk against my skin. Fingers circle and slide up my calves, crossing over thighs and then lingering in places that have me arching and moaning for him. "Please, Jack. Now. Please now."

His lips replace his fingers and I soar straight into the sun with a cry of pleasure that draws his mouth back to mine. His hand cups the tender place he's just set aflame, and I feel myself pulsing against his palm. Before I fall from the height of near madness to solid ground, Jack's touch invites me to rise again. This time, he joins me.

The roughness of leather sliding over my breasts brings me to the brink of fracture. I run my hands up his thighs under a silken tunic to guide him home. Once there, he loses himself as I am lost. I rise to meet him. He drives deeper and deeper, never forcing, but claiming more and more of me. Our hips sear together, igniting a conflagration as bright as the center of a star. We both fall back to earth, bodies scattering in a downpour of golden raindrops.

He finally allows me to rid him of his costume. I kiss my way across the soft, curly hair of his chest, delighting in moans he doesn't hold back.

"I love you, Jack."

He rolls me onto my side, pressing my body against his. "I'm going to hold you to that."

"You have to, because that was ten, and now we own this."

"*Mo grá*. My silly girl, darling beauty." He dips his head to kiss my breasts. I reach down to find him well on the way to an encore when a phone alarm starts chiming on a table next to the bed.

His head collapses on my shoulder. "Shit."

I raise his chin with my thumb. "Am I keeping you from something?"

He grabs my ass with both hands. "Oh, you'll be keeping me." After lingering for a moment, he lets go. "We've got thirty minutes before night security makes their rounds."

I admire the contours of his ass as he slides out of bed and taps his phone. I marvel at his ability to move swiftly around the room given his state of arousal.

He throws my clothes to me. I shake them at him. "You're kidding, right?"

Reaching under the bed, he pulls out his street clothes and carefully returns his costume to a rolling rack next to the set. "We're just moving off from here, that's all."

I yank on my jeans and sweater, not bothering with bra or panties. I have no intention of depriving myself of more Jack as soon as possible. I don't care if it's in the back seat of his Renault.

"Help me with the candles, *Mo grá*." He flips over each candle to switch them off. There's got to be at least a hundred of these LED suckers in the room.

"*Mo grá*? What happened to *Mo chroí*?"

Jack pinches the waistband of my jeans to pull me in, kissing me quickly but thoroughly. "You're both to me, my heart and my love." He gives me a gentle shove. "Candles."

As I set a candle down, a terrible thought hits me. "Crap, this is a hot set. Are we putting them back right?"

His laugh starts as a low rumble that makes me tremble somewhere lower down. "We're not shooting in here tomorrow. Best advice I ever got was to make friends with the prop master and the head of accounting."

"The head of accounting scored you these candles?"

He snorts and then nods to the hot set signs. "Niks put these up to keep any strays out."

I whip around to him, my face as red as the sunsets from his wooing. "Niks knows what we're doing here?"

"Niks found me blubbering like a fool over you. She slapped me out of my misery and told me to get on with loving you."

"She helped you do this?" I wave a hand at the room.

"This was all my idea, but she did say I had to do something grand if I wanted to win you back."

I melt into his arms. "This is pretty damn grand."

We kiss until his phone alarm goes off again. I slap him lightly on the chest. "You set a backup alarm?"

He looks a little shy. "I didn't know where we'd be in the mix when the first went off. This one means we've got to get serious about leaving."

After the last candle is switched off, we scoop up the rest of our things. Jack motions toward the stables. "My car's round back." He slides his hand up under my shirt to give my breast a playful squeeze before dipping eager fingers down the front of my slacks. "Seems you may be up for another go."

I trace the fly of his jeans. "Seems I'm not the only one."

He groans and removes my hand before we lose control in the middle of the sound stage. "Game for a romp under the stars with me?"

"I'm game for anything with you from now on, Jack O'Leary."

CHAPTER
TWENTY-FOUR

Despite the layers of sub-zero rated sleeping bags under us and wool blankets piled on top, the dawn chill drives me closer to Jack. The first rays of sunlight bronze his ever-present beard stubble. A thin line of new red hair begins to peek up from the roots along his forehead. Someone is going to have to endure another dye job before long.

I can't keep my hands off him. I want him inside me before the sun clears the tree line across the rolling fields. I gently rake three fingers along the muscles on his chest while I tilt my head up to kiss and taste the Orion's belt of tiny moles on his jaw. "Hi," I purr as I detour from his chin up to his lips and feel him stir.

Forearms to rival the god Atlas destined to hold the earth on his shoulders capture me until there is no space between our naked bodies. "Stop squirming, woman, or I'll have to take you before I'm fully awake to do a proper job of it."

I run a hand down his ribs, taking a sharp turn inward at his hip bone. He's as substantial as a limb of the hawthorn tree above our nest. I stroke him and throw a leg over his hip so I'm fully open to him. "Your friend down here and I are going to get started. You're very welcome to catch up anytime."

Finding me as ready as he is, Jack slips inside me with a lusty growl. We move together slowly in time with the light spreading over the fields. With an impressive roll and lift, Jack sets me on top of him. My skin shines as golden as his hair in the morning glow that reaches us on the hilltop.

I throw my head back, spreading my knees to take him deeper. His hands travel over my body, bringing me closer and closer to that moment of blissful insanity. Fingers lock on my hips as he arches and releases just as a burst of dawn light splashes across the hawthorn tree. Moments later, my lovely man has me on my back and carries me with him into liquid sunlight.

We're both out of breath as I nuzzle into the hollow of his shoulder.

He nips my earlobe and then recites Donal Cam's lines. "Under stars and on a fresh day dawning will I have thee."

"How much personal experience do you think Deidre draws on for her books?"

Jack grunts and tightens his arms around me. "I think she's close to killing Doolin, so I'd say quite a bit."

We both laugh and watch a little brownish bird with dashes of red above its eye and down its breast. It hops from branch to branch, pecking at the offerings tied to the hawthorn while keeping a close eye on us.

I whisper in Jack's ear so as not to disturb our dawn visitor. "Do you know what kind of bird that is?"

He squints up at the tree. "A linnet, I'm thinking.'

"It's cute."

"You're cute," he says, flicking his tongue in my ear.

"If you keep that up, we're going to be here all day."

He lets out a deep sigh and flops onto his back. "If only we could."

I lean on an elbow. "What are we going to do, Jack?"

He copies my position so we're face to face. "We're going to be in love." When I try to protest, he lays a finger on my lips. "Out loud."

With those two words, all my fears over the repercussions of people finding out about us pale in comparison to loving this glorious man. To borrow Meg's line, I paint a scenario in my head of endless breakfast conversations with Jack, chatting about the intersection of art and life. "I don't care if they fire me. I'll be happy working at a shop and writing in my free time, but I do care if they fire you."

His eyes narrow. "Fire me?"

"Yeah. They might *Doctor Who* you and find some other hot guy to dangle in front of women."

"*Doctor Who* me?"

"You know. Regenerate Donal Cam like The Doctor. Replace you."

He looks even more baffled.

"Please tell me you watch *Doctor Who* or this"—I fan a finger between us—"ends right now."

"I have a canny piece of paper that says they can't regenerate this face for at least five years. And an option for the length of the series." He reaches around, cupping my ass to pull me closer. "I'm not ready to joke about us being done with."

I run fingers through his hair. "I'm sorry."

"Gilly, I'm still battling with understanding why you left me without even trying to weather the storm."

I drop the top of my head against his chest to gather my thoughts and then I look into those crystal blue eyes. "Because I thought the wrong things were most important."

He traps the tear rolling down my cheek on his pinkie and blows it away like the puff of a dandelion.

I twine my fingers through his. "Nothing in my life is more important than you."

He kisses our joined hands. "Even if they could *Doctor Who* me for being with you, I'd not care. You and I could open a cheese and onion pie shop and golf in the Irish rain. That'd be my Heaven."

"And mine." We kiss deep and slow for a long time. "I thought we happened too fast, and it was all about impulse, not reality."

"What are you thinking now?"

I smooth a strand of hair off his forehead. "I'm thinking that right here in my arms is a person who is genuine, who I can trust with everything I feel and dream and want." I drop a kiss on each of his eyelids. "You are loyal and loving. Jack O'Leary, you are the creative partner I've always wished for. I tell my stories with words, and you tell yours by becoming the story itself."

"And it doesn't bother you that my career is about lies and pretend, even if I'm not."

I shake my head. "You're wrong. Your talent is about finding the truth of every character you inhabit."

He takes my mouth with such passion that I claw at his back to bring him closer. Jack breaks the kiss, leaving me wanting. When I move in to continue, he slides his hands up the sides of my face.

"I'm smart with my money. I've got the place in Sneem that's all paid off. It's not big, but there's plenty of land to add on to the house."

My insides begin to bubble. I want this to be going where I think it's going. I wish with all my heart and spirit for Jack not to stop.

His thumbs lightly trace my cheekbones as he continues. "It's for me the way it is for you, love. My future must be with a partner who values a creative life above all else." His grip tightens. "I won't have you working in a shop, but I will have you writing all the stories that I know are swimming around in this darlin' head. I'll read every one of them in front of a roaring fire with you by my side."

Jack's face shifts into soft focus through the sheen of tears coating my eyes.

With that crazy strength of his, he lifts me to my feet but stays on one knee before me. "I never believed love could happen in an eye blink until I met you. There's nothing I've ever been so sure of as you. Share this life with me Gillian Bettencourt, my perfect partner. I love you beyond dreams, beyond hopes"—he nods up to the hawthorn—"beyond wishing. Will you marry me?"

I drop onto his knee and throw my arms around his neck. "You're it for me, Jack. I'll marry you in this lifetime and all that come after." I lean back to look at him. "You will never have to chase me like Nieve. I will know you in every time."

He pulls us to our feet. "Oh, but you are my Nieve. The woman I'd woo a thousand times to keep by my side."

Even the heat of our kiss can't compete with the freezing wind that slaps against our naked bodies.

"Bugger it," says Jack, yanking a blanket around us. He gestures to the hawthorn. "I think we've given the good people enough of a show for now." I keep the soft wool cover while he gathers our clothes.

"Come here, darlin'," says Jack, holding his arms wide for me to fold into before he relinquishes my jeans. I press against him while he raises his cell and snaps a picture of the hawthorn, its leaves etched in gold outline from the rising sun. He nuzzles my neck. "I never want to forget this brilliant dawn."

Once dressed, I lean against the lichen-covered boulder, hugging arms to my chest. "So, tell me, love, what will out loud look like?"

"Blazing normal. I've heard that down Wicklow Way, Daniel Day Lewis still puts his own bins out on Thursdays."

"I'm talking about the read through this morning." A giant shiver blindsides me. Only part of it is from the cold. The rest is anticipating the fallout when our bomb detonates inside The Clan.

Jack drops the pile of sleeping bags and blankets he'd gathered to come wrap me in a hug. "It's going to look grand." He taps his temple. "I see how it is up here. Trust me."

I put my trust into a kiss that could get us in trouble very quickly. Jack lifts me off my feet and carries me to his Renault at the bottom of the hill. It's damn sexy to be carried in the arms of a Celtic god. Not so sexy the way he dumps me in the passenger seat.

"You stay here and quit tempting me with your magic, Witch, while I bring our baggage down."

I admire all the parts of Jack pressing against his jeans as he moves up and down the hill. All the parts that now belong to me. Visions of our lovely red-headed babies who will grow up to be poets, painters, and storytellers, and call Jack "Da" twirl in my head.

He dumps our campsite into the boot of the car and slides behind the wheel but doesn't move. His knuckles whiten.

"What is it?"

Creases line his forehead as he presses his lips together. "I haven't got a ring for you. I should have planned better."

"Yet. You haven't got a ring for me, yet." I lean over to capture his mouth with mine. "And you could not have planned last night any better."

He beams at me. "God, I love you."

"I'll hold you to that," I say, repeating his line.

"We'll go to my place for a wash up and then we walk into work, hands clasped. Yeah?"

"Yeah," I say, leaning over to kiss his ear. I truly am ready to sacrifice my future on *The Chieftain's Son* writing staff for a future with Jack. I'm not pissing away an opportunity for a man. I'm embracing love and a creative life with the partner I choose. Other opportunities will come, or I will make them myself. That's the beauty of being a writer.

Perhaps I'll offer to freelance for Deidre and help her with season breakdowns of the rest of *The Chieftain's Son* series. She wanted to work with me anyway. Heck, I'll do that just for the joy of spending more time with her. Somehow, I know Deidre LaRochelle will understand my decision better than anyone else.

Still, my new gilded reality isn't without the inevitable gut punch of disappointment when I imagine the look of betrayal on Bobby's face and having to say goodbye to the rest of the writing staff.

Jack butchers the words to the song playing on the radio, and I smile. A lifetime of this will be pretty grand. As an engagement gift to myself, I change his contact in my phone from *Cheese and Onion Pie* to simply *Jack*.

TWENTY-FIVE

After a shared shower with benefits at Jack's teeny, two-room mini-house, I don the Christmas gift sweater he bought for his sister that he's supposed to exchange for the right size but hasn't gotten around to yet. I may not have a ring, but at least I'll avoid the walk of shame showing up in the same outfit I wore yesterday.

"We're going to be late," I tap on the console clock of the Renault while we sit in the car park.

"Not yet," says Jack.

My stomach flops over one way and then attempts to right itself. He wants to be last to the table read so everyone will be there for our "out loud" reveal.

"Stop worrying yourself pale." Jack shares his latest social media post at me. "The reactions to this shot is what makes me both Meg and True Time proof." There's the picture of the hawthorn tree in dawn's golden light with the caption: *Woke to this on the best day of my life.* If you look closely, faint shadows stretch beneath the tree. I can make out it's us sans clothing, but for those not in the know, we're just an abstract. There are already over forty-five thousand likes.

"Enjoy the hearts while you can." I make a heart with my hands.

"They might turn to dagger emojis when your lovely lasses find out about me."

Jack flashes me his wiliest look. "What do you Yanks say? 'Bring it on'?"

"I wish I had your confidence."

He takes my hand and squeezes. "Here. I'm giving you a bit of mine."

A car screeches up the road and skids into a spare expanse of gravel. Maureen hops out carrying a large flat donut box and rushes through the front door.

"Someone seems to be back on with her pastry chef." If I were still on staff, we could do some wedding planning together.

"You don't look happy, love."

I pat his hand. "I'm fine." Looking into that chiseled, ridiculously handsome face, I can't help but smile, knowing I get to wake up to this view for the rest of my life. "Actually, I'm brilliant."

"Let's to it then."

Murph doesn't even notice we're holding hands when I fob us in. The walk through the sound stage and down the corridor to the table read feels like a hundred miles or kilometers whatever is longer.

There's the usual buzz ahead. My nerves short-circuit when I see everyone seated at the table for the read through.

"I love you," says Jack just before we step through the door.

Conversations die like the snap of a power outage. It's almost comical the way every pair of eyes, from Bobby's to the writers', to Alan Rafier's, to the actors' and Niks' lock onto our joined hands. I sneak a look at Jack. His smile shines like one of the giant stage lights.

"Good morning, all," he says. "There's a thing Gilly and I would like you all to know."

I never hear Meg coming. She barrels between us from behind, breaking our grip to open a Meg-size space between us.

"Actually, there's not," she says, as if her maneuver will erase the evidence of our joined hands from everyone's memory.

Bobby is first to recover and takes a step toward us.

"What the hell?" His expression is even stormier than I imagined.

Jack rests his hands lightly on Meg's shoulders. "I respect what you're about, Meg, and I do appreciate it, but I can't go along with what you've cooked up for me anymore." He dots a kiss on her cheek.

Questions fly. I feel as if I'm sinking under the barrage, but then I catch Deidre LaRochelle's eye. She sits at the table with a smile that makes her look more beautiful than I've ever seen her. Slowly, she raises fingers to her lips and blows me a kiss.

That's all the encouragement I need to slip my hand back into Jack's. "As he said," I say, raising my voice above the din. We're back in the spotlight. I lay my hands against Jack's stubbly cheeks and pull him down for a kiss.

"I didn't know they knew each other," says Alan Rafier, baffled.

I turn to the group. "I want to thank everyone here from my heart for the opportunity to work on this amazing show. I'm sorry to compromise your trust and mess up Jack's PR." I face my golden-haired fiancée. "But my future is pledged to this wonderful man."

Maureen sits back and plops her feet up on the table. "Which means? Punch up that dialog for me, G."

Jack lifts me off the ground and spins me once before pulling me against his side. "I'm marrying this woman."

Niks jumps to her feet to start the applause. Everyone in the room joins her or pounds on the table. Everyone except Bobby and Meg, who have their heads together in frenzied conversation.

Jack accepts some rowdy thumps on the back while I enjoy more gentle embraces.

Bobby raises his arms for quiet. The stern look on his face stabs me straight through the heart. I hate to let people down.

"Gillian, you realize I have to fire you."

I tense everything to keep from crying. "I understand."

He drives the knife deeper. "I took a chance on you and look where it got me."

What do I say to public shaming? All I can do is nod my head.

"I've lost an incredibly promising writer's assistant."

One more helping of guilt, and I'm going to totally lose it in front of all these people. Jack threads an arm around my back. I feel him tense.

I've got to get out of here before he comes to my defense and puts himself in a worse position than our "out loud" may already have done.

Bobby lifts a stack of scripts from the empty chair next to him and heaves them onto the table. They fan out down the middle like fallen dominoes. "But I've gained a brilliantly talented staff writer."

My eyes fall to the cover of the top script in the pile. *Chieftain's Son Episode 113, The Parting by Gillian Bettencourt.*

Jack lets out a deafening *whoop.*

Bobby is across the room in a flash, lifting me off my feet in a crushing hug. "You're never going to make things easy for me are you, Bettencourt? It's a damn glorious script." He holds up a finger. "There will be notes."

"Oh my God, Bobby. Thank you. Thank you so much."

He moves in for another hug. "I expect free golf lessons."

"You've got 'em."

Benj and Benny double team me. "Welcome to our clan."

Doolin shakes Jack's hand and kisses my cheek. "Do I have your word the O'Leary brood will be off to dual immersion Irish language school?"

I throw my arms around him. "I promise." The O'Leary brood. I love the sound of that.

Maureen stands in front of me, arms crossed. She jerks her chin at Jack. "Why does he get to call you Gilly?"

"Please do call me Gilly." I wipe away tears with the sleeve of my soon-to-be sister in law's Christmas sweater.

Meg squares off with Jack. "I suppose you think this is a fairy tale." She holds up a finger before he can answer. "My bosses at True Time will most likely bust a vein over this. Painting you as the devoted fiancée is not what they had in mind."

Maureen elbows Jack and cups a hand around her ear. "Listen, I hear the sound of a million hearts going *splat* by the roadside."

As Jack blushes and playfully shoves Maureen away, Meg stomps off toward her office. I hope whatever new scenario she's painting doesn't leave me with a black eye. Although it may be a well-deserved shiner, given the spot we've put her in.

Deidre gathers us both in her arms. "As I said, there will be a flock of ginger babies."

"Off to Irish school," says Jack.

"Too right," calls Doolin from his seat.

A huge bang draws everyone's attention. Alan Rafier thrusts a finger at the pile of scripts. "Best to you both, but let's get down to it."

Jack kisses me soundly before taking his place next to Niks. She brushes a kiss across his cheek, and I don't even care. Then she looks straight at me, clasps her hands together as if in prayer and bows. It's a little weird, but I'll take it.

Danna taps me on the back and points to the empty chair next to Bobby. Scripts are passed around, opened, and folded back as I take my place at the table. The room is quiet, but the tune in my head is electrifying. I want to pull Jack up onto the table and dance. Out loud is the way all love and happiness deserve to be. I will never accept anything less.

Donal Cam's husky voice floats through the air as Jack reads the lines I've written for him. "Time and love are the strongest forces a human heart must endure. Through the mists of daybreak and across the ages, I will always find you, my partner in passion, spirit, and laughter. Gillian, my forever love."

When he lifts his eyes to mine, the single tear sliding down Jack's cheek matches my own.

TWENTY-SIX

The tumult on Meg's face as Jack as I take our places in the plum-colored chairs opposite her desk makes me wish I'd brought a Donal Cam sword to this meeting. Since the reveal of our engagement last week, she hasn't spoken to either one of us. Thank goodness Bobby's offer of joining *The Chieftain's Son* writing staff makes me as close to bullet proof as I'm likely to get.

Next to me, Jack sits battle-ready on the edge of his seat. Meg's double pedestal desk is the only barrier between the lion and lioness ready to spring at one another's throats. That makes me the lion tamer. I hope I walk away with minimal toothmarks.

Meg folds her hands. "Bobby wants to paint Jack as the dutiful fiancé."

Her comment is so in sync with what we want that I nearly slap the desk and call out, "Done!" It will be a relief to have her as an ally again.

Jack slips my left hand, the one wearing an engagement ring, through the crook of his elbow, bringing it to rest on his forearm. The opal surrounded by diamond chips twinkles in the beam of an overhead light.

When Meg narrows her eyes at my ring, the body next to me transforms into a pillar of stone. I press my knee against Jack's in an attempt to keep him grounded.

The queen of publicity flattens her palms on the table, targeting us with a glare that could summon hailstones from a summer sky. "I said no to that plan."

A vein on Jack's temple pulses. Before he blows, she holds up a finger. "We're greenlighting Gillian to develop *The Chieftain's Son* podcast with Maureen."

"Great. I'd love to." Maybe this isn't going to be a bloodletting after all.

"And I owe you both an apology for the way I acted that night at Howth. I panicked and left your feelings out of the equation. That was wrong."

Jack shifts beside me and darts a quick glance at Meg before draping an arm across the back of my chair. "A nice offer for Gilly and an apology..." He drops his chin, studying Meg's face. "Why is my gut saying you're buttering us up for news we're not going to like?"

She meets his stare head-on. "Let me paint the scenario I've got planned."

Oh God, one of Meg's scenarios. I nearly crush Jack's fingers.

He grasps the edge of the desk and leans forward. "I think it's best if we're the ones doing the painting."

I slide a finger along the edge of the desk. "Before you lift that paintbrush, you should know I've moved in with Jack."

Meg's chin gives a startled bob.

"In his cottage here on The Clan property and in Sneem." Moving in may be an exaggeration since I'm still basically living out of a suitcase. I do have toothbrushes at both places.

Meg drops her head, staring at the top of the desk for a long brittle moment. Slowly, she raises her eyes to us. "The Clan cottage isn't a problem, but Sneem is a disaster waiting to happen." She jabs a pen at her personalized note pad, leaving a smudge of blue ink. "You've already been seen there together. There's probably press camped out waiting to catch Jack and the mystery girl."

I flash on the grief we've caused Imelda because her delivery boy blabbed about us on cheese-and-onion-pie night. The thought of turning peaceful Sneem into a hornet's nest of paparazzi is a legit concern.

Jack shakes his head. "Are you operating on the notion this is a negotiation?"

Meg taps her fingernail on the desktop. "It's a strategy meeting, Jack. We've got to approach this to benefit the show and appease True Time."

His eyes glaze. I know that look. He's attempting to reconcile his ongoing conflict between Donal Cam's image and Jack O'Leary's life.

Meg jumps on his moment of hesitation. "Bobby and I have met with every department." She thumps a file on her desk labeled *NDA* that holds the non-disclosure agreements we've all signed to avoid leaks from *The Chieftain's Son* universe. "News of your engagement is currently on lock down."

Locked down or not, it's really happening. Jack and I clasp hands, and I'm adrift in his ocean blue eyes. This wonderful man is going to be my husband long after all ten seasons of *The Chieftain's Son* are available on Blu-ray.

He gives Meg a lopsided smile. "That'll be fine until our wedding come fall unlocks it."

The strangled cry from across the desk shatters our ten seconds of bliss. Meg's face doesn't have a drop of color left. "*This* fall?" She leaps to her feet and paces behind her desk. "You can't. A wedding that soon will shred your fandom."

Jack pounds the arm of the chair with his fist. "I won't—"

Meg sits down hard. Twin lines of light from the desk lamp give the appearance that we've shocked streaks of gray through her chestnut hair.

I grip Jack's bicep, signaling him not to speak as Meg takes a shaky breath. A pang of sympathy catches me by surprise. She and Bobby seem to be vying for the workaholic of the year award. Does she have any semblance of a personal life away from the show? On the night she dragged me away from Jack in Howth, she was interviewing Cam O'Sullivan, no relation to Donal Cam, her new assistant. After the interview, she'd been alone at Lobster Lee's with nothing but an overflowing glass of wine for company. For the two years Treat and I were in limbo rather than investing in a real relationship, seeing couples who were obviously in love was painful. It made me acutely aware of what I didn't have.

Do Jack and I make Meg feel that way?

"Here me out," Meg levels her gaze at me. "I need *The Chieftain's Son* to make a splash at Cali Con this summer." She rubs the bridge of her nose. "The show and the man."

Jack twirls his hands for her to get on with it. Thank goodness he's calmed down enough to let her say her peace.

Her intense gaze sends a shiver through my body.

"I need time before you two officially go public." Jack sputters, but she continues. "Teasing the relationship between Jack and Niks already ballooned our ratings, inspired new online fan sites, and my phone is ringing off the hook for interviews. Help me work that scenario for all its worth. All I'm asking is some semblance of subtlety on your part to give me a shot at finishing the success we've set in motion."

The pleading look on her face softens Meg's features, humanizing the publicity machine.

I'm not as gut-punched any more by the trumped-up love between real life Donal Cam and Nieve. It turns out Niks, Marisa, and I have a girl band chemistry I really enjoy. Besides Jack's sister, Bonnie, and his nieces, Niks and Marisa are the biggest cheerleaders for our engagement. I tilt my head at Meg. "How long do you need?" If Niks and Marisa have to make a sacrifice, I can be subtle for a while, at least in public.

She steeples her fingers. "True Time wants us to stay the Jack/Niks course until after the season two finale airs."

"We're done here." Jack shoots to his feet with a snarl, dragging me toward the door of the office.

The look of panic in Meg's eyes enlarges the soft spot I'm beginning to feel for her. Her motives and insane drive exist because of her dedication to the show. The three of us share that.

A bargaining chip suddenly occurs to me. I pull Jack down to whisper in his ear. After I finish, his eyes search my face. When I nod, he touches his forehead to mine for a moment before we slip into a quick but thorough kiss.

I pivot to face Meg and lean back against Jack's broad chest, pulling his arms around me. It may be my imagination, but I swear I catch a fleeting look of longing on Meg's face as she stares at our vertical snuggle. A moment later, the matching grins on our faces send her eyebrows skyward.

My smile widens even more. "We'll play True Time's game until the season two finale drops on one condition."

Meg studies us before tapping a pen to her chin. 'Which is?"

I'm the one calling the shots on the cat and mouse game now. "You help secure us a wedding venue guaranteed to keep out any unsanctioned media attention."

Jack rests his chin on my head. "Shouldn't be too big a bother for you since we'll be well into shooting location scenes for season three by then."

Meg does not miss the mischief in Jack's voice. Her eyes dart back and forth between us with suspicion. She takes what can only be identified as a cleansing breath. "I assume you've already got a specific place in mind?"

I tilt my head back to see Jack's face. His eyes twinkle like sparks from a bonfire. He bobs his chin at Meg, and we say together, "The Skelligs."

If I had to wager, I'd say not much shocks Meg. But this does. By the end of season two, my future husband will be so insanely famous, any hope of a private wedding will be a pipe dream, unless we exchange vows on a rock in the sea covered in puffins with near-impossible access.

I giggle as Jack scoops me up in his arms and lets out a triumphant laugh. "Paint that scenario for us Meg, and we'll buy you the canvas.

EPILOGUE

We honestly intended to honor Meg's timeline. In her P.R. scenario, Jack O'Leary and Gillian Bettencourt will tie the knot on Skellig Michael off the coast of Ireland in June a year from now. The event will be great publicity for the show, so of course Jack and I promise to be one hundred percent on board for Meg's hoopla.

In reality, the Skellig spectacle will be our second ceremony, the public version. The love of my life, with one niece thrown over his shoulder while the other torments our cats, waits for me under a rented white trellis in the backyard of our home in Kerry for a more secret affair. It's barely been a month since we wrapped shooting on season one. Call us impatient or impulsive, but Jack and I chose not to wait another day before making our vows, a year ahead of Meg's schedule.

The writing staff, Jack's parents, and Deidre LaRochelle do whiskey shots at the refreshment table. Doolin rescues the cats from Jack's niece and sets them on top of the low stone wall at the back of the lawn. Niks and Marisa chat up Jack's sister, Bonnie. Bobby, Jack's best man, ever the organizer, checks his watch and attempts to wrangle our small party of guests to their seats. Meg sits alone, looking like she could use a dozen whiskey shots. Saying she wasn't pleased when we let her know about the private wedding is the understatement of the century. After an extremely tense meeting and pressure from Bobby, Meg grudgingly conceded to Jack's point that hiding our marriage wasn't any trickier than hiding an engagement.

My mother fusses with a hot glue gun to put finishing touches on the wreath she fashioned using pale lavender cuckooflowers from Jack's garden for my headdress. "Perfect," she says as she settles it on my head and arranges the trio of white satin ribbons to flow down my back. There was a time I would have opted for a veil, but wearing Irish wildflowers feels right.

Mom hugs me from behind. "You're a stunner, Gillian."

Dad frowns from the doorway between the bedroom and the master bath. "That tub is huge. It's not to scale for the room. Quite the squeeze around to get to the sink."

I blush at memories of sharing the oversized tub with Jack and steal my lover's phrase. "A big man needs a big tub, Dad."

He shakes his head and comes to stand next to Mom and me. Here we are, the Bettencourts three, standing together looking out the window at my future. In a few minutes, I'll alter the team for good. I try to speak, but then get all mushy. Words, the tools of my trade, refuse to come easily.

"I'll love him forever," I manage. "Get out any comments now about this happening too fast. No thinly veiled snark at my wedding allowed."

My parents clasp hands behind my back. It's my father, not my mother who sniffs away a tear. "From the moment I first saw your mother covered in green splatters next to a backdrop she'd just finished painting, I knew I'd found the love of my life."

Mom smiles and shakes their joined hands, bumping knuckles against the back of a simple white Nieve dress I borrowed from wardrobe. I can indulge my princess fantasies when I choose a fancier wedding dress for our Skellig spectacular next year.

"You know how that story ends, sweetheart," says Dad.

Mom laughs. "Vegas, four months later. When Bettencourts fall, they fall hard and fast."

"Are you insinuating I inherited soulmate-dar?"

Dad gives mom the same flavor of smile I see every day on Jack's face for me. "It's better than inheriting the Bettencourt beak." He taps his nose.

"Gilly. Gilly. Gilly," sings Maureen, my maid of honor, as she dances into the room. "Imelda says if we don't get this party started, her cheese and onion pie won't be gooey fresh for the reception." She hands me a bouquet of cuckooflowers to match my headdress.

We make our way to the back door. Mom walks out first, taking the arm of Jack's brother-in-law, who escorts her to the front row of mismatched chairs from houses of various attendees. Maureen goes next, pressing play on the boom box wedged into a flower box under a back window before she flits up the aisle. Jack and Bobby laugh as she twirls before taking her place near the solemniser, a friend of Jack's mom, who will be performing our ceremony.

The beautiful notes of "Give Me Your Hand" settle our rowdy crowd. Dad nestles my hand in the crook of his arm, and we're off. Music twines with the rush of love in my heart for the man waiting for me. When Dad sets my hand into Jack's, I'm overtaken by a lovely sense of peace. This man is my life, my love, my creative partner, my future. My gaze locks on his and in that moment, certainty in each other binds us closer than any ceremony.

Instead of solemnly turning as one to the solemniser, wedding officiant, Jack snatches me up in his arms and spins us. The ribbons from my wreath stream out behind me, and I nearly drop my bouquet. Our gathering of friends and family cheer, calling out encouragement in English and Irish. Jack sweeps me around one last time and dips in for the kiss that's supposed to come at the end of the ceremony.

Rather loud throat clearing and an "All right then," from the solemniser ends the kiss. This is the wedding I want, a raucous affair overflowing with love and friends. This is the man I want, a person bursting with life and not afraid to shout to the skies how much he loves me. This is the life I want, one where creativity and passion will always reign.

Jack O'Leary and I turn to the solemniser and marry.

Thank you for reading! Did you enjoy? Please add your review because nothing helps an author more and encourages readers to take a chance on a book than a review.

And don't miss book two in the *Behind the Scenes* series, PRESS RELEASE, available now. Turn the page for a sneak peek!

Also be sure to sign up for the City Owl Press newsletter to receive notice of all book releases!

SNEAK PEEK OF PRESS RELEASE

The weekly call from my boss is overdue. Every Wednesday, this phone chat with L.A. guarantees loss of appetite and teeth grinding. I regress into a secondary schooler summoned to the principal's office instead of the thirty-two-year-old head of P.R. for a brilliant TV period drama that's currently rocketing in popularity.

I beat samba, waltz, and tarantella rhythms around the phone on my desk to summon the call with no result. Perhaps tapping out "Bohemian Rhapsody," best rock song ever written, will do the trick. Better yet, here in the land where the blood of druids and pagans still flows through my fellow Irish locals, a ritualistic *"ring damn you"* chant may be the wisest choice.

If only I knew one.

The glint of an overhead light catches my new coat of nail polish. I chose a perfect tonal match to my plum-colored skirt and suit jacket. My reflection in the glass office wall is a study in plum. My suit and nails are the exact shade of my leather desk chair. Except for the pale skin of my face, I'd disappear completely into my surroundings, a carnivore poised to pounce on the unaware. Here in my personal jungle of plum, steel, and glass, I am the alpha predator.

Or am I?

I glare at the non-ringing phone on my desk. This call is my weekly judgement, shifting my position to more prey than predator. Och! I'm being as dramatic as a scene in our television show, *The Chieftain's Son*. My overly loud exhale falls somewhere between ironic chuckle and frustrated huff. I prefer to initiate calls instead of being shackled to the receiving end. Control is my goddess, and I gladly worship at her bejeweled sandals.

A backwards shove of the chair gives me freedom to pace between door and desk. My feet pinch from a day in heels. I can't decide if I'd rather down a generous pour of the red blend waiting at home or soak my feet in it.

"Ring, you bloody bastard."

The alarm on my cell trills half-six, day's end for most everyone else here at The Clan, production headquarters of *The Chieftain's Son*. It's my daily reminder to catch people before they leave for the day if I've got a bit of news or instructions for them. My frustration ebbs a bit at the thought of the accolades for our brilliant show. In our first season out of the gate, we scored ten Crystal nominations, the most prestigious U.S. television award, along with additional smatterings of European honors. Everyone on our team in the FYC, For Your Consideration, campaign across multiple awards made final cuts. That's an entire bird's worth of feathers in my cap for the backbreaking work to coordinate the publicity and marketing chores between here in Ireland and Hollywood. Truth is, the challenge lights me up as bright as a Beltane bonfire.

So, why does my gut ping like radar detecting an imminent attack while I wait for the damnable L.A. phone call?

Through the glass wall of my office, I return waves from folks leaving for the day. When I deal with Hollywood, the time difference between here in County Kerry, Ireland, and the land of palm trees and over-priced sunglasses makes their quitting time the beginning of my workday.

Collin, one of our senior writers, pops his head in. "Pub call, Meg. You in?"

"Waiting to chat with L.A. Maybe after."

He flips a strand of black hair out of his eyes. "Bobby's standing the first round."

I hate to turn down a fresh drawn Guinness, mother's milk. "Can't commit, Coll, but thanks."

"Anyone ever tell you, Ms. McGrath, it's no crime to ease up now and then?"

"Every day." Easing up is a non-negotiable for me. High standards make the world go 'round. "If luck is with me, I will walk through the pub door before the second round."

"Here's hoping." He tosses me a parting smile and heads out. From a side view, I notice Collin's belly has shifted from paunch to trim. The once-a-day walk and weekly round of golf Gillian Bettencourt O'Leary, our newest staff writer and wife of our star, instigated with the writing staff is paying off.

Ten more minutes plod along as slow as cattle blocking the lane, and I drop back onto my desk chair. This isn't the first time Dashell Everett, my boss at the True Time Network, ranked a call to his on-site publicist for *The Chieftain's Son* television program a lower priority than morning espresso. With *The Chieftain's Son* debut at San Diego Cali Con, the celebration of the popular arts chock-full of celebrities and high-octane fans, less than a month away, Dash and I have a laundry list of logistics to button up. Or rather, I'll fill him in on everything I've inked in. He'll respond with a few inane questions, one or two ludicrous suggestions, and then sign off with his signature morning yawn.

Maureen, the most manic of our writing staff, swings in on my door like a kid on a playground. Her kinky red hair frizzes in an impressive nimbus to frame her face. It must be a nightmare to run a comb through that maze. She balances a small dessert plate on her palm, maneuvering a flat figure eight with it through the air.

"Megsie, I've brought deliciousness."

I slash an X with my hand. "We agreed to bury the 'Megsie' thing."

She dances around my desk, tempting me with the pastry on her plate. "How about Megalith? Megawatt?" Maureen cuddles up to my chair and waves the goodie under my nose. "Dulce de leche Napoleon with your name stamped in the icing."

I accept the offering of my favorite dessert and set it next to my computer. "Did you think to bring a fork?" Maureen's fiancé is the pastry chef at our fanciest hotel in Waterville, the closest town to The Clan production complex. The man is a god with his sweeties. "Or are you withholding utensils until you explain the conditions of this blatant bribe?"

She spins my chair so we're face-to-face and clasps both hands over her heart as if suffering a mortal wound. "Can't I gift one of my bridesmaids with something to put a smile on her face and crumbs on the lapel of her tailored suit jacket?"

I defy anyone not to crack a smile in the wake of Maureen's Maureen-ness.

"I want your opinion on the sweetie. Grady's thinking to make our wedding cake a three-tiered version of this Napoleon."

I cock my head. "The groom's baking his own wedding cake?"

"You think he'd trust anyone else to do it?"

There's something Maureen's Grady and I share. If you want a thing done the way it should be, you do it yourself.

Her livewire locks tickle my nose as she darts in to give me a peck on the cheek. "You caught me on the bribe. Nothing in life comes without an angle, Megsie." She rests elbows on my desk. "Here's my ask. I know you planned for the two of us to room together at Cali Con, but will you die of loneliness if I have my own digs?"

"Bringing Grady to San Diego, are you?"

"He begged the week off from the hotel, and we thought it would be lovely to tool around California with Jack and Gilly a bit after the convention." Her eyes take on a wicked glint. "You're very welcome to share the room with the both of us, it could be interesting."

The needle on my danger meter bounces into the red at the mention of our star and his hush-hush missus. "Tool around where with Jack and Gilly?" I'm at my wits end trying to keep news of Jack O'Leary's marriage on lockdown. How can those eejits think prancing around together in the land of Paparazzi-on-every-corner is anything but image suicide for Jack? It's vital his female fans continue stoking their fantasies about him being available.

"Stand down, Warden. Bobby'll be with us as well." She crosses fingers on both hands and makes circles in the air. "We'll make sure to keep at least two bodies between the happy couple wherever we go. You have my word not to make your job any harder than it already is."

Truth be told, toolin' around on adventures with the person who shares your dreams sounds grand. Seeing Jack and Gilly together pokes at the fingertip-sized scar on my heart from the few times in the past I'd thought such a connection was possible. Part of me pulls to support the two publicly, but the stronger force says to sit them down and warn: what are rainbows now will disappear when the sun shines bright enough to illuminate fan backlash.

I mentally count our reserved rooms. Our senior writer, Danna, bugged out of Cali Con in favor of staying here and cracking the whip so Collin, Benj, and Benny, the rest of our writing staff, will polish their scripts for the second half of season two. Gilly, Bobby, and Maureen will carve out writing time while we're in San Diego. "You and Grady can take Danna's room."

Maureen bows. "You're a love, Meg."

Before the door closes, I call after her. "Bring me a fork." I jot a quick note to schedule a meeting to discuss "toolin' around" with all parties involved.

My eyes flick to my wrist. The watch I set to Hollywood time is nearing half-ten.

These calls with Dashell Everett make me a dog on a leash. They're infuriating and irksome. It rankles I'm required to pass every business move I make through him. The end of my probationary period with the True Time Network is almost up. Surely, with the splash I've planned for *The Chieftain's Son* at Cali Con, on top of all I've done for the show, Dash will finally sign off and give me free reign and full authority to run things on my own without his constant gatekeeping. To kill time, I adjust room assignments on my spreadsheet.

"Meg, got a minute?"

I almost squeak with surprise when the man himself, Jack O'Leary, star of *The Chieftain's Son* and the face voted most likely to set female hearts aflame, pokes his head in my door. The advantage of glass walls is to see someone coming, which only works if you're looking in the first place.

I'm tempted to lock my door until I get the business with my boss done, but blowing off my lead actor isn't good policy. "Always. Come in."

I wave him in. His new bride, Gillian Bettencourt O'Leary, follows as close as a shadow in his wake. Here's the very pair making my job harder than it needs to be.

"I've got a call coming in, but I'm yours 'til then."

I rub my lips together. I'm not being charitable or fair. Gilly is a rare talent, one of our ten Crystal Award nominees for writing a truly beautiful season-one finale. She didn't scheme to slip between Jack's sheets as so many would. The two fools fell in love.

They plop into my guest chairs, never releasing the hold on each other's hand. Gilly smiles at me. I've got to give her credit. Even after I tried to warn her off Jack, she's been kind to me. It's me having trouble warming up.

"I've got news I thought you should know," says Gilly as Jack trains a loose strand of strawberry blond hair behind her ear. "I've signed with Jack's agency."

I nod my head. "I know, your agent called me."

"Great. Then he told you about the panel he booked for me at The Con?"

I lean forward. "The Con?"

"Sorry, Meg, I mean Cali Con. My parents used to go all the time. They always called it The Con."

I hold up a finger. "Hold on. Did you say 'booked'?"

My tone is harsh enough to make Gilly sit back in her chair. Jack's features harden, a male of the species defending his mate.

I compose myself. "Go on."

Gilly lays a hand on Jack's arm, clearly sensing the protective waves jumping off his skin. "It's the *Pages to Screen* panel on Friday morning."

"Her award noms give my woman wicked clout," says Jack, beaming at Gilly.

"And you didn't think to check with me first?" I regret the snap in my voice. We're not adversaries here. Same team. Same goals.

Then why is the burn in my chest getting hotter? The goddess of control sits at the edge of my desk, crossing her legs and throwing me an over-the-top-of-the-glasses look. *The Chieftain's Son's* presence at Cali Con is my domain. My plans for our show's involvement at the event are flawless. Wrinkles, alterations, or hiccups of any kind take a swing at my perfection.

Jack's blue eyes shift from crystal to storm-cloud gray. He and I got along brilliantly before Gilly showed up. Now, I'm afraid he sees me as the witch who insists on keeping his marriage secret while I force him to play kissy-face with his co-star, Niks Tellefson. It's Jack's dedication to the show, not any loyalty to me, driving him to act out the fauxmance with Niks. I wonder if Gilly and Jack have a voodoo doll of me at their place. That would explain my constant headaches.

"We're checking with you now, Meg," says Jack, his tone confirmation of the diminished warm fuzzies between us.

I've got to fix that. Not just for the sake of the show. I miss the easiness we used to enjoy with each other.

Gilly is so flustered, a stab of guilt pricks at me. For the love of God, she tears up, and I feel like a first-class shit.

"I'm really sorry, Meg," says Gilly in a six-inch voice. "I thought you'd be happy the show increased its representation at the Con."

I take a deep breath and wave my hands. "I am." I manage a smile. "It's grand. I'll blast it out on social straight away so the fans will know where to find you."

Gilly's made every effort to warm to me. The barrier between us is my doing. Our showrunner, Bobby Provost, is close with Jack and Gilly. He's also one of the few people on the show, besides Maureen, that I count as a real friend. I don't want to damage our long-standing friendship by ruffling Jack's feathers and making the new Mrs. O'Leary cry. In truth, I'm frustrated with myself for not scouring the Cali Con schedule for more potential exposure for anyone involved with the show.

My push was for Deidre LaRochelle, author of *The Chieftain's Son* book series and permanent fixture here at The Clan, to represent in a big way at Cali Con. Deidre had slammed the door on that idea. I get it. Deidre's been paying her appearance dues on the convention circuit for over a decade. She's paid up.

I adjust my bruised ego over Gilly's news and initiate damage control. "What do you golf nuts say? Give me a Mulligan. I truly appreciate *Chieftain's Son* scoring another panel seat." I use my pinkie to flick a mascara flake out of the corner of my eye. "I'm wound a bit tight with Cali Con so close."

Gilly reaches across the desk and pats my hand. She doesn't mean to condescend, but that's how my nerves translate the contact. "You're amazing, Meg. Cali Con is going to be killer."

"Amen," I say, rising from my seat. "Now, off with you both. I'm due"—I frown at the phone—"overdue for a call from L.A."

Jack regains the friendly attitude I appreciate and waves a business card at me. "I hired the assistant you recommended."

I recognize the card of Cam Stephens, the latest in a line of assistants I tried out who didn't live up to my standards. After a bit of a struggle, we'd mutually agreed it was a bad fit. I truly believe Cam will do fine for Jack.

"Will Cam be joining us in California?"

"Naw. He'll be coming on board when we get back."

"Fine." I smile at Gilly. "Your appearance news is brilliant, Gillian. I'll update your schedule."

Jack smiles as they slide out the door. "We promise to print it out, save it to our phones, and write it in Sharpie on our arms."

It takes me a second to register his tease. There's the good-natured Jack O'Leary impossible not to like. I should hire him as my life coach.

Arms wrapped around each other, Gilly and Jack glide down the hall. Before they're out of sight, Gilly turns to drink in a long look at me. I expect agitation, but instead, softness unnervingly close to sympathy shows through the glass. There's no call for me to be the object of such an expression.

The two lean their heads together and whisper. Whatever the exchange, it ends in a kiss not intended for an audience.

"Glass walls," I hiss under my breath and look away from them. A flurry of emotions spins through my head, wedges on a wheel of fortune. Unwelcome and unexpected spikes of what I'm loathed to admit is jealousy hit me. What those two have, many would call enviable. I dig thumbs into my temples. I refuse to be envious of Jack O'Leary and Gillian Bettencourt O'Leary. It's a bad investment of energy for me right now. I don't have the time or desire to be on the hunt for what they have. I owe *The Chieftain's Son* my all. It's made a strong showing in its first season, and I'm charged to keep it at a gallop.

I sneak a glance in their direction. The last remnant of jealousy melts into a puddle of wistfulness. Even I admit there is genuine sweetness in their relationship. They are so easy with one another. It's hard to believe it's only been months since they first met. The two seem like an old couple who've already shared a lifetime of love and memories. I lay a hand to my cheek, surprised to find a bit of moisture at my fingertip. The half formed tear sends the skeptic in me on a mini break. How must it feel to be so sure of a partner?

I dismiss the unwelcome sliver of loneliness attempting to sneak into my psyche. There's logic they fell hard for one another. They're an equation of proximity plus the fusion of artistic personalities. The real question here is: how much has love diluted their own individual identities? Ah, there's the peril of love. It takes two people and sloughs off enough of who they are to snug their puzzle piece into someone else's. I never want to be stuck to another person to create a single shadow. *"Me"* has power. *"We,"* signifies a proportional loss of self.

The phone finally rings. I wake the agenda on my laptop as I check my hair. What am I doing? This isn't a video chat. I could be in bathrobe and slippers. Dash would never know.

Snatching the receiver, I commence the meeting. "Meg McGrath."

A sleepy California accent answers. "Mornin', Meg. It's Dashell."

He speaks as if caller ID doesn't exist. "Your mornin', my evenin'." Damn it. There was too much unintended edge to my tone. "You're on speaker so I can type. Are you looking at the agenda doc?"

I hear Dash gulp whatever his liquid morning fuel might be. "Give me a sec to bring it up."

While Dash retrieves the agenda, my computer pings with a message. My heart skitters when I click on the attachment. A gorgeous color graphic rendering of a towering wall of Southern Cal Stadium, the baseball complex across from the Diego Bay Events Center, home of Cali Con, graces my screen. Adorning the massive structure is a building wrap featuring the signature portrait of Jack and Niks as their characters from the show, Donal Cam and Nieve. Letters spelling out *The Chieftain's Son on the True Time Network* shimmer in gold. It's dazzling. It's perfect. The jewel in my Cali Con crown.

"Dash, the final version of the building wrap for Southern Cal Stadium is in. It's grand. I'm forwarding you the latest rendering with the changes we asked for." I hear keys clicking at his end as I read the rest of the message. "According to schedule, it'll be up less than two weeks before the convention starts."

Dash's hum of pleasure flows from the speaker. "It is a beaut'. Nice work, Meg."

I glow with accomplishment.

"We're placing the *Star's Shadow* wrap next to yours. True Time's two hottest shows, lording over the event," says Dash.

Thank goodness we're not on video chat, so I'm not forced to temper the bitterness tugging down the corners of my mouth. I worked blazing hard to secure that prime location. My cutthroat negotiations knocked a show from one of the three big U.S. networks off Southern Cal Stadium to make room for *The Chieftain's Son*. Dash tosses off the building wrap placement for his bit of Sci-fi fluff, *Star's Shadow*, like it happened with no more effort than ordering a sandwich with salt and vinegar crisps.

"Another update, Gillian Bettencourt is slated for an additional panel." I share the addition, feeling my scorecard needs another tick even if her agent is the one who pulled off the booking. "*Pages to Screen*."

"Fine, fine," says Dash. "Add it to your Cali Con playbook."

"Already done." As if I need telling to keep the game plan up to date.

"About that playbook…" Dash clears his throat. "There's a question I must put to you, Meghan. Is it enough?"

I bite my bottom lip to prevent going on the defensive. How can he be asking me this now, less than a month before go time? I've bled, securing panels, press events, party appearances, autograph sessions, hotels, security, transportation, media blitz, appearance fees, and fecking building wraps. What the hell can he mean?

My mind flashes on the possible comebacks my boss expects and settle on a good one. "Is it ever enough? I'll continue to work full-tilt once I hit the ground in San Diego to make sure I grab up any additional opportunities for *The Chieftain's Son*."

"Let me be up front with you, Meghan."

Well, crap. That's two Meghans in one conversation. I am in the principal's office and not for anything good.

"Please."

"You've done quite the admirable job with *The Chieftain's Son*. I know your probationary period with True Time is flashing red, so I owe you clarity about my end of things. I've got a full plate. It's time I step away from my involvement in *Chieftain's Son* so I can focus on upcoming projects and network expansion."

Step away? I do my best not to choke on the adrenaline surging up my middle. Is this the happy news I'm to be trusted to captain the publicity and marketing for *The Chieftain's Son* without requiring Dash to sign off on every bit of minutiae?

"We're prepared to offer you the permanent number two position on the publicity/marketing team for the show."

I did not hear him right. "Excuse me, did you say number two?"

"Yes, you'll stay on board with *The Chieftain's Son*, but I'll put a more seasoned player to head up the department. Like I said, Meg, you've done a fine job with an untested show, but our baby hit the stratosphere. You're still a newbie in the overall game, so I think it's best to move forward with a number one who has a proven track record. Together, you two will keep the show's climb meteoric."

My hands shake. "This isn't fair. I've been instrumental in the rise of *The Chieftain's Son*. Ten award nominations in the U.S. and more if you add in Europe, Dash."

"*Star's Shadow* grabbed ten Crystal noms as well If you'd beat them, I might be inclined to overlook the P.R. mess between your star and his alleged mystery woman that whipped fans into a social media uproar. I know you've been teasing an offscreen Jack O'Leary/Niks Tellefson pairing, but so far, the impact of your hints is a Band-Aid on a broken arm. Jack is our publicity brass ring. We've got to avoid the fallout and potential ratings drop if the public catches a whiff that your fabricated romance is a ploy to dupe them."

My stomach curls in on itself. If Dash knew about Jack and Gilly's marriage, he may fly over here to push me off the Cliffs of Moher. "I've got a game plan."

"I'm sure you do, but there remains the question of your experience and expertise to pull it off. Placing a head of P.R./Marketing in Ireland that isn't as green as your local countryside will head off a disaster."

"I've been pulling it off."

There are a few false starts on his end before he lets loose. The pulse on my throat bangs like it's trying to split my skin.

"You didn't pull off Jack's offshoot project."

"Hold on, Dash. *Secrets of My Ireland* is supposed to be a between-seasons filler to give the fans a steady dose of Jack. You greenlighted the concept and tentative production calendar for the space between seasons two and three. *The Chieftain's Son* shooting schedule was too tight to fit it in between seasons one and two. We can't burn out our biggest draw."

"Timing isn't the issue. Jack hasn't signed a multi-season contract for *Secrets*. I know for a fact piles of movie scripts are landing on his doorstep. If he lands a sweeter between-seasons deal, we're screwed with a one-off."

Shit, I should've pushed Jack harder to sign on for more than a single go of the companion project. I counted on his loyalty to stay on for more. Dash is right. I've committed a classic rookie error. Jack will do what's best for his career, not mine.

I squeeze my eyes shut, searching for a clear thought path. A single question for Dash rises above the static. "What can I do to prove to you the number one spot belongs to me? Give me a challenge, a goal. I guarantee I am as capable as your Hollywood pro."

He's silent for too long. Is he figuring out the cleanest way to fire me or taking my request seriously?

"Dash, it's humiliating and unfair to be demoted to number two given where I've taken the show already. If you won't consider keeping me in the lead position, I may have to bow out."

Holy Mother. Did I just give one of the chief executives at the True Time Network an ultimatum? No denying I'm green, but I do believe I am capable and talented enough to foster an even steeper rise in *The Chieftain's Son* popularity and ratings.

There's an edge of panic in Dash's voice I find gratifying. "Let's back up a little here, Meghan. I need you to stay with the show."

One more Meghan and I'll scream.

"The plan is to marry your *Chieftain's Son* expertise with a proven hand in the overall publicity playing field. I'm drafting a winning team."

Now it's my turn to be silent. Grunts and hums from the other end of the line give me hope. They need me. I'm important enough not to be shoved off Ireland's sea cliffs.

"The offer wasn't meant as an insult. I thought you'd appreciate a mentor."

Is he kidding? Does he expect me to lap up a blatant demotion?

My throat tightens. I will not cry. My mother's *I'm not surprised* expression vaults into my psyche. She believes my job on the show is a lark, a temporary fling. The script my parents wish I d follow is to take a slight taste of a bigger world, then choose to live small. Settle in my home village and market local businesses, marry a man I've known since primary school, and be a loyal daughter. Their script, not mine. I want to be a Jack O'Leary, the kid from a small Irish town who succeeds in a big way. Accepting the life my family perceives for me is the definition of failure.

"I'll be frank with you, Meg. It isn't solely my call. Given *Chieftain's Son* splash and potential for longevity, True Time wants a heavier hitter to take lead on the show. Personally, I feel I owe you the shot you're asking for."

A shot, a chance. I'll take whatever he offers. My knee-jerk ultimatum gains traction. There's some gratification the network doesn't want to lose me altogether.

"Here's what I can offer. First, fill every *Chieftain's Son* panel, autograph session, and other events to bursting. I want lines of fans salivating at the chance to be in the same room as our people. I want to see Jack O'Leary's and Niks Tellefson's faces plastered all over the news coverage of Cali Con. Make *The Chieftain's Son* San Diego's hottest ticket."

"Done." Sounding confident is the first step to being confident.

"Next, I want a twenty percent increase in trial subscribers to the True Time streaming app credited to *The Chieftain's Son* by Sunday night of The Con."

Twenty fucking percent! Dash might as well have asked me to perform the labors of Hercules.

"And a signed contract from Jack O'Leary for three seasons minimum of *Secrets of My Ireland.* You pull all that off, and I'll go to bat for you at True Time."

"Anything else?" I say it as if he's asked me to do something as simple as washing his electric car.

"All right then. I wish you luck, Meghan McGrath." His tone is brittle. We both know his checklist is virtually impossible. We both know he's dangling this sweetie so, in the end, I'll accept the number two position under a fool from L.A. The click of Dash's Hollywood phone is a mouse trap snapping on my future.

I let my head fall onto my hands. I've stepped in it now.

Don't stop now. Keep reading with your copy of PRESS RELEASE

And find more from Leslie O'Sullivan at
www.leslieosullivanwrites.com

Don't miss book two of the *Behind the Scenes* series, PRESS
RELEASE, available now, and be sure to discover all the details on
Sullivan's website at www.leslieosullivanwrites.com

Meg McGrath, a publicist with few but impressive credits on her
resume, finds herself playing in the P.R. big leagues when she lands a job
as head of publicity for *The Chieftain's Son*, an Irish historical drama
based on an insanely bestselling series of romance novels. The show's
buzz hits the stratosphere in its first season, and given her lack of
experience, the network questions Meg's ability to keep up with the
skyrocketing publicity demands of their top tier show.

When her boss threatens to replace her with a new head of P.R. and
demote Meg to an assistant position, she convinces him to make a deal.
If she orchestrates an unforgettable splash for *The Chieftain's Son* at Cali
Con, a massive annual convention of the popular arts in San Diego,
she'll continue at the helm of publicity for the show.

Much to Meg's resentment, in San Diego the network pairs her up with
Cian Malley, the savvy publicist of the network's other top show, *Star's
Shadow*, to show rookie Meg the ropes. Meg's initial game plan is to
simply siphon off the best of her competitor's marketing flair in order to
keep her job – until the heat between them burns down the boundaries
of their professional connection, complicating everything.

Will the sizzle between Meg and Cian inspire her to up her game and
impress her boss, or does her naivete blind her to the real P.R. game
going on behind her back?

Please sign up for the City Owl Press newsletter for chances to win special subscriber-only contests and giveaways as well as receiving information on upcoming releases and special excerpts.

All reviews are **welcome** and **appreciated**. Please consider leaving one on your favorite social media and book buying sites.

For books in the world of romance and speculative fiction that embody Innovation, Creativity, and Affordability, check out City Owl Press at www.cityowlpress.com.

Acknowledgments

Loving thanks to everyone behind the scenes and in front of the camera on "It's Garry Shandling's Show." I am honored to have been a part of this amazing series as the assistant art director and grateful for all the lessons I learned during the experience. It is a time in my life I will treasure forever. An extra serving of gratitude for the writers on the show, especially Ed Solomon, Tom Gammill, Max Pross, Alan Zweibel, and Garry Shandling who never suspected they were Jedi Masters teaching this padawan how to craft a story with innovation, humor, and heart.

Boundless appreciation to Michael, the most amazing tour guide in all of Ireland, for sharing the beauty and lore of the Ring of Kerry.

This wild and wonderful writing journey is only possible with supportive friends and family. Thank you with an exponent for all the encouragement, hand holding, and love to Melissa, Cameron, Rich, John, Sidney, Diane, Flo, Laurie, Rob, Tiffany, Shannon, Gail, Anthony, Lizzy, Sarah, Julie, Katharyn, Shona, and Greg at The Rose and Crown Pub.

A special shout out to my fellow teachers, Eagle-Eagle-Eagle Soar-Soar-Soar who never cease to demonstrate caring and selflessness. Thank you for your devotion to students, and for being a light even in the most stressful and challenging of times.

Thank you to City Owl Press for creating a joyful environment for writers to create their art. I so appreciate everything you do to bring our stories into the world. Special hugs to my editor, Theresa Cole, for believing in *Hot Set* and helping me tell Gilly and Jack's tale.

Finally, I'd like to acknowledge my appreciation to the *Outlander* television series for being the inspiration for the fictional TV show, *The Chieftain's Son*, in *Hot Set*. I'm a lifelong fan of everything *Outlander*. A special thank you to Sam Heughan who had the courage and transparency to share a post on social media about the monumental personal challenges of being in the limelight. Sam, your words touched my heart and sent me on the journey to write this story. Thank you so very much.

About the Author

LESLIE O'SULLIVAN is the author of *Rockin' Fairy Tales,* an adult romance series of Shakespeare/fairy tale mash ups set against the backdrop of Hollywood's music scene. Her *Behind the Scenes* contemporary romance series peeks into the off-camera secrets of a wildly popular television drama. She's a UCLA Bruin with a BA and MFA from their Department of Theater where she also taught for years on the design faculty. Her tenure in the world of television was as the assistant art director on "It's Garry Shandling's Show." Leslie loves to indulge her fangirl side each year at San Diego Comic Con.

www.leslieosullivanwrites.com

facebook.com/leslie.osullivanauthor

instagram.com/leslieosullivanwrites

twitter.com/LeslieSulliRose

tiktok.com/@leslieosullivanwrites

About the Publisher

City Owl Press is a cutting edge indie publishing company, bringing the world of romance and speculative fiction to discerning readers.

Escape Your World. Get Lost in Ours!

www.cityowlpress.com

facebook.com/YourCityOwlPress
twitter.com/cityowlpress
instagram.com/cityowlbooks
pinterest.com/cityowlpress

www.ingramcontent.com/pod-product-compliance
Lightning Source LLC
Chambersburg PA
CBHW020826260626
47169CB00003B/847